MW01487783

Fall Again

Also by Lisa Herrington

Fall Again

Lisa Herrington

Writerly House Publishing

FALL AGAIN

Published by Writerly House Publishing
www.WriterlyHouse.com
www.LisaHerrington.com

This is a work of fiction. Characters, names, places, and events are products of the author's imagination. Any similarity to events or places, or real persons, living or dead is purely coincidental.

Copyright © 2022 Lisa Herrington
First Published April 2022
All rights reserved. No part of this book may be reproduced or transmitted in any form or by any means, electronic, mechanical, photocopying, recording, or otherwise, without written permission.

ISBN: 978-0-9990626-1-6

10 9 8 7 6 5 4 3 2 1

For G. G. & J.

Chapter One

REAGAN GENTRY, DIVORCE ATTORNEY to the stars, had already put in three solid hours of work at her office, and it was only eight in the morning. She needed to keep occupied until she met with her friend, Amber, to share her big news. Amber had recently taken a job with the city attorney's office and moved back to town. It was perfect because they could plan spur-of-the-moment coffee breaks or even lunch once a week.

After graduating from law school and working in different cities, Reagan and Amber had picked their friendship right back up where they had left off. That's what great friends did when they got together, acted like no time had passed between them.

Reagan waited in the busy cafe, happy that Amber had moved back to town and she now had someone to confide in other than her brother. Ryan was busy with his booming business and even more preoccupied with his new fiancée, Sydney.

Reagan had spent a few hours with Ryan and Sydney over dinner the night before in Maisonville. The couple had recently finished renovations on their largest flip home and were glowing with happiness. Reagan sat back and watched as they talked about the property with each other as if she weren't there. They whispered and laughed over private jokes, and she knew it had less to do with the fact they worked together and more because they were in love.

Reagan drank the rest of her iced tea as the couple kissed each other again, and then she grinned over her private thoughts. *Newly engaged couples shouldn't be allowed in public. They weren't fit for the company of others, especially single friends, and family members.*

Their waitress, Olivia, stopped back by the table and refilled their drinks, but Ryan and Sydney hadn't noticed. Olivia leaned in conspiratorially to Reagan, "Sucking face in public should be outlawed. They need to get a freaking room."

Reagan laughed at the smart-mouthed waitress. Olivia was always foul and funny. Truth be told, Reagan didn't mind the couple's public displays of affection. Five years ago, she couldn't imagine her brother happy again. His injuries from his last deployment with the Marines had stolen every ounce of the little brother she'd known, and therapy along with a job he loved had only brought a portion of him back.

The redhead sitting next to him had done the rest.

Watching them together helped fade the difficult memories and hard times they each had conquered in order to claim their happiness.

Reagan shook her head. Maisonville lived up to its nickname with the locals, and even her analytical side could not argue with it sometimes. They called it Renaissance Lake. It was easy to see the new beginning Ryan and Sydney were living. Maybe there really was a little magic in the town.

Ryan and Sydney finally finished their desserts, something Sydney always insisted on and then slowly walked Reagan out to her car. In the middle of the parking lot, Sydney unexpectedly stopped as she tried to talk Reagan into spending the night and more time at the lake.

Reagan made the usual excuses about work and being too busy to slow down because she didn't like spending too much time alone at her lake house. The house was perfect and brought back memories of the only fun times she had during her child-hood, spending days at the lake with their uncle, but it also reminded her that she was single, very single. And she was pretty sure the local charm of the lake wasn't going to fulfill any fantasies for her.

She'd had her shot five years ago and had thrown herself into the relationship the best she knew how, but it wasn't enough. Dr. Seth Young had been building his psychiatric practice and surprised her when he decided to move out of state to take over for a retiring doctor. Her heart turned inside out when he left, and she pulled herself together by focusing even more on her career. Recently he'd surprised her again by moving back to the city. She spent a good bit of focus avoiding him at all her regular places, but she wasn't going to stay at the lake to avoid him. She liked the city. She found comfort in the bright lights and crowds of tourists. The hustle had a beat all its own, and it gave her singledom comfort that she didn't want to explain.

Ryan and Sydney tried harder to talk her into spending the night, and she'd looked back at Miss Lynn's diner and shook her head. Those two were trying to lure her into lake life with good company and comfort food, but she couldn't handle the relaxed atmosphere for too long. The slower pace made her antsy.

Reagan loved them, but she'd left Maisonville as fast as possi-ble, and while waiting on Amber in the early light of the cafe, it was clear that she was where she belonged. It was packed with people and humming with conversation. There were young and old professionals, college students, and soccer moms everywhere. The eclectic crowd had character, and it always made her smile to see the various types of people coexisting happily.

Harmony wasn't something she'd had growing up or saw very often in her career as a divorce attorney. However, she did strive for it in her personal life and at the office. She was a successful divorce attorney and had earned her nickname because when one of the famous football or basketball players decided to get a divorce, she was the one they called. It helped her become one of the busiest lawyers in the city and her firm. It was also the reason she was celebrating with Amber.

Reagan had received word that she would officially make partner in two months, and she immediately called Amber to meet for coffee. Reagan was wearing a tight-fitting red dress with a matching blazer and three-inch stilettos, making her petite frame look longer.

She stood up to greet her friend when she heard Amber's laugh before seeing her. "I bet you're making partner, hot little mama," she said, looking Reagan up and down before she hugged and kissed her.

Reagan wiggled suggestively, and then they both laughed again. Finally, the waiter came over and took their orders. "How did you guess? Can you believe it's finally happening?" Reagan asked as her friend adjusted her larger frame into the uncomfortable metal chair.

"There was no mistaking your excitement over the phone, and you deserved that promotion a year ago," Amber said with conviction. She was a curvy woman with flawless mocha skin. Amber was tall, and *Housewives of Atlanta* attractive. She had more dates than anyone Reagan knew, including the men, and she never stayed home on a Friday or Saturday night. Her confidence drew people to her, and Reagan loved to watch Amber in action, working a room, or controlling a conversation.

Reagan had started her career and was still at the same law firm, Williams, Morrison, and Weisnick, and loved it. It was the coveted spot everyone in their graduating law class had wanted, and she was a perfect fit. Amber had started at another law firm in Baton Rouge but was happy to be back in New Orleans with her closest girlfriend and working for the mayor's office.

While Reagan was the family attorney to the stars, Amber was helping advise the mayor, the council, and other city offices and boards. She specialized in reviewing city contracts and documents that created any legal obligation affecting the city. She was brilliant but sometimes misjudged because of her looks.

"So, how goes it with Alexavier Regalia?" Reagan asked, accentuating the single mayor's name suggestively.

Amber rolled her eyes, and they both laughed again. "He's trying to kill me with the whole let's-modernize-this-city-government-for-the-people-initiative. I swear if he applies for one more federal grant in order to keep his reelection promises, I may jump out my office window."

"Oh, Amber. You know those windows don't open, babe," Reagan said with a straight face.

Amber laughed so loudly several people turned around, but before they became a complete spectacle, the waiter came with their coffees and pastries.

"I thought I heard he was advocating for that new health center?" Reagan asked.

"In case you haven't heard, he's an overachiever."

"Oh, I've heard alright. The mayor has gone out with almost as many beautiful people as you have," Reagan winked at her friend. Alexavier Regalia was of Italian descent and had the beautiful face and thick dark hair to prove it.

"If you ever want to be set up, let me know. He's asked about you before, you know?"

"Um, no thanks. My clients are in the news enough. I'm not looking for my picture to be in the paper, too," Reagan said.

"Then you probably shouldn't wear tight little dress suits that accentuate your ass, girlfriend," Amber said loud enough for the mayor and his two male companions to hear as they walked up.

"Ms. Gentry. Amber. Good morning," he said with that politician grin that got him mostly what he wanted.

Reagan kicked Amber under the table.

"Good morning, Mayor Regalia. So, you do remember my friend, Reagan?"

"Of course," he said and then introduced the head of his technology department and a member of the city council to them.

He didn't linger, but he didn't take his eyes off Reagan while he was there. As he said goodbye, he leaned in and said, "It is a pretty great dress," making Reagan bite her bottom lip as he turned and then disappeared inside the crowd.

"I'm going to kill you, Amber," Reagan said, cutting her eyes at her friend.

"Your ex is back in town, and a little competition would do his ego some good."

Reagan shook her head. She had no intention of dating the mayor or her ex-boyfriend, but there was no reason to argue the point with Amber, who would never agree with her.

The friends finished their coffee and then headed to their respective offices, a block and a half away from each other.

Reagan walked into her office and was greeted by her assistant's strange smile. Nancy was efficient, but she wasn't friendly and rarely smiled unless it was at a good-looking man. Reagan cut her eyes at Nancy as she handed her the mail like she held in world secrets. Then, without a word between them, Reagan walked into her office, reading the return addresses on the envelopes before settling on what to open first.

She looked up just in time to dodge a large bouquet of red roses sitting on the credenza. "What?" she said and backed up, avoiding the card. That's when she felt the second floral arrangement jutting out from her desk and turned in time to grab it before they tipped over.

As she carefully stepped back to take in the room, there were five large floral arrangements, each with a dozen long stem red roses taking up all the extra space in her office.

Reagan closed her eyes and took a deep breath, trying to clear her mind, but the scent of fresh roses surrounded her. Finally opening her eyes, she reluctantly grabbed a card off one of the vases. She knew the flowers were from Seth. He'd tried to get her attention for the last month since she ran into him at his office with Sydney.

Sydney Bell had needed legal help to get joint custody of her stepsons and to help fend off an attack from her ex-husband's new girlfriend. It was challenging but helped Reagan and Sydney become close friends. During that time, Sydney needed to meet with a psychiatrist, and Seth had surprised Reagan when he walked in the door as Sydney's doctor.

Since then, he had done everything he could to get Reagan's attention. He called her office. He called her home. He left handwritten notes on her car. He sent fruit baskets and a singing gram. Every week he had surprised her with something. The roses got her attention. He'd sent five dozen long stem roses to her office for every year they had been apart.

She shook her head as she looked at her calendar. It was the anniversary of the day they had met.

Reagan sat down at her desk, still holding her briefcase and the mail. She wasn't going to see Seth or talk to him because she might have to admit that she loved his attention. In fact, she was fooling herself by pretending she didn't still think about him. After he moved, she had taken off for a week and hidden away from everyone so she could cry alone. Then after seven days, she didn't allow herself to shed another tear. She'd hardened her heart, and it made her a better person. Well, it made her a stronger woman than ever before and the best family attorney in the area.

She was about to make partner. The only way she could keep up the hours it would take to keep her status at work would be to forget about beautiful Dr. Seth Young.

Nancy knocked as she stood in the open doorway.

"Come in," Reagan said.

"Looks like that fella isn't going to give up."

Reagan looked at her assistant but didn't reply to her comment. "Did you need something, Nancy?"

Nancy gave her a knowing smile. She was twenty-five years older than Reagan and still an attractive woman. She certainly had her share of older male attention. "I wanted to make sure you saw your messages before I left for the assistant's office meeting."

"Thanks," Reagan said, giving Nancy a look that told her she was sorry she had to participate in the mundane monthly meetings. Even though Nancy worked exclusively for Reagan, she still had to pay her dues to the head of the secretarial pool. The assistant's meeting was meant to keep everyone on the same page in the office regarding employee events, changes to employee policies, or even building rules. But, what could have been handled in a single email was always drawn out into an hour-long gathering by the head partner's secretary, Betsy. She'd been with the firm and worked for Terrence for only two years but had somehow appointed herself as the office assistants' boss. And she loved to wield her power over the underlings.

Reagan laughed to herself, thinking about how Nancy would torture Betsy. It would be subtle. Probably a sneak attack. But above all, it would be the end of that twenty-somethings career at the firm, and no one would be the wiser. After all, it was why she had the job in the first place. The previous assistant had been a snitch, and Nancy wouldn't put up with anyone tattling on her for anything, including parking in the partners' parking places on their days off. Reagan sort of admired Nancy's rudeness. She had style.

❧

SETH WALKED his patient out and locked the office door. He had a short schedule and wanted to make sure he got to Reagan's office building before being locked out again. He knew she'd still be there after hours because she worked all the time, but her office was locked up tight at six.

It hurt him to see that she didn't have a life outside of work. He had moved back to town and prepared to win back her heart. He knew she was single but had no idea she was determined to stay that way, dedicated to her job and nothing else.

Sure, she loved her brother and his girlfriend, but she barely saw them. They would come into the city and have dinner with her most of the time because she couldn't take off to go across the lake to visit with them, and he'd heard she had a house over there.

Seth had been patient. He'd watched her from afar. But,

honestly, he had spent weeks devising a plan to see her and couldn't have planned it better when she'd walked into his office with a new patient for him.

Being that close to her was all it took. Memories of Reagan in his bed flooded his mind as soon as he smelled the vanilla fragrance on her skin and the almond shampoo she used on her hair. It was a punch to his gut when he saw her that day, and he couldn't wrap his arms around her. She was the most incredible woman he had ever met. He still remembered the red dress she wore the first night he'd met her.

His old professor had invited him to a party for the candidate for mayor. A member of her law firm was hosting the event. She was holding a glass of whiskey, and every time she took a sip, the thin gold bracelet she wore would slide up her arm delicately. He'd felt hypnotized by the action and stared shamelessly at her until she made eye contact.

They didn't run out of conversation all night, but it took him months to get her to go out with him. "I can buy my own drinks," she would tell him. "I can pay my own tab, and when I'm done, I'll call my own Taxi," she'd said, not wasting any time letting him know she could take care of herself. It really did something to him.

The first night they spent together, he let her know that he respected her independence, and although she could do everything on her own, he wanted to take care of her. Seth tried like hell to prove it over the next few years and thought he'd gotten through to her. She'd finally told him that she loved him. Although it was New Year's and she'd been drinking, he knew it was true. They made love until the sun came up. She never said it again.

He'd tried to force her hand and get her to move to Tennessee with him, but she'd thanked him like he'd been her personal concierge or something. She congratulated him on the opportunity and told him good luck. If that wasn't a kick in the pants enough, she finished it with *it's nice to have an adult conversation when a relationship has run its course instead of some emotional breakdown and argument.*

Seth didn't know what to say but had felt the blow in his core. He felt like someone had died as he went through the motions of packing and moving. It was the hardest thing he had ever done.

Reagan didn't speak to him again.

It took him a year to realize there was no taking a girl away from New Orleans.

He worked day and night building his practice in his new state, but the success felt hollow. He knew he would never accept Memphis as his home if she wasn't with him. His career would never be as important to him as Reagan Gentry. He had built a considerable practice and fortune in Tennessee, but after five years, he sold his business without a blink of an eye just to get back to her. She had to give him a second chance. He wasn't going to take no for an answer.

He'd tried subtle. He'd been sweet. But the time had come for him to confront her.

Chapter Two

REAGAN SPENT HER AFTERNOON meeting with a local football star filing for divorce from his second baby momma. The young men needed help navigating the business of divorce, and she wished they were forced to take a class in college. All those hot bodies and careers laden with crazy amounts of cash were like a neon sign hailing an entourage of gold diggers from all corners of the globe. Occasionally it was a high school sweetheart that couldn't hold on to him with all that fame. Reagan had seen it all and found it equally sad because there were usually children in the mix.

Nancy knocked on her door and waited for Reagan to tell her to come in. "Leaving for the day?" she asked.

"Unless you need anything," Nancy said, knowing her boss wouldn't ask for anything that late.

They were always the last ones in the office, especially Reagan. It was usual for her to work until 9 or 10 without eating a proper dinner.

"There are sandwiches and Caesar salad leftover from the meeting today. Would you like me to make you a plate before I go?" Nancy offered.

Reagan held up her coffee cup and shook her head. "I'm good. Thanks."

Nancy gave her a small wave and then left for the evening. They didn't usually discuss any personal plans or have much friendly conversation, so it wasn't out of the ordinary. Nancy dropped the outgoing mail in a basket at the front lobby desk, and before she reached the glass doors to exit, Seth opened and held the door for her.

"Thanks," Nancy said, smiling like a cat. What she would do with a hunk like that would be sinful and possibly illegal in a few states. Nancy laughed at herself and kept going. He had stopped by several times before trying to see Reagan, but she wouldn't talk to him. *Poor lovesick fellow.*

Reagan looked up before Seth was able to knock on her open door. The outer offices were empty, and if he hadn't beaten the cleaning staff back inside, he would have been locked out again. Nancy would not have let him pass.

His eyes locked with hers for a moment. Reagan was wearing a red dress just like the night they met.

"Hey, Reagan. You working all night?" he asked, using that deep gravelly voice she used to find irresistible.

"How did you get in here?" she asked, trying to ignore his sexy smile. "The main lobby door was supposed to be locked at six. Did someone leave it open? That is a fireable offense," Reagan said, getting up from her desk to go check out the lobby door. She had to move so she wouldn't focus on his handsome face and messy, dirty blonde hair.

"Hold on, Rea. No one needs to lose their job over me. I waited until the housekeeping staff came out, started on the windows, and acted like I belonged here. I saw your assistant leaving as I came in. It's not their fault," he reached his arm out to stop her from walking away from him. He couldn't stand the thought of being separated from her again.

She backed up so they wouldn't touch and tried not to inhale his fresh scent. It was a cross between laundry detergent, bleach, and his own warm musky scent. It got to her back when they dated, and it still worked. So, she backed up another step.

"I have a lot of work to do, Seth. How can I help you?" It was her way of blowing him off, but he would overlook it. He knew she would be tough to crack again, but he was in it for the long haul, and it didn't matter how much she made him work for it.

"I have a real problem," he said, and she looked up surprised. "I don't like to eat alone, and I know you don't like to eat alone either. We should go to dinner together."

Reagan rolled her eyes and shook her head as she headed back to her chair. "You don't know me anymore. I eat alone just fine now. And I already told you that I have a lot of work to do."

Seth walked over to her desk and looked into her coffee cup. "Coffee is not eating." He cut his eyes as he smiled at her. "And there isn't any nutritional value in those crackers out of the machine down the hall."

"I don't eat those anymore," she said, ignoring his cute facial expressions as she sat behind her desk. It was her fortress. No one got through the mahogany desk.

Seth took a seat across from her. "You don't? Are you telling me that you've also given up those chocolate-covered mini donuts too?"

Reagan bit her lip but couldn't stop her smile. Those donuts were all she had the first time he'd spent the night at her place. She made him coffee and served him those donuts for breakfast, and he never let her forget about it or the lack of nutrition in her diet.

He single-handedly taught her to eat vegetables, which her parents had never done. They were not role models, and she quickly became the caregiver where her little brother was concerned. She always had to take care of him and herself from a young age.

Seth cleared his throat. He knew he was losing her when she got that far-off look in her eyes. But, boy, how much would he love to get into her head and find out what she hid in those memories. She never talked about her family, except for her brother, whom she loved, and never spoke about her childhood, except for summers with their uncle. It was a mystery. One he wanted to solve over long lazy Sundays in bed with her.

"Let me take you to dinner, Rea," he said, looking into her eyes.

She stared back at him but didn't say anything. She was great at negotiating because she knew when to speak and keep silent. But Seth was a patient man. He'd already waited five years for her, and he could wait a few minutes for her to acknowledge that he was serious.

The awkward pause hung in the air. Reagan smiled at Seth, and he smiled back at her. She leaned back in her chair, and he put his arms on the armrests of his. Then, finally, she broke. "I have a high-profile client I have to finish some work for, and I can't leave until it's done." She grimaced like she regretted telling him, no, but he couldn't be sure if she meant it.

"Still working for the arrogant class?"

"Arrogance is often confused with confidence. You of all people should understand."

"I'm not arrogant," he said, locked onto her stare.

Reagan laughed and didn't take her eyes off Seth. Then, leaning forward in her chair, she lowered her voice when she spoke. "But you are overconfident, and it could easily be confused if someone didn't know you."

"Let me take you to dinner, Rea," Seth said again.

That time she looked away at the papers on her desk. "I can't. I have to finish these," she said with less conviction.

Seth stood up and leaned on her desk. "I could order us something, and we could eat here. That way, you get to finish your work."

She stood up to match him. "You don't have to do that. I can finish this in an hour and then grab something on my way home. You don't want to hang around here while I type and make notes."

"Sushi or Pad Thai?" he asked, ignoring her last comment.

"Spicy Pad Thai sounds really good."

"You're not going to lock me out if I go pick it up, are you?" he asked.

"I told you, you don't know me anymore," Reagan said, and the mischief from days gone by danced in her eyes. She had only ever done that once, and she'd been furious at him.

"You can say that as many times as you want, Rea, but you and I both know that I know you better than anyone," he said, pausing for emphasis. She looked nervous for a second, and if he hadn't been staring at her, he would've missed it. There was a chink in that tough armor of hers, but he didn't want to make her feel uncomfortable. Instead, he circled back to his plans to pick up the food. "I'd have dinner delivered, but it would take too long. I'll be back in less than thirty minutes," he said. "I'll text you when I'm at the office door."

Reagan nodded, and he sent her a text message to make sure she hadn't blocked his number.

Her phone dinged.

She stared at her phone. She couldn't believe Seth hadn't changed his number after all those years.

He noticed how overwhelmed she looked when she didn't say anything except that she got the message. Was she surprised that he still had the same number? He'd kept it the same for her. In case she ever needed him. It killed him that she never had.

She walked him to the lobby and input the code to unlock the door. He gave her that stalwart smile of his, then leaned down and kissed her on the cheek before leaving.

Reagan felt the heat on her face as she slowly walked back into her office. She'd expertly avoided him for weeks and was disappointed that she'd let her guard down so easily. She tried not to think too hard about what it meant. After all, it was only dinner. She had skipped lunch and was indeed hungry. It certainly didn't mean things were going back to the way they were.

Seth was the one that moved away. He had taken a job out of state and left her. He hadn't been in love with her like she'd been with him. He was back in town, but it had to be another vertical move for his career. It was what he had lived for, and now it was what she lived for too. So why couldn't they have dinner and agree to be friends?

She sat back down at her desk and picked up the documents she'd been reviewing. Then she sat the papers back down. Who was she kidding? She had spent an enormous amount of time thinking about Seth Young. He was the one and only person she'd ever fallen in love with, and she almost couldn't pick herself back up. After he'd left, she was heartbroken beyond reason, and the only thing that helped her was work.

Reagan sank everything she had into her career. She had no life outside the office, and she'd been okay with that until he'd shown up again. She shook her head and then laid her forehead down on her desk.

She was acting ridiculous.

Seth couldn't possibly want to get back together with her. Maybe he simply had something to tell her, and after dinner, they would pretend to be friends? She could have one meal with him, and afterward, the notes and flowers would stop.

He was career-minded and probably needed to clear the air so they could work together if they needed to, like Sydney's case. Sydney had been ordered by the court to have a psychiatric evaluation. Seth was filling in as the court-appointed doctor. Reagan was shocked to see him that day and then relieved because she knew Seth would be fair. In actuality, he helped resolve the entire case. The lawsuit was mediated out of court, and everything worked out in Sydney's favor.

Since that case ended, Seth had tried to meet up with Reagan on multiple occasions, but she'd rebuffed him each and every time. His efforts had to be about their work relationship. He was a psychiatrist and excellent at his job. He could tell things about people before they even knew what was going on with them. He had to know she wasn't interested in a romantic relationship with him or anyone. Her career was blowing up, and the referrals were coming in constantly. She was in high demand, and it was why she would be a partner in the firm. Reagan couldn't slow down and give up her success. She would be the first female and the youngest partner in the firm's history. She'd earned it.

Seth had a demanding job, and she was super busy. So this wouldn't be a big deal. Right?

She nodded as if to answer herself as she cleaned up her desk.

It was only dinner.

Chapter Three

SETH WAS SURPRISED THAT HIS tactics worked on Reagan. She hadn't responded to one single attempt he'd made before, and he'd honestly thought the personal note on her car would have gotten to her before anything else. No matter what, he wasn't going to let the chance get away from him.

He knew that if he took too long, Reagan would refortify her walls and keep him out. She had barricaded her heart, and he planned to ply her with Thai food.

He called the restaurant and placed the to-go order so it would be ready when he arrived. He was then back at her law office in less than thirty minutes as he'd promised. Reagan opened the door, and when he walked in, he was surprised that she'd cleared her desk for them to eat.

"I seem to remember a conference room where we could spread out," he said. Of course, he had no intentions of "spreading out," but instead, he wanted the opportunity to be close to Reagan, and to do that, he would have to get her away from that ridiculous desk.

She shrugged her shoulders, picked up one of the bags of food, and led him down the hallway to the conference room they'd met in for Sydney's case. It had a single long table and eight chairs. Seth waited for her to sit and then took the chair next to her.

Reagan didn't say anything when he sat down, but he noticed how she sat hugging the chair arm furthest from him. Was she afraid that he might touch her? He smiled and opened the take-out boxes, displaying the aromatic food.

She held her stomach and smiled.

"I sure missed this food. Remember how we used to eat there once or twice a week?" Seth said, passing her some chopsticks.

Reagan pulled one of the containers closer to her and took a bite of noodles as she nodded. "I haven't eaten Thai food in years," she said, leaving out the fact that she'd stopped going because it reminded her of Seth.

He stopped eating and looked at her. "Me either, Rea."

Reagan didn't make eye contact as she took another bite. Her head told her that he would discuss their working relationship, but her heart disagreed. She quickly changed the subject. "Tell me about Tennessee. It must have been different living there?"

Seth ate several quick bites before he answered. "It's beautiful there. Not a lot of sailing going on. I had to get used to the fact that the Gulf of Mexico wasn't close anymore and that I couldn't do any saltwater fishing like I'd grown up doing most of my life."

He took another bite of food before adding, "The weather was a lot different too. Did you know they get all four seasons? And not all in one day like we do here. So I saw fall leaves change in the fall and then light snow in the winter."

"I wasn't referring to the topography or weather. What about your job and the people?" she asked.

He smirked at her for pretending to be direct. Reagan had a question she wasn't asking, and while he didn't know what it was, he was confident she would lead him there. "In general, they were very nice. Hospitable. Of course, plenty that needed counseling too."

"So business was good?"

Did she really want to know about his career?

"Fantastic. I quadrupled my practice, and if I could have gone without sleep, then I could've done even better."

"Wow. That good?" Reagan wiped her mouth with her napkin and looked directly at his ring finger. "So, no wife? No kids?"

"Not yet," he said, locking eyes with her.

Reagan's heart dropped. "So, there is someone?"

"Absolutely."

Reagan didn't expect it to hit her so hard. She tried to hide it and took a drink of her water. She was always in control of her emotions, but they hit her like a freight train. Why then had he sent her flowers and messages? She quickly excused herself and hurried to the restroom, locking the door behind her. Standing with her back against it, she could feel her heart pounding in her chest. She was over him. She'd been over him for years. *Wasn't she?*

She felt Seth's soft knock on the door.

"Rea? Baby, are you okay?"

She blinked several times, trying to call back her watering eyes. *He called her baby.* "Fine. I'm fine. I just got something in my eye. I'll be out in a minute."

Five minutes later, she returned to the conference room where Seth had finished his food and had cleared their trash away. He also had a large slice of chocolate cheesecake on the table with two clean forks. Her food was still sitting there, and the idea of eating anymore made her stomach roil.

"Hey," he said, watching her closely.

"Hey." Reagan avoided looking at him as she sat down and closed her container of spicy noodles. When she pushed it away, she felt Seth move in closer.

"Chocolate?"

"You know that's not fair."

"What?" he asked, faking innocence.

She took the fork and the first bite of cake. Seth watched as she leaned back in her chair like she wasn't strong enough to sit up with such ecstasy.

"That's good," she said barely above a whisper.

Seth moved his chair even closer to her. "I didn't mean to upset you, Rea."

"You didn't."

He covered her hand with his. "Then why the tears?"

"No tears. Just tired. I had a tough week and haven't slept much. That's all. I haven't stopped to eat dinner at a normal time in months. And I was thinking about my brother and how I should probably call him to hang out. You know, with Sydney too."

Seth smiled. Reagan was good at hiding her feelings, but not to him. Hopefully, he hadn't made her cry, but she was clearly upset. He could always tell when she was covering something up on the spot. She explained herself too thoroughly and then asked direct questions so she could distract him.

"So, who is the soon-to-be Mrs. Young? She must be from here if you moved away from such a lucrative business. I know work is important to you, and you couldn't wait to move up there."

"Work isn't that important to me. At least not more important than her."

Reagan watched him smiling like crazy and wondered if anyone would ever smile over her like that someday.

Seth got out of his chair and knelt beside her. "Sweetheart..."

Reagan shoved her chair away as she stood up. "I'm pretty sure you shouldn't use terms of endearment with me if you're going to get married, Seth Young!"

"I shouldn't?"

Reagan gritted her teeth, and he tried not to laugh at how angry she was at him.

"You know you shouldn't do that and stop trying to hold my hand," she said, putting her hands behind her back. "And what were you thinking sending me all of those flowers?"

"I like to call you sweetheart, and I'm not sure I can stop." Seth stood up and crowded her into a corner.

"I need to know. I need to know who she is, Seth," Reagan said, not recognizing her own breathy voice.

Seth leaned in closer and whispered into her ear, "You know the only person I've ever loved is you, Reagan Gentry."

Reagan couldn't believe his words and quickly looked away from his eyes. Seth gently lifted her chin and then kissed her harder than she had ever been kissed. When they came up for air, Reagan searched his eyes. "You loved me?"

"I love you. I have never stopped loving you. I came back for you."

Reagan licked her lips and took a deep breath. She needed to sit down. Stepping past Seth, she leaned against the table. With her hand on her heart, she stared up at him. That wasn't what she'd expected.

"So, you're saying there isn't anyone else?"

"There hasn't been anyone else since I met you. I was set up a few times with different women in Tennessee, and I never went out with any of them a second time. It wasn't fair to them. I couldn't stop thinking about you."

"But you never called. Not once."

"You all but shoved me out the door, Rea," he said, standing in front of her and leaning down, so they were face to face.

"No. You're the one that took the job out of state without consulting me. You left me."

"I tried to talk to you about it, Rea. Don't you remember? I asked you to take a few days off to fly up there with me. I also had the offer in Texas, but you made some joke about everything's bigger in Texas, especially the egos."

"You know I didn't mean that. I have friends in Texas. I love

Texas. But I'm not leaving New Orleans to live there. Besides, my brother needed me."

"Ryan was better."

"But I didn't know if it would stick. I needed to be here to look after him. He's the only family I've got."

Seth shook his head. The conversation about leaving New Orleans with her would always go round and round. His Louisiana girl was never going to leave her hometown.

"I would've stayed for you, Rea."

"I would've never asked."

And that was the crux of their problem. He loved her. He wanted her, but he needed to hear her say she needed him too.

"I see that now," he said, straightening back up.

"Seth," she said his name like it was a lifeline. She stood up and leaned into him.

Neither of them knew what to say to the other. Seth had spent weeks trying to get Reagan to talk to him. Could he ever get the answers he wanted? Would she ever need him like he needed her?

He wanted to stay and force her to discuss everything, but that wasn't how Reagan worked. He'd blindsided her with how much he loved her and how he came back for her. She was going to need some time to process it all.

His true nature was to take control, but that had never worked with Reagan, except in bed. They never had any issues with sex. But he couldn't think about that, or he'd never be able to leave. He needed to go to plan his next step, and she could have time to consider all he'd said. He'd meant every word of it. He was going to marry her.

"Reagan, I should let you get back to work."

Her shield was instantly back in place. "Yes. I do need to finish."

He didn't want to leave, and she didn't want him to go, but neither of them would admit it.

Seth kissed Reagan on the forehead and reached around her

to pick up his phone. "Walk me out, Reagan, so you can lock up behind me."

She did as he asked, and that time when he left, she physically felt like a piece of her was missing. *How was she going to keep him away?*

Chapter Four

REAGAN WORKED UNTIL ONE in the morning. By the time she got home, she was too tired to do anything but peel off her blazer and dress and climb into bed. No matter how tired she was, she couldn't fall asleep. Finally, after five years of missing Seth Young, he was back in town and told her he loved her?

Then why did he leave so quickly after professing his feelings?

She knew the reason. Everyone in her life left her. She wasn't the kind of person that made them want to stay. She heard the comments behind her back at school and at work that she was the ice queen.

They didn't know her. She honestly felt everything, maybe more than most. When she was young, she cried herself to sleep every night. It took her some time, but she'd learned to compartmentalize all those emotions so that she could protect her little brother. She knew he would be scared if she were, which made her work harder. She had considered it a skill, hiding all those feelings that other girls wore on their sleeves.

She didn't want to hide her feelings from Seth, though. Could she make him understand? She'd often wondered what would have happened if he'd stayed. She even had dreams of him coming back to profess his love for her. But never in her wildest imagination, well maybe her wildest imagination, but never in her reality did she think it would happen. But he was back. He said he loved her. He said work wasn't more important than her. *Didn't he?*

Reagan kicked off her covers and searched for her silk robe. She couldn't lay in bed and think, she needed to pace. Reagan did her best thinking on her feet. She found her robe and slippers in the closet and then headed straight to the kitchen for a small glass of whiskey. She would drink and pace.

If Seth was in love with her, why did he leave so quickly after dinner? He'd spent the last month trying to get her attention with all that stuff, and the minute he had her alone, he'd bolted. Seth wasn't a weak man. He also didn't have a hard time expressing himself. He was a freaking Psychiatrist. He talked for a living. Maybe he listened for a living? She wasn't sure anymore.

Reagan added more ice and more Jim Beam to her glass. It would take more consideration than that first glass was going to inspire. She walked around the kitchen island and slowly walked back into the living room around the sofa.

Damn it. If Seth loved her, then he should have stayed to talk. But, of course, she wasn't sure if she could have handled that either.

Reagan knocked a throw pillow onto the floor and kept pacing around the armchair and then in front of the large window that overlooked the city lights. She finished her drink and then went back to pick up the pillow. She didn't like things out of place.

She sat down on the couch and then laid across it, covering up with the chenille throw blanket. Had she pushed Seth away five years ago? Had she driven him away after dinner too?

SETH WALKED into his apartment and dropped his briefcase, coat, and keys onto the entry table. He couldn't get Reagan off his mind, but of course, that had been the situation for years.

He stripped off his clothes, leaving them on the bathroom floor, and took a hot shower. He did his best thinking in the shower.

He thought about how he'd gone to Reagan's office, prepared not to take no for an answer. He was going to see her and talk to her. But, just because it didn't go quite as he'd expected, it still was progress. So why was he so miserable?

He turned the hot water up higher. As steam circled him, he leaned his head against the tile. She should be there with him. It was Friday night, and she was still up at that damned office working her ass off. She needed to take better care of herself. She was tired, and he could see that in her face. She was still the most beautiful woman he'd ever known, but she needed some pampering. Pampering and affection were his specialties.

Reagan didn't get enough love as a child. He was sure of it. So, Seth would make sure she got more than her share as an adult. He'd already been patient enough. He'd waited five years. He wasn't sure he could wait much longer.

After his shower, Seth dressed in sweatpants and a t-shirt and made himself some coffee. The caffeine had little to no effect on him, and he often drank it before bed. Then he grabbed his paperback book off his nightstand and headed to the couch where he would get through a few chapters trying to distract his brain from Reagan.

By one, he'd finished over half the book but still couldn't stop thinking about her.

I could drive by the office and make sure she's gone home. Seth told himself, knowing that it wouldn't be enough. He would go up and talk to her if she was still there, and if she wasn't, he would go by her condo.

It was 2 a.m. when Reagan heard the light knock on her front door. She sat straight up on the couch. Had she fallen asleep? Was someone really out there? Why didn't they ring the doorbell?

She heard it again and quietly went to look out the peephole as she tied her short robe tighter. It was Seth wearing a beige trench coat and what looked like gray sweatpants.

She unlocked the deadbolts and opened the door.

They locked eyes, and the next second he was kissing her inside and closing the door behind them.

Seth left his shoes and coat on the entryway floor, and Reagan stumbled out of her slippers as they fell onto the couch. He was on top of her and kissing her thoroughly when she finally whispered, "Seth, wh-what are you doing here?"

He stopped kissing her neck, to then kiss her lips before he spoke. "I know it's been a long time, baby. This is called making out."

Reagan laughed and shoved his shoulder softly. "No kidding."

Seth pulled her robe closed, trying to help her keep covered, and then looked into her eyes. "I didn't want to leave you tonight. Then I worried that you'd work too late. I regretted it the minute I walked into my apartment. We have a lot of catching up to do."

Reagan nodded her head and kissed him softly on the lips. "Maybe we could talk in the morning?" she said, pulling her robe open and wrapping her arms around him.

It was late Saturday morning when Seth woke up in Reagan's bed with her arms and legs tangled around his body. He pulled her in closer and then dragged the blanket around them. She snuggled in tighter, and he wondered if she knew what that did to him.

Seth was mostly a level-headed man, but he could lose his mind over her. Protecting her, taking care of her, and making her happy were the most important things in the world to him. They were good together. Actually, they were great together.

He fell back asleep and didn't wake up until Reagan ran a warm cup of coffee under his nose. She set it down on the nightstand as he pulled her on top of him. She was wearing that flimsy robe again, and he rubbed his hands down her backside, making her shiver.

She gave him a sexy smile and then rested her chin on top of his chest. "You know, not much has changed in my kitchen over the past five years. I'm afraid I don't even have those little donuts for breakfast. Only coffee."

Seth rolled them over until he was on top of her and kissed her nose. "How do you live, woman? Aren't you ever hungry?"

"I pick stuff up or have it delivered. What can I say? I eat enough."

Seth ran his hand over her flat stomach. "You look great on the outside, but your insides must be rioting for some healthy food."

"I eat salads now."

"Salad bought from a drive-through window. That's not healthy, Rea."

"We've been over this before, Seth Young. I didn't have a stay-at-home mom to cook me perfect little breakfasts and dinners. And I was lucky to grab it on the run."

"One day, you're going to tell me more about that, but for now, I'm going to cook you one of those perfect breakfasts."

"I hate making groceries, and you know it." Reagan bit her lower lip in defiance.

"Well, that's your problem right there. Outside of New Orleans, no one calls it *making groceries*. That makes it sound like work. How about we go buy some groceries instead?" Seth laughed as he pulled her off the bed with him.

She had it right the first time; making groceries was more appropriate because searching for them was work. She didn't correct him. Instead, she got dressed and they headed to the downtown market together. Seth held her hand as they walked through the produce section, and he hand-selected locally grown tomatoes. They weren't in a hurry, but it didn't take long for him to pick out everything he needed for a proper brunch.

At home, Reagan poured them each an orange juice and then

sat at the bar as she watched him prepare an avocado and tomato salad and eggs Benedict from scratch. She washed the dishes afterward, and he dried and put them away.

"Do you have plans for today?" she asked avoiding looking at him. She wasn't shy, but he knew she wasn't sure what to do with him yet.

"My only plans are to spend time with you, Rea."

Reagan grinned as she pulled off her shirt. "I was thinking about going across the lake to visit my brother and his girlfriend. But first, I need a shower."

Seth couldn't wipe the smile off his face as he pulled off his sweatshirt and followed her into the bathroom. He hadn't planned the day, but he liked the way it was starting.

Of course, he hadn't seen Ryan in over five years, and the last time they spoke, it didn't go well. Ryan was a protective younger brother and had spent many years in the military. He could probably kill a man a hundred different ways. He'd said something like that when he found out that Seth was leaving town.

It didn't matter because Seth would never leave Reagan again, and he was ready to face Ryan and do whatever it took to earn his respect.

Hopefully, her brother didn't hold grudges.

Chapter Five

TRAFFIC WAS LIGHT ON SATURDAY mornings, and it only took thirty-five minutes for Reagan and Seth to make it across the lake to Maisonville. Seth insisted on driving Reagan so that he could make sure she didn't rush them across the lake and then rush them around. He leisurely ordered coffee through a drive-through before they headed onto the long bridge. He was going to make sure she relaxed.

Reagan smiled after she drank some of her hot coffee. "I didn't even know I liked hazelnut coffee," she said.

"Try mine," Seth insisted. "It's butter pecan."

Reagan took the paper cup from his hands and took a sip. It was good. Really good. She handed it back to him and shook her head.

"And?"

"It was delicious. Everything last night and this morning."

"Why does it sound like there's a *but* at the end of that statement?" Seth asked, setting his cup down and resting his hand on her leg.

Reagan put her hand on top of his and stared at him. "My metabolism works well enough, but I can't keep this pace."

"There is no pace, Rea. This is called relaxing and enjoying yourself. You could use a few more calories, and I'm certain you don't take any time off."

Reagan smirked. She didn't need more calories, and she wouldn't admit the weight loss was from being heartsick. "Are you kidding? I worked to lose the fifteen pounds I'd gained from dating you after you left. I know better than to eat leisurely all day long. Besides, I am busy. I'm going to make partner in October."

Seth moved his hand up her leg a bit and squeezed it gently. "I'm proud of you. I know you've worked hard, and you've earned that success. But Rea, delicious food is good for your soul."

Reagan moved Seth's hand back to her knee and gave him a stern look. "It's all coming back to me now. You plied me with food while we dated. Don't think I've forgotten the warm cookies at midnight or the pancakes in bed."

He hadn't forgotten making love to her after serving her food in bed. Her silence let him know she was thinking about it too, and suddenly the air was vibrating. Seth took a deep breath when he saw her eyelids get heavy with desire, and he'd wished they hadn't decided to go across the lake.

Reagan leaned in closer to him as she spoke. "You know my brother remodels old homes, and I bought the first one he finished. It's beautiful. It's on the water and has a porch with a nice stone path leading to the dock and boathouse. It's super quiet and private and has a king-size bed."

"I need to see this new house of yours. I mean, if you're sure we have time."

Reagan whispered, "I'm so very sure."

Seth was thankful to be nearing the end of the bridge because he wasn't sure he could keep his hands off her for much longer. Reagan must have felt the same way as she sat back in her seat, all flushed. She gave him directions to her lake house and grinned as he drove up the long winding driveway.

"Reagan? Why are you still in the city?" he asked, taking it all in. "This place is amazing."

"I could never commute. I love my penthouse. I bought the place to support my brother, but it's too big for me," she said, unlocking her door to get out of the car. Seth met her around the car and leaned in to crowd her close before kissing her.

They both were breathing heavily as he whispered, "Show me around, Rea."

Reagan slid her hand into his and walked with him up the stairs. The house was slate blue with cedar-colored shutters. It looked brand new but also fit into the landscape. The oversized furniture on the porch was also cedar-colored and blended well with the setting.

She unlocked the front door and held his hand, pulling him inside. She didn't bother showing him anything else as they went straight to her bedroom and bed, dropping their clothes on the way down the hall.

Reagan slipped into his button-down shirt an hour later while Seth grabbed the quilt from the bed. He was only wearing his jeans, and she tried not to ogle his washboard stomach. She'd lost weight since they'd broken up, but he seemed to have put weight on in muscle. She hesitated as he pulled open the back doors and started toward the pier.

Reagan looked past him at the water, and he knew she was second-guessing herself. It didn't often happen with other things, but she was critical of her body. Seth wrapped Reagan in the quilt and picked her up to carry her outside.

"You're gorgeous, Reagan, and it does something for me to know that your half-naked under this quilt."

Reagan made an exaggerated gasp, trying to hide her real surprise. Seth never said things like that before, and she liked his forward behavior. It did something for her. She wrapped her arms around his neck, trying not to think about how hard it would be to let him go again. She had to keep things casual.

He held her until he reached the outdoor furniture and then had a seat with her still in his arms. Finally, she wiggled free, holding the quilt around her waist so she could turn on the gas fireplace built into her outdoor coffee table. She then sat back down beside Seth, and they quietly watched as several egrets landed on the edge of the pier.

"Rea. This place is heaven," Seth said. When he turned around to see her face, she was smiling bigger than he'd ever seen her.

"My brother did a great job with this house."

Seth kissed her on top of her head. "Yes, he did. But you made it feel like a home with all the furniture you've bought."

"You really like it?"

"Everything about it, Rea," he said, pulling her in tightly, so there was no space left between them. She had a hard time accepting compliments, probably because she rarely got them outside of her job. He understood that she worked hard for the money and stability and to earn approval. However, he hadn't thought about how she didn't have anyone outside of Ryan to be proud of her.

Seth's parents had always been loving and close to him. They still told him how proud they were of him and all his accomplishments, never criticizing any of his decisions.

He kissed Reagan's forehead, and they sat quietly for a while, watching the birds, the lake, and the afternoon sun making its slow descent in the sky. He kept his arm around her, and she rested her head against his chest as she leaned into him. Neither one of them wanted to move.

"What time is your brother expecting us?" Seth finally asked.

"I told him I would text him when we were on our way."

Seth smiled at her. It was time to go to Ryan's house. He couldn't avoid the inevitable. He had to face Ryan and any questions about Seth's intentions with Reagan. Seth wasn't going to let her go ever again, and one day they would all be family. *Family.*

He and Ryan used to get along well. At least before Seth planned to move. When Ryan found out that Seth was moving away and leaving Reagan, he had some serious opinions about the decision. Ryan drove into the city the day the moving trucks showed up and let Seth know that he didn't deserve Reagan and it would be best if he didn't come back.

Ryan didn't know at the time that Reagan had broken up with Seth. And Seth was sure that Reagan never knew that Ryan came to see him that last day either.

He hadn't seen Ryan again until four weeks ago in Reagan's office with Sydney. What a hell of a day that was for them all. *Of course, it was going to be a hell of an afternoon too.*

They headed over to Ryan and Sydney's house, and as they pulled into Ryan's driveway, Reagan reached over and honked the horn of Seth's SUV. Ryan and Sydney came outside to greet them as they exited the car.

Ryan hugged his sister, and then Sydney hugged her. After that, they both nodded Seth's way. "I was wondering what time you would finally get here," Ryan said, teasing Reagan.

"Stop, Ryan," Sydney said, squeezing his arm. "Don't let him fool you, Reagan. He's been marinating chicken and steaks all day so he could grill out either lunch or dinner. And we've been preoccupied watching college football and laying on the couch."

Reagan laughed at Sydney telling on Ryan. He'd met his match with her, and it made Reagan almost as happy as it did him.

They all went into the house for drinks and headed outside to grill and eat together. It was the first time Reagan had been across the lake for more than a quick dinner in ages. She never lingered. She never relaxed long enough for a cookout. It was great.

"Sydney and I have decided to move up the wedding," Ryan blurted out. "No, we're not pregnant yet," he said and reached over to hold Sydney's hand.

"But we want to be as soon as possible," Sydney said, staring into Ryan's eyes. He was truly happier than Reagan had ever seen him.

He finished explaining. "So, we've decided to have a small ceremony with family here at the lake."

Reagan's eyes watered as she congratulated them. "I'm so happy for you two."

She got up and hugged Sydney and then her brother.

Seth congratulated them both too.

"Are you going to do it here at the house?" Reagan asked.

"It's going to be at our home, but that's our other news," Ryan pulled Sydney over closer to him as he put his arm around her. "We've decided to move into the large white house that we recently finished."

"You know, the haunted mansion around the bend?" Sydney added and then leaned in and kissed Ryan on the cheek.

It was the most beautiful house on the lake, and Reagan knew after their last dinner that both Sydney and Ryan were over the moon about the place. It suited them and the big family they would have, including Sydney's stepsons.

Reagan held hands with Seth as they all talked about the new house. Reagan laughed and leaned into Seth comfortably as she explained some of their childhood adventures riding bikes by that old place after the original owners moved out. Ryan had never admitted to Sydney that he thought the house looked scary when he was a child.

"I knew the haunted mansion made you nervous. Admit it. That's the reason you always got me to go with you when the work crew wasn't there," Sydney teased Ryan.

"You figured me out," Ryan said, rolling his eyes and then winking at her.

Sydney kissed him on the cheek. "Alright. Now that you've admitted it, I'll stop calling it that. From here on out, it will be known as the Gentry House. As long as I can decorate it during Halloween like the Haunted Mansion?"

"I think that's a great compromise," Reagan said, joining forces with her soon-to-be sister-in-law.

Ryan gave his sister a stern look. "Don't let her fool you. She didn't want the boys to be scared at the new house, so she made me swear to never refer to it as haunted, although she'd tortured our workers for months."

"That may or may not be true, but I'm not going to admit to anything," Sydney said. "Besides, it's time for dessert. Want to help me, Reagan?"

Sydney smiled at Reagan. Because of Reagan and Dr. Young, she was free to be with Ryan and have shared custody of her boys. It made her happy to see Reagan and the doc happy together.

Ryan was a little more skeptical. He hid it well with his hospitality, but when Reagan and Sydney went inside to get the dessert, he took the opportunity seriously.

Seth watched as Ryan opened another beer and handed it to him. He opened another one for himself and then sat directly across from Seth.

"I've been wanting to thank you for what you did for Sydney," Ryan said.

It was completely the opposite reaction than he'd expected from Ryan the first time they were left alone all day. Seth nodded and took a drink of his beer.

"But of course, I will still beat you to death and hide your body where no one will find it if you hurt my sister again."

That was the Ryan he knew.

Ryan locked eyes with Seth and then clinked his beer bottle into Seth's and took a drink. *Was that it? That couldn't be it.*

"You do know, Ryan, that she broke up with me back then."

"You dated long enough to know better. Reagan has a hard outer shell; at least, that's what she shows most people. Those that are close to her see the soft center. If she broke up with you, it was a test, and you failed. I saw how she was with you. You're the only person she's ever brought home, so to speak. It was the real deal to her."

Ryan was right. Seth had let his own arrogance drive the situation. He wanted her to quit her job and follow him. He'd felt ridiculous as he'd mulled that over in his head for years. It almost cost him everything. It took him five years to get the nerve to come back for her. He didn't know what he would've done if she'd been with someone else. He couldn't think about her with anyone else.

"I shouldn't tell you this, but after you moved, she took a week's vacation from work. She'd never taken a week off before and never has since."

"Where did she go?"

"That's just it. Reagan didn't go anywhere. She stayed locked in her apartment the entire time. When I checked on her, she said she was sick and wouldn't let me in. I could tell she was upset, but after everything I'd put her through, I owed it to her to let her take as much time as she needed."

Seth sat his drink down. He couldn't believe what Ryan was telling him. *Could it be true?*

"I called her every day until finally, she told me to leave her the hell alone; she was going back to work the following Monday. I was so happy to hear her angry voice that I gave in."

Seth stood up. It killed him to know how badly he'd hurt her. Then, before he had time to process everything Ryan had said about Reagan, she walked back outside holding a plate full of chocolate cake.

He turned and took the cake from her to set it on the table. He then grabbed her and kissed her hard on the mouth in front of Sydney and Ryan.

"Miss me?" she asked, a little embarrassed.

Seth nodded at her and had a seat. He didn't talk much while they ate cake, and when they all finished eating, he leaned in to tell her he was ready to leave.

The guys cleared the dessert dishes from the table as Reagan and Sydney put away the remaining leftovers. Sydney insisted they leave the dirty dishes, and in less than five minutes, Seth and Reagan had said their goodbyes and were in his SUV backing out of the driveway.

It wasn't the typical southern long goodbye where they lingered on the porch for a while. Instead, it was a walk straight to the car where Reagan had to roll down her window and wave quickly.

"I wish we'd brought clothes to spend the night here," Reagan said. "It's been nice today. Hasn't it?"

"Yes, Rea. I liked seeing Sydney with Ryan. They're a good fit."

"They are a good fit," she agreed. She wasn't sure if Seth was upset about something, but she was surprised about the quick departure from her brother's house. She leaned back in her seat and quietly looked out the window.

Seth was quiet because he felt the pain he'd caused Reagan. He knew Ryan was right. Reagan did have a soft side, and all Seth had to do was look to see it. He reached over and put his hand on Reagan's leg again. When he was near her, he needed to have his hands on her. It made him feel like she was his. Like they belonged to one another. It was one of the things he missed the most.

"Rea, why don't we plan to spend next weekend at your lake house? We could pack a few groceries and have a sort of private weekend retreat."

Reagan nodded, placing her hand over his.

They stayed like that for most of the trip back to the city, only commenting randomly about the food they ate or Ryan's building skills and remodeling business. Then, finally, Seth pulled into the garage parking under Reagan's building, and they walked together up to her apartment.

Once inside, she offered him a drink, but he was the one who poured whiskey for each of them while she went and changed into her silky pajama shorts and a tank top. When she joined Seth in the living room, he was sitting on the couch and looking out at the city through her large wall of windows.

Seth looked distracted, and for the first time all day, Reagan was nervous over the impending conversation. She wasn't good at personal relationships because she second-guessed herself constantly. She wasn't like that at work.

She watched Seth for a moment. Had he changed his mind?

Reagan knew she wasn't easy to be with, but she was trying. Did she say something or do something that made him question his quick decision to move back and put his feelings on the line for her?

Seth leaned over and handed her the drink he'd poured. She noticed he had almost finished his glass, and he didn't usually drink alcohol. Instead, he liked warm beverages, coffee, hot tea, or even hot chocolate before bed.

It took her a few minutes as she drank a few more sips of liquid courage and finally broke the silence. "Is everything alright, Seth?"

Chapter Six

Reagan watched as Seth took a deep breath before he turned toward her. The pained look on his face made her stomach hurt. *It was going to be bad.*

"I love being with you, Rea. But..."

Reagan threw her blanket on the floor and stood up. "Don't say it, Seth Young. Dammit. I knew it. I knew things were going too well and too fast. I remember how spooked you got over me suggesting we live together after we'd dated for so long. Then you took off and moved out of state."

Seth stood up too. "Rea...."

"No. Don't, Rea, me. You didn't have to go with me to my brother's house. I am not expecting to get married or have kids. We could've had sex, and you could've left last night."

Seth reached out to hold her hand. "We weren't done until this morning."

Reagan took her hand back as she cut her eyes at him. "You know what I meant. You could've left afterward. I'm not the kind of woman that gets her feelings hurt."

Seth again tried to reach for her, but she took a step back. He held up his hands in surrender and then put them behind his back as he stepped closer toward her. "Rea, I didn't stay for breakfast or go with you today out of obligation. I wanted to be there. You don't understand."

"I think I do. You haven't said hardly anything to me since we left Ryan's, and you look like someone stole your puppy. I'm not all shiny and new like when we first met. I have figured a lot of things out about myself over these last few years, Seth. I don't like to play games. I need honesty. I am not the kind of woman who wants to guess what you want or feel. I need you to be direct."

Seth nodded. "Babe, I'm trying to be direct, but you keep interrupting me."

Reagan bit her bottom lip. She'd interrupted him before he could break her heart, but she would give him ten seconds to say what he needed to say. Then she was going to kick him out.

Seth reached over and tucked an errant strand of her hair behind her ear as she stared at him. "I love being with you, Rea. You are funny, brilliant, and sexy as hell. That's why I can't keep my hands off you. But--" Seth paused to make sure she wasn't going to interject again. "But I need to know more about you. You always ask me questions about my work, college, life growing up, and family. You have met my parents and seen my baby pictures. You know everything about me. I want to be able to say the same thing about you."

Reagan's eyes burned. She took a deep breath and ignored the emotion. "Both my parents are dead. I don't even know if they had baby pictures of me. You know that. We talked about that before. I mean, all the important stuff."

Seth couldn't stand the space between them. He reached over and pulled her into his arms and held her tightly against his chest. She fit perfectly under his chin.

"Rea, you told me they were divorced and how they each passed away within a year of each other. But you've never told me how it happened, what you did afterward, or how you coped with any of it. I want to know your whole story. I want to know things your friends don't know about you."

Reagan knew she was in trouble because he didn't even know

she didn't have friends. At least not anyone but Amber. She'd always been what she called a surface friend with people in school and at work, meaning she never got into deep conversations with others or offered up real personal information about herself. So it had never been a big deal to her until that moment. Seth seemed hung up on her life story, and she didn't want to talk about all those difficult years. And he still looked like someone had stolen his puppy, so she was pretty sure she wasn't going to get out of it.

She wriggled free so that she could drink the rest of her whiskey, and then she walked over to the couch with her chenille blanket. Seth sat next to her and pulled her legs into his lap, carefully tucking the blanket underneath them.

He looked at her expectantly, and all she wanted to do was snuggle up and forget most of her childhood had ever happened.

She thought about how wonderful Seth's family was and how he'd grown up in a two-story traditional home with everything, including a dog. She had never shared the information with him because she didn't want him to look at her differently. She was from the wrong side of town and worked hard to move herself and her brother away from that environment.

She remembered one of the last conversations she'd had with her mother before she died. It was more of a fight after she'd found out that Reagan was gambling to win money to help pay for college. Her mother didn't approve and, in her afternoon alcoholic state, yelled that she could take the girl out of the trailer park, but she couldn't take the trailer park out of the girl. She'd never lived in a trailer park, just poor neighborhoods, but she still felt like that girl sometimes, and no amount of designer clothes, shoes, or penthouse finery would change that for her.

She swallowed hard and looked over at Seth, who was staring at her and patiently still waiting.

Chapter Seven

SETH USUALLY MADE SITUATIONS like that easier for Reagan, but he knew she would take it if he gave her an easy out. He could suddenly see how they could've discussed everything years ago if he'd asked and then waited for the complicated answers. But it was hard to see her struggle. She was usually the calmest person in the room during stressful situations, which was why she annihilated everyone at poker and was great as an attorney. She'd perfected her serene expression and remained even-tempered under challenging circumstances.

As he watched her, she wasn't calm and collected.

Seth ran his warm hands under the blanket across her warm legs, and Reagan responded by sitting up and tucking her legs under her as she pulled the blanket up to her chest. He wanted to hold her, but she was used to handling difficult situations alone. She wouldn't open up if he tried even to hold her hand. He hoped he would understand why after they talked.

"My parents fought a lot. It didn't leave room for anything else like parenting. So, I taught myself to read when I was three, and by the time I started school, I was an honest-to-goodness bookworm. I would read all the time, and the librarian would let me check out more books than the other kids because I was reading a book a day. I would check out stuff to read to Ryan, and then once he was asleep, I'd hide out with my books."

She avoided looking at Seth and looked past him as she continued. "They fought about everything. Money was the worst. We barely had enough for bread and peanut butter sometimes. There weren't any family moments like trips to the park or zoo. I would walk Ryan to the park sometimes, but we had to be careful, so no one asked if we were alone. People could be so nosy, and they would call the cops if they thought we were unsupervised. At the time, I would get mad if they questioned me because I took care of Ryan all the time.

"Our mother wasn't a cook either, so see, I'm not the only one. She would make hamburger helper or box macaroni for us sometimes. Mostly we had peanut butter sandwiches. Birthdays and holidays were never a big deal. We didn't have any grandparents or other family except for Uncle Trey, and he was my dad's brother. He would come over on Christmas Day and always bring gifts for us. He would also cook a ham, and my mom would make box macaroni and cheese to go with it."

"Did they ever get along?" he asked.

"Not in my lifetime."

"You've never been to the zoo or aquarium?"

Reagan smiled. "I went to the zoo and the aquarium on a field trip with my school. Ryan and I both did. I liked both places."

"You've only been to the zoo once in your life?"

Reagan looked confused at his question. "Yes, and the aquarium."

She didn't understand why that was strange to him, but she also didn't ask. If he thought that was weird, she guessed it must have been.

Seth thought about how often his mother took him to the zoo, aquarium, and museums. She paid for family memberships every year so they could go anytime they wanted. Most of his neighborhood friends did too. Unfortunately, Reagan was from a different neighborhood.

Seth sat quietly, and she continued. "The best times for us were always the summers when we got to stay with Uncle Trey at his lake house in Maisonville. When I was twelve, I was able to talk my parents into letting us visit him. Uncle Trey loved the idea. After that first time, he would come to get us whenever we were out of school. He taught us how to cook hotdogs and marshmallows over a campfire. He also went bike riding with us and took all the kids he could pile into his truck to the old drive-in movie theater."

"I'm surprised your mom would let you go for the whole summer." Seth remembered how hard it was to talk his parents into letting him go away to summer camp for two weeks.

"Mom and Dad worked odd jobs and hours when they worked. They didn't want to deal with each other when they were off, much less with us. By that time, they were separated and fought over who would take care of us. We mostly stayed at mom's house, but they would fight over the days we were out of school. Finally, I explained how it made sense for them to let us go to Uncle Trey's, and so they did it. I'd taken over getting Ryan up for school in time to catch the bus years earlier. It didn't take long for me to figure out that the less they had to do for us, the easier our lives would be. I would sneak granola bars out for breakfast or make peanut butter and jelly sandwiches for us. We both probably had a thousand peanut butter and jellies in our childhood. I didn't cook back then either." Reagan smiled, making light of her situation.

"No one showed you how, Rea. You were too young to have to take care of your younger brother."

"Mom wasn't very maternal. Besides, I loved Ryan the minute he was born. It was what I think I was born to do. I don't think he would've made it without me." She probably wouldn't have made it without him either.

"What about your dad?"

"He worked a little and did drugs a lot. He didn't talk to me very much. I would watch him when Uncle Trey came around because he would laugh and talk. It was funny to see them together. It was the only time I ever saw my dad happy. They loved each other, and Uncle Trey was a character. He could make anyone laugh."

Reagan smiled at Seth. "Uncle Trey's the one that taught me to play poker."

"I wish he were still around, so I could not thank him for that one," Seth said.

"Don't feel bad that you can't beat me. None of the guys in college could either. That's how I mostly paid for school," she said, biting her bottom lip. "I'm not really proud of that, but I'm also not as ashamed as I probably should be."

"You did what you thought was right to pay for school," Seth said.

Reagan rolled her eyes. "I knew poker games in the dorm basement weren't right, Seth. When I found out about the games, I managed to get myself invited and then flirted my way into getting them to let me play. No one took me seriously, and I made a thousand dollars that first time. Before long, I was the one organizing the whole thing. I needed more of the wealthier kids to play so I could put away more cash. Once I got them hooked on it, then I managed weekend tournaments several times a semester."

Seth locked eyes with Reagan and then asked, "Why didn't you ever tell me that story before, Rea?"

"Because your family is like a Hallmark Channel movie, including the dog. They support you in every way. That's pretty intimidating, Seth. You were also this all-American athlete and earned a full scholarship to college even though your family could have paid for it. I didn't have those options."

"That's funny, Reagan. You were intimidated by my family and me? You're about to make partner at the best law firm in town. You're independent. You have a nicer house than me. Make that two houses. And you've always made more money than me. Want to talk about intimidating?"

Reagan rolled her eyes and smirked at his comment. "It's

sweet of you to say that, but on the inside, I'll always be the girl that couldn't afford a new dress."

Seth reached over to pull Reagan's hand into his. "I wish you could see yourself the way I do. Besides, I don't think I've ever seen you in the same dress twice."

"I work hard not to be an outfit repeater."

"That's a thing?"

"It is for me."

Seth had never thought about why she dressed so well, and it made him a little sad. But he was glad to know about her college poker games and the real motivation behind her incredible skill. "I've always thought you were resourceful, Rea. I guess I didn't realize how far back that trait began for you."

She nodded, and without any further prompting from him, she added details. "My earliest memories were of my parents arguing. Then, when I was seven and Ryan was four, they seriously started going at it. It scared Ryan a lot, so I would make a tent over our bed and read books to him until he fell asleep. Then, as time went on, my dad would leave for a week or two after they had a big fight, and mom wouldn't get out of bed. So I'd make us sandwiches for breakfast, lunch, or dinner.

"I got us up and dressed for school every day, and then when I went into the sixth grade and moved schools, I'd still sit outside with Ryan to wait for his bus with him. His bus came before mine, so it was okay. When Uncle Trey found out, he tried to come around more. My parents got mad and told him to mind his own business, so we went a couple of years without seeing him. Those were the worst of times. When I was in middle school, my parents finally split for good. It was easier then to manipulate them. We didn't see dad as much, and our mom was pretty checked out most of the time. It was tough, but once we got to spend the summers with Uncle Trey, things got a lot better."

Seth sat there keeping his professional stature. He was a great therapist, but her background was difficult, even for him. He didn't want to think of Reagan as a child taking care of herself and her little brother. He'd never had a clue that she scraped and fought her way to success and hadn't been given a single thing she didn't earn.

He had his Ph.D. and MD, yet he hadn't figured out that she was closed off because of childhood trauma? Of course, Reagan hid it with everything she had, but he still felt like he should have picked up on it. He'd thought she hadn't had enough affection, but he had no idea how much worse it was for her.

He focused on the things he did know. Reagan and Ryan were close, and both their parents and only other relative, Uncle Trey, were all gone. "You were in college when your father passed away? How did he die?"

"Yes. It was my sophomore year in college. He had a heart attack." Then, anticipating his next question, she added, "Our mom died ten months later, right after Ryan graduated from high school. He didn't like school and had already told me he was going into the military once he'd graduated. I'm not sure if he told her or not. She smoked like a chimney and always had a bad cough. Ryan went into her room to check on her, and she looked like she was sleeping, but she wasn't. She had passed away sometime during the night. They did an autopsy and found that her lungs were covered in cancer."

"I'm sorry, Rea. I know that had to be hard on you and Ryan."

"It was weird knowing I'd never see them again, but for some reason, I knew they wouldn't live a long time. They both were such unhappy people that it felt like they were dying a little bit inside every day. I don't know what we would've done without Uncle Trey. He paid for both of their funerals. Honestly, he was more of a parent to us than either of them. He died a year after I graduated from law school. It was the hardest thing. Ryan was out of the country, and I had to make all the arrangements myself. Ryan was there for the actual service, though. Uncle Trey had a ton of friends, and they all wanted to meet up at his house after the funeral. I've never seen anything like it."

Seth pulled Reagan into his lap and held her tightly. As she leaned into him, it wasn't clear which one of them needed the hug more. But he was sure that Reagan was the love of his life. Leaving everything he'd built in Tennessee so he could be with her seemed right. Now he wasn't sure if he was worthy.

How could he have dated her for so long and not known her? Reagan wasn't loved enough, yet she could love more fiercely than anyone he'd ever met. She found the courage as a young child to take care of her little brother. Reagan was resourceful enough to feed Ryan and watch over him when someone should have been taking care of her. How could she ever be intimidated by Seth's family or his status in life? She was so much more.

"I can't breathe, Seth," she said, half laughing. Seth was kissing her all over her face. Somehow, he'd maneuvered her below him, and he was all over her. When he lifted his head to look at her, he saw tears in her eyes. He'd loved her for years and yet never realized how tender-hearted she could be when no one was looking.

He felt like he was seeing her for the first time.

Chapter Eight

SETH STAYED AGAIN SATURDAY night, but Reagan had to go into the office on Sunday. He wasn't happy about it, but she knew how to comfort him. They made plans to have dinner later, and he agreed to let her get dressed for the day so she could go to work.

She couldn't stop thinking about the last 36 hours she'd spent with Seth. She knew she needed to work, but she also needed to be alone to think about what it all meant.

As she unlocked the glass doors in the reception area, Reagan was surprised to hear voices. She was usually the only one that came in on Sundays. However, when she made her way around the lobby and receptionist desk, she saw her least favorite partner, Mathew Nunan, rearing back in his chair, laughing with the mayor and his intern who was in there with them. She couldn't explain it, but she suddenly felt like she wasn't supposed to be there. She quietly tried to walk down the hallway to her own office, but Mayor Regalia saw her and immediately walked out to greet her.

"Reagan, I didn't expect to see you. Shouldn't you be home being pampered?"

"Apparently, things are a lot different at my home than at yours, Mayor."

All the men laughed at the comeback that she knew wasn't that funny. *Had she caught them doing something?*

Mayor Regalia waved at the other two men as he put his hand on the small of Reagan's back to walk with her down the hallway to her office. She could have shrugged him off, but she had learned that sometimes it was easier to ignore overly flirtatious behavior.

"I've been meaning to call you and ask you out for dinner, Reagan," he said while he inappropriately ran his hand up and down her lower back.

Reagan was surprised at his forward behavior and then wondered if she just hadn't noticed it in the past. Her radar was up since she'd had such incredible sex with Seth that weekend. Of course, the mayor was charming, and he always seemed to have a soft spot for her, but he dated a lot of prominent women in town. She didn't fit his type. His wife had passed away two years ago, and late last year, he was photographed at dinner with beautiful single women all the time, but he'd never had as much as a cup of coffee with Reagan.

"Thank you for asking me, Mayor, but—."

"Call me Alexavier, Reagan," he said, smiling that practiced grin at her.

"Thanks for thinking of me, Alexavier, but I don't go out much."

The mayor leaned in and whispered, "You're picky. I like that about you."

"No, I mean yes, I am picky, but that's not it. I'm dedicated to my work, and I don't have a lot of extra time to go out."

"You're an amazing and beautiful woman, Reagan, and you don't have to be alone. In fact, I'm having a party in a few weeks on a friend's houseboat and only inviting a few people. Amber is coming, and your partner Mathew is going to be there. I'll make sure you get an invitation."

"You don't have to do that, Mayor— Alexavier."

Alexavier wrapped both his warm, strong hands around one of her hands and leaned in even closer. "I'm not going to take no for an answer."

He winked at her and headed for the door. Before he made it into the hallway, he grinned, showing his perfect politician smile. "I'll see you soon, Reagan."

When he turned around, she shivered and wiped her hand on her leg. Was he always that cheesy? Reagan shook her head and picked up the stack of papers she had in her locked drawer. It was going to take some doing to get her work finished after all the distractions she'd had that weekend, and so she began to proofread.

It was already dark and 7:00 pm when Reagan's phone rang. Seth had sent her several texts, but she hadn't looked at her phone until his call. "I'm sorry, Seth. I've had my head down all afternoon and didn't realize the time."

"It's getting late, Rea. I was worried."

Reagan wished she hadn't promised him dinner. Unfortunately, she didn't have the time, and she would have to break plans with him.

"Honestly, I had my notifications turned off. I have a ton of work to finish by tomorrow morning, and I'm only halfway through it."

"Would you like me to bring you something?"

"That's sweet, Seth, but could I get a raincheck and have dinner with you tomorrow?"

"You really have a lot of work?"

"Yes. When I got up here today, Alexavier was here with one of the partners. It took me a little while to get my head focused." She didn't want to admit that she'd been researching the mayor through the social pages. He'd never paid so much attention to her before, which made her curious. Why was he suddenly talking to her?

Seth didn't like Mayor Regalia. He'd met him the same night that he met Reagan before winning the first election, and Seth thought the man was presumptuous. Seth wasn't confusing the meaning of arrogance either. He smiled, thinking about Reagan's comment. But he did remember how the then-candidate for mayor was very interested in Reagan and if Seth hadn't been there, he was certain Regalia would have dominated her time, and the bastard was married.

Seth had mentioned something about him to her back then, but she absolutely couldn't see it. Seth had seen on the news that the mayor's wife passed away of cancer during his last term. Then noticed various pictures of Regalia and online articles of him with single beautiful women. He was relieved that Reagan was never in a picture with him, but he had a feeling it wasn't because Regalia had given up. He simply hadn't made the rounds back to her yet. Seth tried to remain calm, but it would've helped if she wouldn't refer to him by his first name. "I'm a little surprised the mayor was hanging out in your office on a Sunday."

"I don't think he was hanging out, as you say it. He was discussing something with Mathew Nunan. I'm pretty sure I interrupted them. Anyway, I got started later than I'd planned, and I can't start my week off by being behind on paperwork." She knew she was over-explaining, but she needed Seth to understand.

Seth took a deep breath as he sat down on the couch in his apartment. He needed to show Reagan understanding and let her get her work done, but she explained too much, making him suspicious. Of course, Seth wanted to storm up to her office to verify she was alone, but he had no reason to act like a Neanderthal. She would set him straight if he did and most likely not let him see her the next day either. Besides, Reagan didn't seem to like the mayor much, and by her own account, she hadn't dated in the last few years. He needed to check his jealousy at the door or at least on the phone with her.

"Rea, promise me you won't work too late?"

Reagan wasn't used to being worried about, and she smiled over his words. "I promise, Seth. See you tomorrow?"

"Tomorrow, Rea," he said, trying not to think too hard about her and the mayor.

Reagan said goodnight to Seth but had difficulty concentrating on her work after he hung up. She was hungry, but more than anything, she'd wanted to spend more time with him. Two nights and she was already hooked on not sleeping alone.

She scolded herself for being so weak and then turned on her desk lamp to refocus herself with the added light. Ten minutes into proofreading, she heard loud knocking on the front receptionist door. Had Seth decided to surprise her with dinner, after all? Reagan was sure she wouldn't get any work done as she went to unlock the door. But she was thrilled that he hadn't listened to her.

Reagan hurried around the receptionist's desk area and was stopped in her tracks when she saw it wasn't Seth, but instead standing at the door was Mayor Alexavier Regalia.

Chapter Nine

REAGAN SMILED AT THE MAYOR as he held up a bag of what she assumed was takeout food. There was no way to tactfully leave him out there even though she knew inviting him in wasn't the best idea.

"Hey there, beautiful lady. I was picking up some dinner and thought about how you were still up here alone. I couldn't eat knowing that you probably were skipping dinner to work."

Alexavier strutted into the office while Reagan hesitated with the door open. Unfortunately, he didn't turn around to notice, so she closed the door and locked it behind her.

"You didn't have to do that, Alexavier. I'll be done soon."

"I know I didn't have to, but I wanted to do it. I should have taken you to dinner before now."

Reagan knew the only way to handle a man like Alexavier Regalia was by being direct. She twisted her hair up into a messy bun and stuck the pen she'd been using into her hair to hold it up. Then she looked directly at him to say, "Alexavier, your social calendar has been full for the last year, and I couldn't in good conscience get in the way of your love life."

"So, you've been paying attention to me," he said with a bigger grin on his face.

Reagan rolled her eyes and had a seat at her desk as he sat down in front of her. He glanced down at her paperwork, and she discreetly removed it so it wouldn't compromise her client's confidentiality. He was the mayor, but her football client was even more famous.

Alexavier smiled understandingly at her actions. "Tell me why again, you don't work for me?"

Reagan locked her paperwork up inside her cabinet and then gave him her full attention.

"I'm a family law attorney, and I love what I do. I would never enjoy being a municipal attorney. Besides, I love this city and get pretty fired up over the politics that rule it. And if I'm honest, I disagree with the city council regularly."

"Then we would get along a lot more than you think," Alexavier laughed.

"Well, you have one of the very best attorneys I've ever met already working for you."

"Yes, Amber is great."

"We went to law school together. She's brilliant. Don't you think?

"Yes. I've heard Amber is doing a great job for us." Alexavier didn't have much to say about Amber and quickly changed the subject. "If I can't talk you into working for me, then maybe some steamed wontons and Kung pow chicken will help us become friends?"

Alexavier pulled the Chinese to-go boxes out of the paper bag as Reagan watched. Then, she decided she would never get rid of him if she didn't eat. So, Reagan made room for their food on her desk. Next, she offered him a water bottle, and he accepted as he handed her some chopsticks.

Dinner took thirty minutes, and the conversation was easy between them. First, he explained how he practiced law for ten years before going into politics. Then how much he loved being mayor and finally being able to help the city he grew up in to become a better place to live. Next, Reagan told him how much she enjoyed her work at the firm and how one of her law professors had mentored her and helped guide her to the job.

Alexavier helped clear the trash away when they finished eating and thanked her for indulging him by accepting dinner. He was a perfect gentleman, and Reagan felt guilty for thinking the worst when he'd shown back up at her office.

She walked him to the door, thanked him for dinner, and he gave her a quick wave as he left for the elevator. She watched his athletic frame walk away until he was out of sight. He was a very handsome man.

Reagan shook her head and then went back to work. Eating dinner gave her the energy she needed to finish by 10:30. It was a decent hour when she crawled into her bed after showering and smiled that for the first time in years, she had the option to talk to Seth before she fell asleep.

"Don't tell me you're actually home already, Rea?" he knew she was because she was one of the only people he knew that still had a landline at her house, which showed up on his caller ID.

"I'm at home and in bed too."

"Want me to come over?" Seth offered.

His deep voice made her laugh. "I do wish you were here, but I need some sleep. You know how terrible I am when I don't get enough shut-eye."

Seth knew she didn't sleep much. "You're the only adult I know that can work eighty hours a week and still manage to get enough sleep at night."

"Time management is my middle name." Reagan teased. She rarely slept more than four hours at night, even as a kid.

Seth's gravely chuckle made her stomach do flips. If she couldn't have him in her bed, then at least she could talk to him as much as she wanted.

"What did you do tonight, Seth?"

"I ate a can of soup and a grilled cheese sandwich while I watched a couple of episodes of NOVA that I had on the DVR. Did you get your work done?"

"Yes, all of it," she said, leaving out the part where the mayor brought her dinner. Of course, It wasn't technically a lie since he didn't ask her about dinner. *Right?*

They talked for twenty minutes more before getting off the phone. Reagan was content as she thought about Seth until she drifted off to sleep.

The following day Reagan got into the office early, but when she went to make herself a cup of coffee, the machine wouldn't work. She took it apart and couldn't tell what was wrong but could see that water wasn't making its way into the reservoir. So she grabbed her purse and headed to the kiosk downstairs because she couldn't start her day without a steaming cup of caffeine.

She locked the office door behind her as she thought about Seth. Was he truly back in her life that easily? She could get used to having him a phone call away even if she never got to sleep again.

In the elevator, Reagan's phone rang once and then stopped. She knew the damn box was made of steel but also guessed it was half led since she never had a good enough signal inside it. As the doors opened, she had a message from Amber.

At first, it sounded like Amber accidentally dialed her during a meeting, but when she listened to it again, it seemed more like a party was going on in the background, and two of the city council members were there. Reagan knew it was them because one of them, Teresa McDonald, had a high-pitched voice and a lisp that was distinct from anyone else Reagan had ever met. McDonald loved to talk, and every time there was a camera around, she made sure she was in front of it. The other council member, Bruce Cannon, also loved the sound of his own voice, but he couldn't talk without sounding like a backwoods preacher. Reagan had more than one backwoods preacher as clients, so she considered herself an expert with the comparison. The call went on for almost five minutes, and then she could hear Amber walking away and then opening a door into a quiet area before she whispered into the phone, "I can't talk now but save this message." Then Amber's phone disconnected the call.

Reagan immediately listened to it again. They discussed the new affordable health care facility that was passed by the council. The South Louisiana Community Health Care Facility was another campaign promise of Alexavier's during his re-election campaign. He had explained how he only truly understood what people went through with their medical bills because of his wife's terminal cancer. He guaranteed to find more affordable options for the city. The SLCHC Facility was supposed to be the way to fulfill the needs of the area.

Reagan had been impressed with how steadfast Alexavier proved to be with getting things done for the city. He'd grown up in Mid-City, and his family had lived there for generations. She didn't, however, understand the importance of Amber's message.

It sounded like the city council members were happy with the decision, and she knew the mayor had liked the facility as one of the choices, so wasn't that a win for everyone? It certainly was rare for the mayor and city council to agree so much, and it looked like the city was going to benefit the most from the camaraderie.

Reagan saved the message on her phone and decided to call Amber when she got back up to her office with her cup of Joe.

At the front of the line were Mathew Nunan and the mayor. *Two days in a row?* She'd never noticed them being so friendly before, but she figured she didn't pay much attention to Mathew anyway. Alexavier walked directly over to her and offered her a large coffee with cream and sugar. It was precisely the way she liked it.

"Good morning, Reagan. Lovely as ever," he said as he handed her the cup.

She was wearing her black pinstripe skirt and a champagne-colored silk blouse and double-checked the lid to ensure she didn't spill. "Good morning. Thanks for the coffee."

"You're welcome. Anytime," Alexavier said, smiling genuinely at her, unlike the politician grin he gave most of the time.

Could she have been wrong about him?

"Alexavier, I was wondering about that Community Health Care Place that you were trying to get for the city?"

"The South Louisiana Community Health Care Facility?"

"Yes. I remember you talking about them during your re-election campaign."

Alexavier looked at Mathew and then back at Reagan. "I'm trying to get a more affordable program, and they might be a good fit. But there are also a few other good options too. It's up to the city council now."

He held his coffee cup up like he was going to make a toast. "Here's hoping we get a solution," he said and then took a drink.

Reagan drank from her cup and grinned when Mathew quickly tried to do the same but dribbled a little on his chin and tie.

As they headed to the elevators, Reagan leaned in to whisper to Alexavier. "I think that's a great idea for the community, Alexavier. Thanks for all your hard work."

Alexavier couldn't stop smiling at her after the compliment, and he made small talk as he and Mathew headed back to the office with her. The mayor also made sure he held the elevator doors for her to walk through first and jumped ahead so that he could open the office door for her too. He again was a perfect gentleman, and Reagan wondered if she had imagined the smarmy behavior before. After all, he'd only ever acted considerate all the other times she'd ever seen him. And Amber would've let her know, and him, if he was chauvinistic or misogynistic around her. Reagan felt a little judgy over questioning his behavior. He was a good man.

Reagan smiled at Alexavier as he talked, and she almost walked right by Seth, who was sitting in her main office lobby. He had two cups of coffee and scones in his hands as she awkwardly said hello.

Seth kept a smile on his face, but she could see his jaw tense as he greeted her and shook the mayor's hand. She introduced Seth as her friend to Alexavier. Both men looked surprised to meet each other, and their handshake was a little too firm and even a bit too long.

Alexavier said goodbye as he walked down the hallway with Mathew, and Reagan walked with Seth into her private office. She closed the door behind them and went around her desk to have a seat before she looked into his eyes. He was stealthily quiet.

"Don't look at me that way, Seth Young," she said, pulling her long hair over to one shoulder.

"I guess I didn't realize we were only friends."

"You caught me off guard. I didn't expect to see you. What was I supposed to say?"

"At the very least, I figured I was your boyfriend."

Reagan pushed the coffee away and sat forward in her chair. "I wasn't sure if we were announcing that after one weekend."

"My mistake, Rea," he said as he took the lid off his coffee and drank half of it.

Reagan couldn't believe so much could happen in one morning, and it was barely 8:00.

She walked around her desk and sat in the chair next to Seth as she reached out to hold his hand. She rarely showed affection in public, and he figured it was part of her childhood baggage. He was surprised to have her sitting so close.

"Don't be mad at me, Seth. Nothing is going on between Mayor Regalia and me. He's a professional acquaintance. That's all."

Seth had missed her last night and talking to her before he went to bed was torture since he couldn't touch her. He got to her office as quickly as he could, but she strangely wasn't there. He couldn't believe he beat her into the office. She worked all the time. Then it looked like she and the mayor were together, walking in with identical coffee cups and chatting happily with each other. He didn't like the way it looked. He knew he was acting ridiculous, but he had a gut feeling about Regalia that was different from everyone else in the city. He didn't like the guy, and he certainly didn't like the way he looked at Reagan.

He kissed Reagan on the lips, and when there was a light knock on her door, he laughed at how fast she leaped into a standing position.

Nancy, her secretary, walked in, and behind her was Mathew Nunan and the mayor.

Seth clenched his teeth. Couldn't he get a break? Or at least ten minutes alone with his girl?

Chapter Ten

NANCY WALKED PARTIALLY INTO the office, grinning at Seth. Reagan couldn't help but notice the sparkle in her secretary's eyes. The woman was such a flirt. "Sorry to interrupt you," she said, but before she could say anything else, Alexavier and Mathew took over.

Mathew held his hand out to Seth. "Hi, I'm Mathew Nunan. I apologize for the intrusion, but I think we went to high school together."

Seth stood up and shook Mathew's hand. "Seth Young. I didn't grow up here. I'm from Diamond Head, Mississippi."

"St. Stanislaus?" Mathew asked.

Seth stared at Mathew. "You too?"

"I was only there for two years. My sophomore and junior years '98 to 2000, then my folks and I moved to New Orleans," Mathew said.

"Yeah, man. I was there. You must've been a year ahead of me."

"I knew it when you walked by. You were on the sailing team. Everyone called you Shark because you were a beast out on the water."

Seth smiled as he scrubbed his jaw, and Reagan watched as he relaxed a bit. "I haven't thought about that in years. I don't go out on my sailboat much anymore. I go fishing more than anything else."

Alexavier was strangely quiet. When Reagan looked over at him, he was smiling at her. She couldn't explain why, but the entire interruption seemed off to her. Since when did Mathew care if he saw someone he went to high school with for two years in Mississippi? Reagan didn't even know where he went to college. Mathew had never been that pleasant. He was a few years older than her and a partner in the firm. Didn't he have work to do? Surely, the mayor had a full schedule. She absolutely did, and her first appointment was going to arrive any minute.

It was time for her to shut the reunion down. "I'm sorry, everyone. I have a client coming in soon. As if on cue, Nancy came in to let her know that her 8:30 was on his way up.

Everyone piled out into Nancy's waiting area, including Seth. He gave Reagan a quick wave and said goodbye to Mathew and Alexavier. Reagan closed her door and went to have a seat behind her desk.

She barely had time to consider how weird the whole meet and greet was because her appointment was there. But when she got the chance, the first thing she was going to do was call Amber.

It was mid-afternoon before Reagan had a break. She flopped back down in her office chair and asked Nancy to bring her a diet coke. She needed the hard stuff, and since whiskey was a bad idea during the day and coffee wasn't doing the trick, she used her backup.

She sat there with her cold drink and contemplated how strange her day had been from the very beginning. Days like that were why Mondays had such a bad reputation. She'd tried to call Amber twice, and both times her phone went to voicemail. She checked her messages and email, and she was surprised not to have anything from Seth.

She hoped his day was turning out better than hers, and that's when she heard Nancy raise her voice. "You can't go in there!" she yelled.

Reagan looked up in time to see a massive muscled guy with a bald head and long beard crash through her solid wooden door. She was going to stand up, but as he stepped up to her desk, she thought it was better to stay seated.

He pushed Reagan's laptop and papers off her desk while Nancy called building security. "I have had about enough of you," he yelled, his baritone voice carrying throughout the entire office. "Becky won't let me see the kids and filed a restraining order against me. I can't even walk on the sidewalk in front of my own damn house without being arrested."

Terrence, head partner and Reagan's mentor ran into her office behind the large hulking man. He had a golf club in his hand and tried to get between him and Reagan. The hulk wasn't going to have it.

"I got no beef with you, brother," he said. "Get out of here, so I don't have to hurt ya. Me and her got some things to work out." He backed Terrence out of the room and shut the door, locking it.

Reagan was suddenly very alone, but still, she sat there behind her large desk. It was usually her security blanket, but she knew it wasn't going to keep the man out if he wanted to get to her. Still, she didn't move and didn't say a word.

He yelled and threw one of her winged back chairs into the wall. "I didn't want any of this. I loved my family. She came and talked to you, and now she won't talk to me. You put all this into her head. She had me arrested in front of the kids," he said, and then he called Reagan a couple of choice names, and then he threw her other chair. When he ran out of things to throw, he lunged toward her. That's when six of New Orleans' finest police officers rushed through the door and overpowered him.

It was like watching Godzilla go down. He hit the floor so hard it vibrated the room. Still, he kept threatening her. "You better remember this face. When I get out, I'm coming for you.

When you least expect it, when you're all alone and walking to your car, you better know, I'm going to get you!"

He continued yelling as they carted him, literally all six policemen carried him out.

Everyone in her office and everyone on the entire floor of her building was standing out in the hallway watching the crazed man being dragged away.

Reagan was frozen in place.

Terrence knelt in front of Reagan. "Reagan. You're okay. He's gone," Terrence said and held her cold hands in his. "Someone get me a blanket or a coat!" he yelled. "Reagan? It's okay. Everything is going to be okay," he kept saying, trying to get her to speak to him.

He wrapped a long black coat around her and kept trying to warm her hands. She sat there stoically, but she couldn't speak.

A few minutes later, Nancy brought Reagan a cup of hot tea, and a police Sergeant came into the room with two of the police officers that removed the hulking man.

"Did he hurt you, ma'am? Do you need an ambulance?" he asked.

Reagan shook her head. The policeman looked at Terrence. "Did he hurt her?"

Worry filled his eyes as Terrence looked Reagan over. She finally looked back at him. "I-I'm okay, Terrence. He became unraveled, and I didn't know what to say or do."

Terrence patted her hands and then stood up. "Maybe we can do this later?" he asked the policemen.

They all looked directly at Reagan.

She picked up the teacup, but her hands slightly trembled, and she didn't want anyone to see it. She sat it back down, spilling a bit of it onto her desk. "It's okay. I can talk."

She explained everything that happened from the time she heard Nancy yell at him until the police officers came into the room and stopped him. They wrote everything down.

As she spoke, her professionalism took over, and she was able to discuss it as if it happened to someone else and she was a key witness. She didn't leave anything out. "The funny thing, I mean if there is a funny thing in this situation, I don't even know who he is or his wife."

The policeman said, "Robert Salinas."

Nancy spoke up. "You met his wife a few months ago. Becky Salinas."

Reagan shook her head. "Becky Salinas paid for a consultation, but that was it. She didn't retain me for any services. She was too scared to file for divorce."

The Sergeant took all of Reagan's information, and after thirty minutes of interviewing and taking pictures of all the damage, they left.

Terrence had his assistant take notes simultaneously, and once the police officers left, they also took pictures of all the damage in the office. Robert Salinas destroyed everything but Reagan's desk and desk chair.

Reagan stood up for the first time since the incident and held onto the desk until she had her balance. Terrence helped her put on the oversized long black raincoat, and she picked up her phone and purse, leaving her briefcase and everything else on the floor.

"We'll get everything cleaned up for you, Reagan. So don't you worry," he said. "And we're going to talk about some better security too."

Reagan hugged him. "Thanks, Terrence. I'm going to go home now."

"Let me have someone take you," he said.

She reached out and held his hand. "I'm fine. I'm going straight home. I don't want to leave my car here."

"You shouldn't be alone right now, Reagan."

Reagan hugged him again. He was such a sweet man. "I'm tougher than I look," she said and then smiled at her remark.

Terrence walked her out to the garage and her car. He was sick over what had happened and considered how much worse it could have been. When he got back up to the office, Nancy met him in the hallway.

"Nancy, you should go home too," he said.

"Thanks. I have a couple of things to do, and then I'll take off," Nancy replied. She was terrified over what happened to Reagan and felt helpless knowing the man was locked in the room with her and raging uncontrollably. She also knew Reagan would go home, but she wouldn't ask for help. Nancy knew because she'd been strong-willed like Reagan her entire life too. Rarely asked for help, even when she needed it. Their similarities were the reason they worked so well together. When Nancy needed a job, Reagan was the only person that considered hiring her. She'd never questioned her age or ability after not working for ten years. Nancy looked after Reagan even though she didn't know it, and that's why she made two phone calls on her boss' behalf before she left their devastated office for the day.

She hoped Reagan would understand it wasn't the time for her to be alone.

Chapter Eleven

REAGAN SLID DOWN THE DOOR inside her apartment with her keys still in her hand and hugging her purse. She didn't remember the drive home or unlocking the door, but once inside, she couldn't stop shaking. Tears fell down her cheeks, and it made her angry that she could hold it together during the near assault in her office, but as soon as she was alone in her home, she was paralyzed with fear.

How had it happened? She'd grown up in a violent home. She had been a family attorney for years and handled some of the most difficult people and situations. As a child, she'd learned how to avoid her parents and, as an adult, how to watch out for nutty clients or their exes. But she'd never ever been blindsided like that.

Robert Salinas was a scary man. She hoped his wife did file a restraining order on him. But it had been months since Reagan met her. So why the hell was he suddenly blaming her?

Reagan tried standing on her shaky legs and used the door to help steady her. Suddenly, there was an urgent knock at her door. Her pulse raced, and her mouth went dry.

"Reagan! It's me. Open up!" Seth said.

How did he know? She couldn't believe he was there. She

unlocked the door, and as soon as she opened it, he was inside with his arms around her.

Seth looked down and saw Reagan holding her keys and purse. *How long had she been there before he showed up?* He picked her up and carried her to the couch without a second thought. He sat down with her in his arms.

Seth didn't ask her any questions, just held her for the longest time.

Finally, Reagan managed to ask, "Who? Who told you?"

"Your secretary called me."

"Nancy?" Reagan couldn't believe it. How did she even know his number? "I'm glad you're here."

"I'm so glad you're okay, baby." Seth held her tighter.

There was another knock at Reagan's door, and then they heard a key opening the lock. Only one other person had a key besides Reagan, but her heart still felt like it was beating out of her chest.

"I'm here, Rea," Seth said, looking at her.

Ryan came flying through the door. "Are you okay, Reagan?" he asked, rushing over toward the couch. He knelt on the floor, so he was face to face with her.

"Who is the bastard that came after you? I can promise you he won't ever do it again."

Reagan knew her brother would protect her at any cost, and she loved him for it but also knew she couldn't let him. "He's a sick man, Ryan. They arrested him. I'm pretty sure he's going to be locked up in the psych ward after today."

"He was a client of yours?" Ryan asked.

"No. His wife. Well, she actually came in for a consultation. She didn't want to move forward at that time, and I didn't really know the situation. I thought she was afraid of him, but she also said she loved him, and I didn't think she would follow through with leaving him," Reagan said. "Boy, was I wrong."

Ryan kissed his sister on the forehead. "I think it's time we set up some outside cameras here at your place and your office. I could do it for you, but you really should hire a service so they can monitor it all. I should have thought of it sooner considering your profession."

Reagan shook her head as she pushed up and out of Seth's lap. "I appreciate all this attention, but I'm fine. And I'm not going to have cameras everywhere, so I don't have any privacy."

She walked over to her kitchen island and pulled the decanter of whiskey over to her. When she tried to pour some of it, she used both hands because she was still trembling.

Seth reached over to still her hands, and then he took the decanter and poured her drink. "Here, Reagan." He watched how her hand still shook as she sipped from the glass. He looked over at Ryan to see if he noticed, and it was apparent from his expression that he did.

"I'm fine, you two. Stop hovering. You're making me nervous," Reagan said.

They both smiled at her, but neither of them moved away. Reagan could feel her body relaxing slightly from the alcohol. "I'm going to take a shower," she said, and then she slipped out of the room.

Ryan poured himself and Seth glasses of whiskey, and then they both went into the living room.

"Hell of a day," Ryan said.

"Did she call you?" Seth asked.

"Who? Reagan?" Ryan asked and then laughed. "No. Her secretary called."

Seth nodded, thinking about the situation. "Why did you laugh?"

"Let me ask you a question. Has Reagan ever called you for help before? I mean, you dated for several years. If she had a flat tire or her battery was dead, did she call you?"

Seth stared at Ryan. He was right. After the last big hurricane, Reagan had two flat tires during rush hour and was stuck on the side of the road waiting for AAA to come and tow her. She texted him that she would be late but didn't tell him what had happened until it was over. He thought it was strange, but he hadn't put it all together until Ryan pointed it out. He'd thought she was efficient and responsible, but more than anything, he could see now that she was alone. She was an island and never reached out to those closest to her for even the smallest amount of help. Everyone needed someone, but not Reagan.

"Why?" he asked, staring at Ryan, who had to be the only person on the planet other than Reagan to know the answer.

"Sorry, man, that's a Reagan question that I can't help you with."

Seth's eyes turned to slits. "Can't?"

"Won't." Ryan corrected. "Reagan and I didn't have the same upbringing as most. We had to work a little harder to blend in, and Reagan was a master at making things look fine."

They heard her opening the bedroom door.

"And that's all I'm willing to say about that," Ryan said before his sister came into the room wearing silk pajamas and towel drying her hair.

"You sure you're okay, Reagan?" Ryan asked as he placed his empty glass in the sink.

She nodded.

"And you aren't going to give me the bastard's information?"

She shook her head. He understood. She wanted to tell him, but she wouldn't.

"Then I guess I'll go home and leave you to Seth." Ryan hugged his petite sister. She rarely went without her high-heeled shoes, and he'd forgotten how small she was. "I can't promise that I'm not going to put some cameras and extra security in for you, Rea."

"That's not necessary," Seth said, standing behind the brother and sister. They both looked over at him.

"I'll take care of it," Seth said, looking at Ryan.

Ryan shook Seth's hand and then kissed his sister goodbye, and as soon as Seth locked the door, he could feel her eyes on him.

"I don't need you to take care of anything, Seth. I'm a big girl."

Seth reached for Reagan's hand and then pulled her over to the couch, where he covered her up with her favorite blanket. "You need to rest. You've been through a traumatic situation, and it can wear down your immune system. You won't realize it at first, but the amount of adrenaline your body produces in moments like that can feel like a car accident the next day."

Reagan stared at him as he made her a glass of water and rummaged through her cabinet for some ibuprofen.

"I know you didn't eat lunch, and it's almost dinner time. What are you hungry for, Rea? I'll order dinner," he said as he handed her the medicine and the water.

Reagan took both pills and shrugged her shoulders. She didn't know what to say because no one had ever taken care of her before, not really. She was feeling speechless, like when the idiot busted through her office door.

Seth reached over and took the glass from her hands and sat it on the table. "I think the deli has that squash soup that you like. How about half a sandwich and that soup?" he asked, but it was rhetorical. He picked up his phone and placed the order before sitting with her.

"Would you like to read a book or watch some television?" he asked.

Reagan fidgeted with the blanket as she watched him fuss around her. "I'm not sure. I don't ever have free time, and I don't have a book to read, at least not for pleasure. TV, maybe? I don't know what's on, but the noise might be good."

Seth smiled at her. It was a big step for her to let him take charge. He picked up the remote, but the batteries were dead. So he went into the kitchen drawer for batteries and then went back to the couch to help her pick out a show. Forty-five minutes later, their food was delivered.

He got out a tray and delivered dinner to her on the couch.

He wouldn't let her get up to do anything, and she was embarrassed having him wait on her.

"I'm fine, Seth. Really," she said.

They watched HGTV for a while and then flipped over to a Hallmark movie. Seth laid down on the couch behind Reagan and pulled her tightly into his body after he tucked the blanket around her. She would never admit that she liked the sappy movies as she snuggled closer to him. He was sure his man card would be revoked, but he would watch them all day and night if it made her relax. It was a moment for them, and he knew it.

Reagan fell asleep a little after ten, and Seth carried her into the bedroom and put her to bed. She didn't stir all night, but he laid awake thinking about the close call she'd had and how to keep her safe.

What if Robert Salinas made bail? Seth had seen violent men pass their psychological reviews before and then make bail only to go directly after the person they were arrested for assaulting in the first place. The worst part about it was their second attempts were usually successful.

Seth didn't sleep, worrying that Salinas would go after her again.

Chapter Twelve

AMBER CALLED REAGAN FOR the third time and couldn't believe it was still going straight to her full voicemail. Reagan never forgot to charge her phone, and she never turned it off. If she were in court or meetings, she would silence it. After regular working hours, her not answering didn't make sense.

What was going on?

Amber couldn't wait to talk with Reagan and headed to her office. But, when she pulled into the downtown parking garage, she was shocked to see Reagan's parking spot empty.

Had Reagan left work before six o'clock?

Amber decided it must have been dinner with Seth that took Reagan away, and so she headed home resolved to talk with her friend first thing the next day.

At daybreak, Reagan sat up straight in her bed. She'd had a nightmare and had to look around the room to get her bearings.

Seth was sleeping next to her and didn't stir. She pulled her sheet up to her chest and watched him breathing. It calmed her, and she slipped out of bed to wash her face and locate her phone.

When she walked out of the bathroom, Seth was standing there. It startled her for a second, and then she laughed. "You're like a helicopter parent," she said and then kissed him on the cheek.

"I like hovering around you," he said in his deep morning voice and pulled her in for a kiss on the lips.

"Let me go, helicopter. I need to find my phone," she said, avoiding his sultry eyes.

"It's on the counter in the kitchen, but I couldn't find your charger," he said, following behind her.

Reagan picked it up, and it was dead. She looked around and suddenly realized she didn't have her briefcase with her charger in it. So, she went into the bedroom and dug around in her wardrobe cabinet until she found an extra block and charging cord. She got it plugged in and noticed that Seth was still following her around.

"What are you doing?" she asked.

"Making sure you're okay, sweetheart."

"You know I'm fine. I'm sure I have a ton of messages, though. And I need to get into the shower so I can get to the office and start the cleanup from yesterday."

Seth reached out and held her hand. "I think you need to take a day off, Reagan."

"I'm not a take-the-day-off sort of girl."

She was walking around picking up things out of order and then walked over to her linen closet to get a towel. Seth followed her every step.

"I know you don't usually take days off, but you've also never had someone come after you and threaten your life while he destroyed your office."

"I don't need you to remind me. I was there, remember? I'm not letting a deranged man missing a chromosome dictate how I do things. I'm not going to miss work and let clients down because of him. I don't need my office. I can use the conference room for my appointments."

Seth followed her into the bathroom and sat on the side of the bathtub as she finished her rant. "Maybe you should talk to someone about what happened yesterday? I could get you in to see one of my partners."

Reagan stared at him like he had two heads. "Why would I talk to a stranger about it? I haven't even talked to you about it."

"Exactly."

"What is that supposed to mean, Seth?"

"I think you know. I want you to talk to me."

"I think you know. I'm also not a talk-it-out kind of girl either."

They were at an impasse, and neither was going to give. At least Seth knew she wouldn't at the moment. He walked over to the shower and turned on the hot water. He took off his shirt, and then she took hers off.

It was one thing for her not to confide in him about the incident, but she wouldn't take her walls down for him for a second. She mistakenly thought getting naked was enough, but he was patient.

It would be enough for the moment.

REAGAN'S PHONE didn't turn on until she was in her car. It sounded like it was malfunctioning with message alert after message alert rolling in, causing her phone to vibrate and blink. Reagan left it plugged into her phone charger and headed to the office. She would have to attend to it later.

There weren't many cars in the parking garage, and Reagan tried to ignore the threats made against her as she parked and hurriedly headed to the elevator. She was not going to let the Robert Salinas incident affect her. She stepped into the elevator, but before the doors closed, a man she didn't know stepped inside.

Reagan gave him a tight smile but couldn't ignore the moment her palms began to sweat. By the time the elevator opened to her floor, Reagan couldn't catch her breath. She stepped out and gulped for air. The hallway outside her office was going black, and her eyes filled with tiny dots of light. Holding onto the wall, she managed to remove her blazer and then ripped off the necklace she was wearing from around her neck.

Reagan had no idea how long she stood there, but thankfully she was alone and able to pull herself together before anyone else saw her. She wiped her brow with the back of her hand and was surprised that she'd been sweating. *First her palms and now her forehead?* She didn't sweat.

Cooling down, she put her blazer back on but threw the necklace into her purse as she straightened her skirt and marched into the office. It was eerily quiet, and her palms started to sweat again as she neared her private office area and saw the damage again.

Terrence stepped out from behind the door with a man wearing a tool belt, who turned and measured the size of her office door and the opening. "Reagan? I'd hoped you would at least take the day."

Terrence was a rock but also thoughtful. Of course, he was there early, getting everything taken care of for Reagan. Terrence cared about the firm and its employees but especially her. She was like a daughter to him, and he looked out for her even when she didn't know it.

Reagan smiled at Terrence but didn't answer him. Instead, she reached out her hand to the contractor and introduced herself. "Hi, I'm Reagan Gentry."

"Ms. Gentry," was all he said.

Terrence gently pulled her into the hallway so the man could finish taking his measurements. "Seriously, Reagan. I could have handled your appointments today."

"As if," Reagan said. "You need two of you to cover your own schedule. I couldn't ask you to do that."

"You would never have to ask," Terrence reached his hand out to touch hers. When she looked into his eyes, she could see the worry. "Seriously, Reagan. What are you doing here?

Reagan took a deep breath. "I'm fine. Really. Besides, I would go crazy if I stayed at home all day and had to think about everything that happened."

Terrence nodded and then walked her back into her office. "This is Barry, and he's going to get the place back into shape. Right, Barry?"

"Yes, and happy to do it. Any changes you would like, ma'am, before I get started? Maybe cable the place out so we can install some cameras and perhaps a help button like they have at the bank?" He chuckled but stopped when they didn't laugh.

Terrence told him to wire her office and the rest of the common areas for cameras and then helped Reagan gather her briefcase and papers so she could relocate temporarily into the conference room. Shortly after, Nancy came in, and they set up a desk for her in the adjoining room next to Mathew Nunan's secretary. It wasn't ideal, but it would work until their offices were put back together.

Reagan looked at her messages and was surprised to see how many people from her office had called to check on her. She didn't socialize with the others very much and thought they didn't like her. She had never forgotten when Mathew and another attorney called her the Ice Queen behind her back when she first started at the firm. She thought the others felt the same. The messages suggested differently.

She also had multiple calls from Amber, but only the one vague message from her earlier in the day. Reagan realized she didn't call Amber back like she was supposed to, nor did she tell her friend about the threats she'd received from Salinas. Reagan immediately picked up the phone and tried to call, but Amber's phone went to voicemail. She left a message for Amber and sorted the recovered items from her office.

An hour later, as Reagan prepared for her first appointment for the day, her phone rang. "What the hell happened to you yesterday? I heard the police had to escort someone out of your office building. Did someone finally shoot that snake, Richie?" Amber's voice filled up the phone.

Richie was one of two male assistants in Reagan's office, and he'd flirted like crazy with Amber in the past. "Richie is in a committed relationship, according to my secretary, and doing fine. It was the husband of an almost client of mine."

"Oh. My. God. Reagan. Honey, are you okay?" Amber had no idea it involved Reagan.

"I'm fine, Amber. He didn't touch me. He lost his mind and tore up my office. It took six NOPD officers to take him down, but they did it. Then they hauled him out of here like a rabid animal. But I'm fine."

"I'll be the judge of that. Meet me for lunch?"

It didn't take but a few seconds for Reagan to consider that idea. "I'm not sure I'm up for eating outside anywhere."

"No? How about we meet at Ruth's Chris and ask for one of those private rooms. I need to talk to you, and it needs to be private."

"Amber?"

There was a long silence on the other end of the phone. Amber rarely took a breath between sentences, and Ruth's Chris, even at lunch, was out of her price range. Reagan was worried. "Amber?" she repeated her name.

"I need to run something by you. Okay?" Amber said quickly.

"Yes, of course. I'll be there at 11:30."

Reagan was thankful when Nancy came in to tell her that her first appointment was on his way up. The only way she was going to make it through the morning without worrying what Amber had gotten herself into was to keep busy.

Two long appointments later, a quick chat with Terrence, and it was time to head to lunch. Reagan took the stairs instead of the elevator. Sixteen flights would be a lot more difficult going up, but she didn't feel as trapped as she had in that steel box. As she exited into the parking garage, she saw a couple of people from her office and put on a calm face.

She had to get it together.

She was fine until she got to the restaurant and couldn't find parking. That was always the case downtown, but she wasn't in the right frame of mind to park several blocks away and walk. She circled for twenty minutes and got lucky when a large truck pulled out of a spot directly across the street from the front door.

Reagan walked in, and Amber was standing there waiting for her. Amber wore the black pantsuit that she said was business in the front and party in the back because it accentuated her voluptuous behind. It always got her a lot of attention, and Reagan smiled as two men walked by, staring at her friend.

Amber hugged her tightly. "Good to see you're in one piece. You didn't let on how bad things got yesterday. I heard that it was a huge ordeal and that the perp locked himself in your office with you. He could have killed you, Reagan."

The hostess was standing there listening to every word, and Reagan looked at her rolling her eyes. "My friend is a bit dramatic. Is our table ready?"

The hostess nodded but looked unsure who to believe, Reagan or Amber. She walked them to a small room that was big enough for a square table, four chairs, and a plant stand holding a small fern. She told them their waiter would be there in a moment, and without another word, she hurried away.

"I think you scared the daylights out of her," Reagan said.

"Millennials grew up on the Internet. Nothing I say can be as harsh as the stuff they copy off YouTube."

Reagan laughed at her honest friend. The waiter came in, took their orders, and vacated quickly. She wondered if they scared him too.

As soon as he left, Amber began, "Please tell me with all the cray-cray yesterday that you still have the message I sent you?"

"I do. But I have to tell you that I listened to it twice and didn't hear anything that sounded out of order, except that it sounded like you were drinking at seven in the morning," Reagan said.

"It was Joel's birthday. You know the guy from accounting?"

"Drinking at seven, Amber?"

"There wasn't any drinking. Apparently, cake for breakfast is popular, kind of like Joel." Amber winked. "I happened to be in the right place at the right time to catch Teresa McDonald and Bruce Cannon running off at the mouth. So, we ate cake and waited on the coffee to brew. You know caffeine deprivation can be as powerful as drinking."

"Tell me about it." Reagan clinked her diet coke with Amber's tea glass. "But I still didn't hear anything inappropriate," she said before she took a drink.

"That's because you don't know what I know," Amber said and then reached into her purse and gave Reagan a hundred-dollar bill.

Reagan looked at her friend and shook her head. "Thanks, but it's not my birthday."

"I know, smart ass, but I need to retain you as my attorney so I can speak freely."

Reagan took the money and then took a notebook out of her purse and wrote the time when she got there. "You don't think this is a little extreme?"

Amber shook her head and waited for the waiter to drop off some warm bread and then leave before she locked eyes with her friend.

"I think I've uncovered inappropriate behavior with the city council," Amber said bluntly.

Reagan sat down her diet coke. "That's serious."

"You're telling me. Unfortunately, I don't have all the evidence I need to prove it, but I'm considering turning them into the FBI."

Reagan was suddenly not hungry. If her closest friend turned information into the FBI and it wasn't true, she would never work in the city again. And if it was true, she still might not have a job. Snitches didn't do well in New Orleans.

"Let's slow down. Tell me what you found, and I'll tell you if I think it's enough to put your career on the line."

Amber crossed her arms and sat back in her chair. She looked mad, but it didn't matter to Reagan. She cared more about Amber than to let her defensive attitude stand in the way of her being a good friend and intelligent attorney.

"Don't get testy with me, Amber. You gave me a hundred bucks, and I am in high demand. That wouldn't normally buy you ten minutes."

Amber laughed at that comment. She would never get rich working for the city, but her friend was killing it enough for the both of them.

"You know that the mayor's been working to pull the city into this century with tech, right?"

"Yes. Every time I park in metered parking or run through a yellow light and have my license plate photographed, I'm reminded."

"It's a great thing. I mean, it's efficient, and the city is seeing a great deal of revenue from those light cameras, but I digress. Alexavier is focused on his tech department. Like, I mean really focused on getting that stuff done. We've filed tons of paperwork with the federal government and received a good deal of federal funds to help pay for the upgrades."

"Sounds like everything is going well," Reagan said, confused.

"Yes, but you see, he also ran on a platform to help bring in affordable health care for the community."

"I remember. You were also talking about that on the message?"

"Yes, but here's the thing. We opened the bid as we were supposed to, but it hasn't closed yet. We have had several come in, and they're sealed until next week's deadline. But Teresa and Bruce were talking like it's already a done deal.

"In the beginning, the mayor mentioned a facility that would be called South Louisiana Community Health Center that he liked, but there was no guarantee they would even be interested in New Orleans. It didn't seem probable that the majority shareholder, Community Health Care Centers, would bid because they were spread thin with three facilities in Texas and one they built last year in North Louisiana. However, Mayor Regalia mentioned several that he felt were good choices, and I could tell he was getting excited that we had the ball moving on the project.

"The job was opened a week ago, and they had a few weeks to get all the paperwork in. But I heard from a confidential source that the CFO of SLCHC has been enjoying football games in the Superdome and living it up in box seats next to Teresa McDonald and Bruce Cannon.

"I started investigating further, and Bruce Cannon, who hasn't taken a vacation except to Flora-Bama with his wife and kids, has all of a sudden taken his entire family to Italy. He has six kids. They flew first class. Teresa McDonald is divorced and owns a small cleaning business. She does okay, but she recently put her elderly mother into the city's most expensive assisted living facility. Yet, she couldn't afford the building rent for her cleaning business and had to move the headquarters into her home last year."

Amber stopped to take a drink, and the waiter showed up with their food. Reagan took the time to try and mentally sort out the details Amber had given her.

"Are you saying that the mayor has something to do with this too?" Reagan asked.

"No. He's a really good man. He always wants to be a part of everything we process on his behalf. He asks lots of questions and tells us to be completely transparent so no one can ever question his administration's ethics. I think he would flip if he found this out."

"Well, it could be prison time if they're doing what you think," Reagan said as she ate some of her salad. "I think you need to take this slowly, Amber. I wouldn't want you to jump into this, and there possibly be another explanation."

"I've thought of that too. I don't want everything the mayor has done for the city to be tainted with their crime. If I wait too long, then more damage could be done."

Reagan sat her fork down and reached over for Amber's hand. "I have a great private detective that I use for some of my cases. He doesn't work cheap, but he's thorough. Let's finish eating, and I'll give him a call for you. Maybe you should let me be his contact for now? I think you need to stay anonymous for as long as you can. If they're doing what you think they're doing, then you have to be careful."

"Thanks, Reagan. I'll try to stay quiet until you find something out," Amber said.

"No, Amber. You can't just try. You cannot say anything, to anyone, about this until we know for sure. After yesterday, I can tell you that desperate people behave badly."

Amber nodded her head. She couldn't see Teresa or Bruce as dangerous, but she figured there was no reason to argue with Reagan about it. She understood Reagan had been through something traumatic even though she hid it well. "You know, Reagan, you never did tell me if that guy is still in jail or if he made bail yesterday."

Reagan shrugged her shoulders. It wasn't until Amber asked about Salinas that she realized what had been niggling at her all morning. Why hadn't she called to see if Robert Salinas bailed out of jail? She hid her emotions well, but could she honestly compartmentalize that situation like everything else in her life?

Chapter Thirteen

REAGAN WENT BACK TO her office conference room with all the information Amber had given her on her mind. She called her private detective, Jerry, but had to leave him a message.

Grabbing her laptop, she typed out the notes from her lunch with Amber. Something didn't make sense, and she couldn't put her finger on it. Typing it out and then making a timeline would help clear her thoughts. It was the way she'd always sorted out big cases. But, of course, her job was to represent her client and do what was best for the whole family, which almost always involved kids. Divorce could be more complicated than some criminal cases. Still, this wasn't her area of expertise. So as soon as possible, she would talk Amber into consulting with Terrence.

Jerry called Reagan back, and she set him into motion. She'd already decided to pay for his services herself. Of course, Amber would insist on paying for it, but she was stressed over the situation, and taking the small financial burden away from her might help.

Seth had left a message with Nancy for Reagan to call him, but Terrence stopped in to speak with her before she got an opportunity.

"How are you holding up?" he asked.

"Great as usual," she said.

Terrence sat down, and what she'd thought was going to be a fly-by *how ya doing, kid* was going to be more. His warm almond-shaped eyes always caught her off guard. He was a sincere and caring boss and friend.

He smiled at her as he seemed to examine her face. She knew she didn't look different than before the incident because she was skilled at keeping a placid expression. She began as a very young child, practiced it with poker, and perfected it as an adult and attorney. She would never let anyone see anything she didn't want them to see.

Still, Terrence acted like he knew something else when he looked at her. "Reagan, no one would think less of you if you took a few days off. I must admit, after yesterday, I felt like I might need a short vacation myself. Mr. Salinas caught me off guard. I had always thought we were safe here with the building security and the layers of walls and glass surrounding our office.

"After that man broke through with no more than a little fury and determination, I had to question my belief that this was our actual fortress. He could have hurt you." He paused and reached over to pat her hand. "Or much worse."

"I understand, Terrence," Reagan said, trying to gather her thoughts because she had considered the events over and over in her head most of the night. "But he didn't hurt me, and you have to wonder why? I mean, he had the opportunity. He was certainly physically able, and I wasn't in a position to stop him. Instead, he chose to destroy my office, the chairs, the walls, and maybe even my computer. I have to believe that was a conscious choice. He had no intention of harming me. He was heartbroken and couldn't control his temper."

Terrence continued to stare at her. "You can't truly believe that, Reagan. It took six of the biggest police officers I've ever seen to take him down and out of here."

Reagan smiled calmly. "Yup, but he didn't touch a single hair on the top of my head." That was saying something because when she wore her hair down, it was a long force of nature on its own.

Terrence stood up, and to anyone else, it would look like he was satisfied with the conversation, but Reagan knew, felt, he didn't believe her.

Terrence didn't believe her, but he wasn't going to call her out on her lie. Instead, he decided to let her keep her facade up and tell everyone she was fine, but he knew the truth.

"Well, it's my duty as head of the firm to make sure nothing like that ever happens again. So, I'm going to look into some high-tech security as well as the low-tech kind. I'll keep you posted," he said.

As he began to walk out, Reagan stood up. "Terrence? Any word on my office?"

Terrence smiled at her. She was his favorite in the office, and he worked hard trying not to show the favoritism, yet his smile gave him away now and again. "I believe the contractor will have you back in there by the end of next week."

"Thanks," she said and worked hard to keep the look of relief to herself. She liked the privacy of her office. Unfortunately, the glass walls in the conference room couldn't give her the solitude she needed, which was crucial for the crazy hours she kept.

It was three when Reagan sat down to call Seth back, and as she was dialing his number, Mayor Alexavier walked into her conference room office.

Why was he in her office so much?

"Reagan? Do you have a minute?" he asked.

Reagan nodded as he walked in and sat beside her at the conference table. He had his eyes locked on her, and she couldn't break the stare between them.

"I heard some disturbing news today, and I had to come and talk to you myself," he said, and Reagan could feel a lump forming in her chest.

She felt herself slightly nodding again and couldn't believe her body was betraying her. Physical control was even more important than words when trying to hide your emotions. She had written the damn handbook on it, and in front of the handsome mayor, she faltered.

"Is it true, sweetheart?" he asked.

Reagan was stunned at the endearment and licked her lips like a desperate schoolgirl. She closed her eyes over her ridiculous behavior. Then she realized how that must look too. *What the hell?* Where was her stoic behavior now when she needed it most?

She opened her eyes and gave him a slight smile. Amber must have told him about the city council today. She'd said she would try to keep it to herself, but Reagan had a feeling Amber had already planned to tell Alexavier.

Mayor Regalia reached over and patted her knee. "Were you attacked in your private office yesterday?"

Reagan's mouth went dry. She suddenly couldn't form words without a drink of water. As she opened her water bottle, her body betrayed her more. Her shoulders fell, and she nodded for the third flipping time as she took a sip.

"Son of a —," he said as he stood up and paced a few feet. Then he apologized for cussing in front of her. "Where was your security? How did that lunatic get up here in the first place?"

Reagan didn't know what to say because she was surprised by his behavior.

"I don't like you being put in danger like that, and I hope you don't mind, but I'm going to have a talk with Terrence over the lack of security in this office."

"You don't have to do that, Alexavier," she said and couldn't believe her own breathy voice.

He sat down beside her again but moved his chair a little closer and held both of her hands in his as he spoke. "I know I don't have to, but I want to do it. You take care of those around you, but who looks after you? I'm not in the habit of butting into things. But I can't explain how protective I felt when I heard you were almost hurt."

"I-I'm fine. Really. He didn't touch me."

"Well, at least I won't have to kill him now," he said bluntly and then seemed embarrassed. "I apologize, Reagan. I shouldn't have said that out loud.

Reagan had never seen that side of Alexavier before, and she had to admit that strong men were very attractive. Nevertheless, her stomach felt twitchy since he'd walked into her makeshift office. She was a little out of her depth. She hadn't been on a date in over a year, and now Seth was back in her bed, and was the mayor hitting on her?

"Alexavier?"

He smiled at her like he could devour her. "I like to hear you say my name," he said.

Reagan bit her bottom lip hard. She was in a glass-walled office with the freaking mayor ogling her, and she was pretty sure she was flirting too.

"I'm flattered. I'm really flattered, but we're in my office," she said.

Alexavier squeezed her hands warmly. "I understand, Reagan. I'm a private man too."

He let go of her hands and straightened out his slacks, pulling his blazer together and buttoning it up as he stood. Reagan's face heated when she realized how excited he was to be near her.

She took a deep breath and stood up. "I didn't mean to—."

Mayor Regalia locked onto her eyes as he quietly said, "I know. We will pick this up in private. Let's have dinner."

Reagan looked away, trying to understand what the hell she was doing. She cared about Seth, so why wasn't she shutting the mayor down?

"I can't tonight."

She looked up, and that was when she saw Seth standing outside the conference room watching her and Alexavier together. Mayor Regalia followed her eyes and saw Seth too before Seth walked away. He reached over and pulled Reagan's chin gently toward him. He was grinning at her. "I see. I have some competition."

Reagan opened her mouth to speak, but nothing came out.

Alexavier kissed her on the cheek and whispered, "I think a little healthy rivalry is good for the soul. You should know, Reagan, I don't give up easily, and I play to win."

She was shocked at his declaration and barely managed a slight nod as he headed to the door. "I'm going to talk to Terrence. If you need anything, *anything*, you call me on my cell. Is that clear, Reagan?"

"Yes," was all she said as she watched him leave. She sat down, putting her head in her hands. Maybe she should have taken the damn day off.

Chapter Fourteen

NANCY WALKED IN A FEW minutes later and gave Reagan the note that Seth had left for her. "I tried to run interference, but that man walks fast."

"It's alright, Nancy. That's why offices shouldn't be made of glass. Things can be misconstrued, looking in from the outside."

Nancy nodded and then went back to her desk. She could tell Reagan needed a few minutes.

Reagan picked up her things and headed to her car. She'd already put on a show for everyone, and she wasn't going to read Seth's note in public too.

"I'm gone for the day, Nancy," she said and hit the staircase door with force.

Inside her car, she slowly opened the handwritten note. "I can see that I interrupted something important. I'm still cooking dinner, and it will be ready at 7, but at my apartment instead of yours. If you cannot make it, I'll understand that you have made another choice."

Reagan leaned her head against the steering wheel. She didn't want to hurt Seth. She didn't want to date the mayor. She needed something that both of them had, but neither possessed fully on their own. She needed to talk to someone smarter about those sorts of things.

She called Amber.

Fifteen minutes later, Reagan was sitting at a table in Gordon Biersch and waiting on the love guru to show up. She watched as her tall curvy friend walked through the room confidently with every eye on her. Amber disproved the myth that all women needed to be a size 2.

"Sweet friend, you sounded like hell on the phone. Have you ordered for us yet?" she asked, looking Reagan over as she had a seat.

"No. I haven't been here, but a few minutes and the female waitress has ignored me."

"Hmph," Amber said as she stood up and pulled her tight skirt down before she headed straight to the bar.

One of the bartenders hurried over before Amber got there so he could help her. Reagan loved to watch Amber work her charm. The bartender gushed and talked as fast as possible while he had her attention. He made the drinks she ordered, and Reagan laughed when she saw him write his phone number down on a napkin and slide it to Amber with the glasses.

"We don't need the waitress. Bradly is going to take care of us," she said with a wink.

"You are good," Reagan said as she licked some salt off her margarita.

"So, tell me, what's got your hose in a twist?" Amber asked, laughing at herself.

"I don't wear hosiery," Reagan teased back.

"And that is a travesty because you are missing all the sexual undertones of a man seeing you in thigh highs."

"Oh my God, Amber. Stop. We're in public."

Amber laughed even louder. "Then you better get down to business. I'm having another Margarita after this one, and you know two drinks remove my filter."

"As if you have one in the first place," Reagan said, but she knew she only had a short time to talk, or her friend would have four men sitting at the table with them.

Reagan explained that she'd called her private investigator, and he would get back to them ASAP. Next, she described how sweet Terrence had been to her, which had to be the reason she felt vulnerable when Alexavier came into her office. Finally, she told Amber word for word what Alexavier had said and then how Seth almost walked in on them.

She watched Amber, who never tempered her facial expressions. First, she was sympathetic, then shocked, and at the end amused. Reagan suddenly wasn't sure she could handle her friend's assessment or advice at that moment.

"What was I thinking, Amber? I mean, I kind of liked Alexavier flirting, but why didn't I just tell him about Seth? What am I going to do about Seth?"

Amber sat her almost empty glass down. "First of all, how awesome is Terrence? He is absolutely the reason why your office is the coveted place to work among all attorneys."

"He's golden," Reagan said, placing her hand over her heart.

"I am a little surprised about you and Alexavier, though. Slut." Amber cracked up laughing as she licked the last of the salt off the rim of her glass and then waved over at the bartender, who quickly made her another then brought it over personally.

Reagan's mouth was still opened in pretend shock at her friend calling her a slut. It was fake because Amber never missed an opportunity to say that word whenever they were alone drinking and talking about men.

"Close your mouth, Reagan. I'm going to give you some advice about yourself," Amber said and then winked at her friend as she stopped for a minute to flirt with the bartender. As soon as he walked away, Amber smacked her lips.

"Amber," Reagan said, admonishing her friend.

Amber batted her eyes innocently and then lowered them at Reagan. "Don't correct me; you're the one with a trail of men wanting to rescue you."

"Rescue me? That's insulting."

"Well, let me impart some knowledge on you, sister. You are a tough cookie. I know you know that some of the assholes in our field call you the Ice Queen, but that's because you're always so strong and don't need any help, unlike the rest of us."

"I'm not a bitch, though," Reagan said, trying to reign in her hurt feelings. The Ice Queen remarks still bothered her.

"Of course, you aren't. You are the sweetest person I know, but they don't know you the way I do. On top of that, you're gorgeous."

"Whatever," Reagan said, rolling her eyes.

"Don't whatever me. You didn't have a sister or apparently much of a mother to let you know it, so let me explain this to you. You. Are. Hot! I mean, like all the boys want you hot, but they're also a little afraid of you. Look in the mirror and then look at a Victoria's Secret catalog. You have model looks but wear a few too many clothes." Amber took a drink and waved to the bartender to bring Reagan another.

This would get ugly if she didn't hurry the conversation along.

"Thanks, Amber. According to the best friend's handbook, you're obligated to say things like that when I'm down, but it's still sweet of you to say it. Now, what's your point?"

"It's not sweet of me to say. It is a fact. The point I'm trying to make is that you're like top ten percent of the world beautiful and don't know it. Therefore, you don't know how to use it to your advantage, which is a shame with that big brain of yours. Anyway, you're always buttoned up so tight that everyone is intimidated by you, not only professionally but socially. Enter in stage left, the psycho yesterday. While everyone was relieved you were okay, it also turned some things around because, for the first time ever, you were vulnerable. I heard you didn't cry or anything. However, someone did see you trembling and mentioned someone else wrapped you in a coat, and well, that brings out the protective nature in certain men."

"Certain men?"

"Really possessive men. And let's face it, strong women like us are hot for strong possessive men."

"Lord, you truly believe the reason I behaved the way I did today with Alexavier and Seth is that I need a mouth breather to fight my battles and drag me home by the hair of my head? Did you start drinking before you got here?"

Amber put her hand over her mouth to stifle the loud squeal coming out of it. When she composed herself, she made eyes across the room at the bartender again. "Look, this is the first time you've ever asked me for drinks to talk about men. Do you realize every time we have done this, it's been because I needed to talk? So, I am not going to waste this opportunity. Everything I have said is true. And I wouldn't call the hot mayor a mouth breather or your doctor ex-boyfriend. But should either of them want to drag me home by my hair or not, I'd be game."

Reagan cut her eyes at Amber. "You did not say that in front of me."

"You can't be jealous because you can't make up your mind, and well, neither of them are talking to me," Amber winked at her friend.

Reagan laughed and drank more of her margarita. She loved Amber, but she was a bit crazy at times. "It's not that I can't make up my mind. I want Seth, but I'm not sure he's up for the real deal. I mean, he says he is, but words are not the same as action. As far as Alexavier goes, I'm baffled. He can't be interested in me like that. I'm sure he's fooling around. I mean, we're barely friendly with each other, and we've only talked a few times."

"Yet, he canceled an appointment when he heard what happened to you and went straight to your office to see that you were alright. Then he asked you to have dinner with him. Lucky duck," Amber said as she fingered the salt that remained on her second empty margarita glass.

Reagan stared at her friend. "Wait a minute. Do you have a crush on Alexavier?"

"I am a grown damn woman," Amber said and then laughed loudly again. "Damn straight, I have a crush. What's not to like? That thick wavy dark hair or those coal-black eyes? I'm a big fan of his strong jawline too. He's pretty much the entire Italian package. But alas, I am not his type. He hasn't even blinked my way. He sure hasn't asked me to call him Alexavier. So, I would like to live vicariously through my bestie, and you better not leave out a single detail, especially when he takes off that perfectly tailored suit."

Reagan shook her head, watching Amber give her best *poor-me-someone's-not-attracted-to-me* speech. "Are you done yet?" she asked. "You know that may work with someone who doesn't know you, but I know you. You may not get every man but my dearest friend, you are never without one."

Amber licked her lips, and on cue, the bartender was back with fresh drinks for both of them. It was unnerving how she could do that to adult men.

Reagan leaned in. "Yes, that's exactly what I was talking about, and you know it."

Amber held her glass up to clink with Reagan's.

"Have you ever thought that the reason Alexavier isn't interested in you is that you work for him? I'm sure that fraternization within the city attorney's office would be frowned upon," Reagan said.

"It could be, but most likely it's because I drank a little too much at the office Christmas party right after I started. When Mayor Regalia walked down the hallway past the restroom I was in, I pulled him inside and mauled him. I thought it was my date who I'd told to follow me. Imagine my surprise when he pushed me away, and I had my top off and his pants unzipped. Not my most shining moment."

"Oh, Amber. You didn't?" Reagan scrunched up her nose. She'd reminded Amber about the drinks in New Orleans. "Why haven't you told me this story before?"

"Seriously? It's embarrassing enough now," Amber said.

"Besides, he accepted my apology and was a perfect gentleman about the entire humiliating event."

"But you like him?"

Amber smiled. "I do like him, but that's it. Like. He's a good man, and I think you two would be good together. I've seen the way he looks at you, and that's something serious."

Reagan rolled her eyes. "I had a moment of weakness there in the office with my nervous breakdown in the elevator and then Terrence mothering me to death. Alexavier caught me off guard. I thought you'd actually talked to him and that he was there to discuss your hypothesis about those two city council members. I had no idea he was there for me. Anyway, I have no plans to go to dinner with him. And you're wrong; I'm not into possessive cavemen. I'm an independent woman."

"You're only saying that because Doctor Young doesn't quite make the cut where cavemen are concerned."

Reagan was ready to defend Seth and explain that he was assertive in the right ways, but the bartender that Amber had been flirting with for the last hour was removing his apron. His shift was over, and he was heading their way.

Amber moved over so he could sit beside her while Reagan stood up and took a quick look at her wrist. "Oh, look at the time, I'm late. You two have fun," she said.

As she grabbed her purse and hurried to the door, she heard Amber yelling, "You're not even wearing a watch!"

Chapter Fifteen

IT WAS 6:45 WHEN REAGAN pulled into Seth's parking garage. She felt guilty showing up so close to dinner time and hoped he would let her explain the scene he saw earlier that day.

She'd ran by her house and changed into a slinky silk dress that wasn't more than a long slip, but after her talk with Amber, she'd hoped it would help her case.

She'd thought about what Amber said over drinks the entire drive home and then over to Seth's apartment. Amber was partly right because sometimes Reagan secretly dreamed of not being in control. She did like powerful men, but she wasn't looking for someone that was domineering. Assertive would be more like it. Self-assured too. She loved Seth but needed him to be more direct.

How did he honestly feel about her? Where could their relationship go after they wrung it out the first time? And would he leave again?

She took the stairs and gently knocked on the door of Seth's apartment. When he answered the door, his face was red. He barely said hello as he stepped back to let her walk inside. He didn't offer to take her trench coat, so the whole reveal of the slip dress was ruined. It was the only game she had since she wasn't exactly a seductress like Amber. She decided to keep her coat on.

The apartment looked clean, and she could smell the delicious food he had prepared. She climbed up on a barstool and watched him open the oven and take a large iron skillet out. The silence was awkward, and she was nervous being there when she didn't feel wanted.

He opened the oven and threw in a small loaf of French bread. When he turned around, she could see that his face hadn't lost any of the anger.

"I'm going to go ahead and go. I can see this was a mistake," she said, hopping down off the barstool. She practically ran to the front door, but he was behind her as she reached for the handle.

Reagan felt the heat rolling off his body, and she closed her eyes. The week started out like hell, and she had no idea how she would keep it together if he said things were over for good.

"Please come sit down, Reagan. We need to talk," he said. He gently wrapped his arm around her waist from behind and pulled her back to his front. It only lasted a moment, but it made her stomach feel hollow.

She did as he asked, but she moved slowly, feeling his eyes on her the entire time. He pulled the bread out of the oven and placed it on a plate that he covered with a white cheesecloth towel. He stirred whatever he had in the pan and then put the heavy lid back on top.

Finally, he walked over to Reagan and offered to take her coat. She wasn't sure about removing it but thought he might feel like she wanted to leave if she kept it on. When she stood and peeled the long coat off, she could hear him take a deep breath.

He didn't say anything as he walked away and hung her coat up on his coat rack by the front door. Amber didn't know what she was talking about because men weren't waiting in line for her. When Seth walked back into the kitchen, he opened the microwave and pulled out a bowl of white rice. He sat it on the counter in front of her then looked into her eyes. "You look incredible, Rea. You know blue is my favorite color."

Reagan barely nodded her head. She was hoping for the

compliment, but he seemed miserable paying it to her. "Thanks," she whispered.

He finally removed the lid and told her he'd made crawfish etouffee for dinner. She was surprised. When they had dated before, he barely cooked anything beyond the spaghetti that he loved to eat almost every night.

"It smells delicious, Seth. Thank you for cooking." She watched as he made her a bowl. He then poured her a glass of white wine and made himself a glass of ice water. She helped him carry everything to the table, and within minutes they were eating the fragrant food.

They didn't talk during dinner.

Twenty minutes later, Reagan was rinsing her dishes and a few other pots that he had left in the sink during his meal preparations. He set his bowl in the sink but pulled her away from doing any more of the cleanup.

Seth led her to a chair in the living room, and Reagan tried to prepare herself that he would end things for good. It was the first time he hadn't sat next to her since they had gotten back together. Her stomach had that twisted feeling, but she kept her emotions in check.

He watched her closely, and she figured he wanted her to talk first, but she wouldn't. If he planned to break up with her, he would have to start the conversation.

"Reagan, I think you know what I walked into at your office today. I can't say that I'm surprised, but I didn't expect you to lead me on while you were interested in the mayor. It was embarrassing and hurtful, and I never figured you for a mean person.

"I-I'm not mean," she whispered.

"I'd tried to call you late morning to see if you wanted to get lunch, but you were out. Then I tried to call you again to check on you this afternoon, but Nancy said you were with a client. I had heard that Robert Salinas was out on bail, and I wanted you to know as soon as I knew. But I couldn't reach you. I had no idea it was because of Regalia."

The color drained from Reagan's face. "He's out?"

"Yes," Seth answered. "But you seemed preoccupied with something else."

"Nothing is going on between Alexavier and me. I swear."

Seth couldn't stand for her to call the mayor by his first name. It was too intimate and made him angry. He didn't say anything for fear she would see his temper. Instead, he looked away from her out the sliding glass doors in his living room. It took a lot to get him mad, but he'd been on edge ever since he saw the mayor flirting with her, and he didn't want to lose control.

It wasn't easy to see how angry she'd made him. Reagan tried to explain again. "Seth? I am not interested in the mayor. We're barely friends, and we haven't been friends for very long. He found out about Salinas coming to the office and came over to check on me. That's all."

"He definitely looked friendly today," he said, finally looking up, and she wished that he hadn't. He had looked angry before, but now it was worse; he looked like he didn't feel anything.

"I don't know what else you want me to say, Seth. I am not interested in the mayor in a romantic way. We haven't seen each other outside of work, and we don't know each other very well. So, I think you have the wrong idea. I'm not his type."

Seth looked her up and down. She was sexy as sin in that silky blue dress that looked like lingerie. He couldn't help his comment. "I'm pretty sure you're everyone's type."

"What is that supposed to mean?" She stood up. "Are you implying that I'm easy or something?"

She used her hands as she talked, and Reagan only did that when flustered. It didn't happen often. "I didn't do anything wrong, Seth. I don't deserve the third degree. I haven't been on a date in over a year. This is ridiculous." She grabbed her coat and purse and stormed out the door.

Seth wasn't fast enough to stop her, and when he got to the elevator, he realized she had taken the stairs. So he picked up his pace and was on her heels when she bolted out the exit door into the garage. She stopped short when she saw her car. All the windows were broken, and the paint had been destroyed. The word bitch was scratched across the hood, and then a red liquid that looked like blood had been poured all over it. It was something out of a horror movie.

She screamed when Seth came out the stairwell door behind her. He instantly pulled her into him and looked around the garage to see if the vandal was still around.

It was empty.

"Shhh, Rea, it's me," he said, trying to comfort her.

"Who?" Reagan asked. It was the only thing she could say.

"Baby, please let's go back upstairs so I can call the police."

Reagan looked at him. "You don't want me there. I knew it from the minute I walked in. I can call them from my cell phone."

She was shaking but grabbed her phone to show him she could take care of herself.

"I do want you there. I don't want you in this open garage when I don't know if the person or persons who did that are still around."

Reagan gasped. She hadn't thought of that, and she quickly turned and tried to open the door to the staircase. Seth grabbed it first and held it for her. Then, together, they ran back up the stairs and into his apartment.

It took forty minutes for the police to get there.

No other vehicles were damaged, and the detective that showed up said it looked personal based on the amount of damage and the writing.

Of course, it was, Reagan thought.

Seth told them about the attack at her office and let them know that Robert Salinas was out on bail. The officers took the information and then asked her a few routine questions like whether she could think of anyone else who might be holding a grudge or want to scare her.

By the time her car was towed, it was almost midnight. Seth

offered for her to spend the night, and she declined. He then drove her home and insisted on walking her upstairs to her place.

Once inside, Reagan went directly to her bedroom and changed clothes. Seth made her a cup of hot tea.

When Reagan walked into the living room and saw the tea, it made her emotional, and her eyes watered. "Thank you. I didn't know I had tea."

"You didn't. I brought some with me tonight."

Reagan nodded. He liked hot drinks before bed. It turns out she did too.

She slowly moved closer to him on the couch, and when he wrapped his arm around her and pulled her closer, she curled up next to him, where she fell asleep.

It was the middle of the night when Reagan woke up in her bed screaming. Seth tripped over the end table as he ran into her bedroom to check on her. She had her covers pulled up to her neck, and her eyes scrunched closed. She was shaking all over, and he had to shake her to make her open her eyes to see him.

"Reagan! Wake up, Rea!" he yelled.

When she opened her eyes, she blinked several times, focusing. "Seth?"

He pulled her into his chest. "Yes, baby. It's me. I'm here."

"I had the worst dream."

Chapter Sixteen

IT TOOK TWO HOURS FOR REAGAN to calm down enough to curl up on the couch with Seth. He made her some toast with Nutella, one of the few ingredients in her kitchen, and some hot tea with honey. When she finished most of it, he pulled her in close and covered her with the comforter he'd taken off her bed.

She said she couldn't remember everything about the nightmare, but someone was chasing her. She was pretty sure it was Robert Salinas. She didn't admit that she was a child in her dream, but she trembled for an hour as he tried to talk to her and distract her from it.

Finally, she fell back asleep, and he didn't take her back to her bedroom. She'd scared the hell out of him when she screamed, and he wasn't there with her. Instead, he laid down on the couch behind her and fell asleep for a couple of hours until the sun came up.

Reagan woke up to Seth already awake and lying beside her. "Please tell me you weren't watching me sleep."

"You're beautiful when your sleeping," he said and kissed the top of her head.

"Did you get any rest? I know you have to work today, and

I've kept you up all night. I'm sorry," she said. She felt guilty not telling him everything about her nightmare, but she could psychoanalyze herself. She didn't want him to do it.

She felt incredibly vulnerable and was sure that was why she was a child again in her dream. The worst part about being a kid for her was being defenseless.

"I'm fine, Rea," he said. "How about you? How are you going to get through work today with so little rest? Don't you need your eight hours?"

Reagan laid her head on his chest. "That's a fairytale. Perpetuated by my brother. I haven't had eight consecutive hours of sleep since I was born." She took a deep breath before she continued. "But I was considering taking the day off. I'm going to call Terrence and tell him what happened and then have Nancy cancel my appointments."

Seth tried not to look shocked. *So, she was going to take a personal day off?* He knew the destruction of her car had rattled her. Of course, Reagan had handled it like she was handling a case once the police officers arrived. She was professional and concise as she spoke, but Seth knew she was devastated over the violation of her property because that was the first new car she'd ever bought herself.

"I think that's a good idea. Do you need me to take the day off too?"

"I couldn't ask you to do that, Seth."

"Sure you can. Just say, Seth, I need you. Could you take the day off with me?" he said, holding her chin and pretending like her mouth was moving up and down.

She smiled back at him when he was done. "It's really sweet of you, but I'm probably going to be a couch zombie for half the day. Then I'm going to need to get a rental car to use until my car is repaired."

"I'm sorry to be the one to tell you, Rea, but that little Mercedes is not repairable."

She poked out her bottom lip as she contemplated what he'd said. "I guess I could go look for a new one."

"You shouldn't go anywhere alone after last night," he said, using his deep voice that got her attention.

She nodded and then rolled over the other way and pulled her blanket back up. He knew she was upset, but she wouldn't talk about her feelings to him. People paid good money to tell him their problems but not Reagan. No matter how much he wanted to hear it.

She laid there quietly for a while and then went to find her phone to call the office. While she called her office, Seth called his assistant and took the day off too. He then called her brother and told him what had happened to her car.

Ryan brought up a good point. Someone must be watching Reagan to be able to vandalize her car and not get caught. She hadn't been with Seth for long and rarely went over to his apartment. *Were they still following her?*

Seth wasn't going to let her out of his sight. He and Ryan planned to talk later about how to protect her best until the police picked the criminal up for good.

Reagan walked into the living room with her blanket still wrapped around her. She always kept her place on the cool side and said it made for better sleeping. Seth pulled her down onto the couch with him and picked up the remote so they could watch the morning news. It wasn't long until she drifted back off to sleep and he laid there comforted that she was safe and resting for a while longer.

It was late morning when Reagan woke up and then dressed for the day. Seth had ordered them brunch, and they ate together before they made plans to go car shopping.

Reagan called the police detective to see if there was news about her car, and all he could tell her was that the garage cameras were too foggy from the humidity, and they couldn't get anything off them. He also said they couldn't locate Robert Salinas because his last known address was the house he'd shared with his wife, and she'd kicked him out.

It wasn't good news, and Reagan didn't want to share it with Seth immediately, so she called her office instead. As she followed Seth out to his SUV, she spoke to her secretary. Nancy gave her an update on her scheduled appointments for the rest of the week and then gave her opinion about the office repairs. Unfortunately, Reagan's office was a giant mess behind some hanging plastic sheeting with the walls demoed and flooring pulled up. Nancy told her that it looked impossible for them to finish by the end of the week as they had estimated.

When Reagan got off the phone, Seth reached over and held her hand. They were sitting in the parking lot of the Mercedes-Benz dealership, but she shook her head.

"Babe, I think it's too soon to worry about a car. I'm going to be your personal chauffeur for the next few days, and between Ryan and I, you won't have to worry about driving."

She nodded, and he pulled out of the dealership parking lot into the afternoon traffic. She worried Seth because she didn't argue over him trying to take care of her. Instead, she was quiet and putting up those walls she hid behind.

He offered to buy her a dessert coffee, as she called it, and then he drove her around listening to the radio and site-seeing old neighborhoods in the city.

After a while, she told him what the detective said and what Nancy had told her. She didn't offer up how she felt about it, but it was a beginning.

"Are you worried about your office getting done?" he asked.

She shook her head. "I'm sure they'll finish as soon as they can, and honestly, the conference room is fine. I mean, I like having the privacy of my office, but at least it's a good space where Nancy can be close.

She sat there and drank her coffee for a few minutes and then told him to turn onto another street near City Park.

They paused at a stop sign when she admitted, "I have something I need to tell you, Seth."

He looked up to see a large Cadillac, circa 1990, coming up behind them and quickly veered off to the side of the street to get out of its way so he could give her his full attention.

He reached over and held her hand, but she gently pulled hers back into her lap. They hadn't discussed the argument they had from the night before, and she couldn't forget about it. She had a lump in her throat, but she looked him straight in the eyes so she could admit she'd had dinner with Regalia in her office on Sunday Night. "I swear I didn't plan it. I truly wanted to have dinner with you, but I didn't feel like I could leave the office. When I heard the knocking on the receptionist's doors upfront, I honestly thought it was you."

Seth felt the jealousy slam into him, but he'd had a lot of practice as a therapist that helped him master his own emotions. "Then what happened?"

"Nothing happened. I mean, except that we ate Chinese food in my office and talked about work. It lasted maybe half an hour. He was a perfect gentleman and then left."

Seth nodded his head but didn't trust his words. He believed it was innocent on Reagan's part, but he didn't have faith in the mayor.

"I was going to tell you the next morning, but then you came in, and the whole coffee inquisition happened. I didn't think it was the right time, but I don't want to keep secrets from you. So I hope you can understand."

Seth didn't want to understand, and he sure as hell wanted to lash out at someone, but it wasn't Reagan that he blamed. He reasoned with his jealousy that she was giving him her trust by telling him the information she could have kept secret.

He reached over for her hand again, and she watched as he kissed the back of it and then put her hand on his leg. She looked calm, but on the inside, she was relieved beyond measure.

As Seth began to pull out onto the street again, she asked him to turn left. Then, she showed him a duplex where her father had lived. After her mother and father divorced, he'd moved to the country and found odd jobs as a farming hand, a dishwasher, a painter, and any cash-paying positions he could get. "He couldn't afford the place in the country after one of the big hurricanes caused a lot of people to move out there. It drove the property values up. So he found that duplex, where he lived until he died. It was run down from the beginning. He never did anything to fix it up because he couldn't keep a steady job, but then again, he barely ever could support us growing up." she said, not making eye contact.

"So, you and Ryan visited him there?"

Reagan stared at the little duplex like she was thinking back to that time. "Momma let us visit him a few times in the country, but when she saw that he had a single mattress on the floor for us to sleep on and slept in a sleeping bag himself when we were there, she put a stop to it. I never spent the night again, but I think Ryan stayed a few nights in high school. Our mother always accused our dad of having a drinking and drug problem. I never saw him drink. She also said he blew all his money on his vices, but I never saw that he had any money."

Seth reached over and picked up her hand and kissed it several times. She'd never talked about either of her parents, and he knew it was a big deal for her to share the information with him.

Reagan pointed him toward the entrance to City Park. "We didn't spend the night, but we did spend time with him at the park. He liked City Park, and he would watch us while we played. He was more of a stranger than a dad."

Seth suddenly understood she had tested him with the story about the mayor. She needed to see his calm reaction before opening up about her family. He was thankful he'd earned her trust. It meant everything to him that she shared something she guarded from everyone else.

He pulled into a parking spot. "Want to get out of the car and walk around a bit?"

Reagan nodded. He was sure the beautiful park brought back old, sad memories, and he wanted her to replace them with happy times in her life with Seth.

They held hands and walked around a populated area of the park, watching moms with their babies, toddlers, and dogs. Seth enjoyed watching Reagan makeover the dogs. They sat on a bench until they finished their coffee, and Seth kept watch for anyone that didn't fit into the atmosphere of the park.

He saw one older man that seemed to be watching the younger moms with their kids, but then his grown daughter with her kids, his grandkids, showed up, and they had a picnic. He also noticed a gardener who wasn't actually gardening, but he kept busy probably to keep his coworkers happy.

Reagan stood up to throw away her empty cup, and Seth was on his feet walking to the trashcan beside her. When they got to his car, he pulled her in for a kiss. "I like hanging out with you, babe," he said.

Reagan leaned in and hugged him.

Once they left the park, he drove them to the market to pick up items to cook for dinner. Reagan was quiet as he picked out what he needed to make her spaghetti. "I've got a new recipe," he said, and she smiled.

She hadn't talked since they left the park, and although he wanted to know everything about her life before they met, he understood it was going to take some time.

It was too early to begin dinner, and once they got back to Reagan's place, she jumped on her computer to check her work email. Seth sat with her at the table and went through his email on his phone. He returned a few emails and made some notes to work on others later. Reagan rapidly typed emails and then seemed engrossed in something she said had to do with work.

She was focused on her computer but evasive toward him when he asked if everything was all right. "Yes. I'm sending an email to Amber," she said. Then she followed it up with, "I probably should call her. Do you mind if I go into the bedroom and talk privately?"

Seth watched her facial expression, it didn't change, but something about her demeanor made him suspicious. He watched her walk out of the room as she dialed her phone. Then she closed the door, and Seth heard the television come on. *Was she afraid he would listen to her?*

Chapter Seventeen

AMBER PLANNED TO CALL REAGAN to discuss the city council members but found out about the vandalism to her car. She was upset for her friend, and before her call went through, Reagan was calling her.

"Great minds think alike," Amber said. "I was dialing your number just now."

Reagan laughed. They called each other at the same time often, and the deep connection meant a lot to each of them.

"Have they picked up that Salinas guy?" Amber asked.

"No. The police officers haven't been able to locate him," Reagan said, talking as if it was a minor detail.

"Are you freaking out yet? I know you're not, but you should be freaking out now, Reagan."

"I'm fine. It will all get sorted out soon."

Amber wanted to dig in deeper about the vandalism and the attack on her friend, but Reagan wouldn't stay on the phone long if the subject were about her. Discussing the suspected fraud was the only way to talk to her.

"I just found out the announcement will be made tomorrow that the South Louisiana Community Health Care Facility won the option and will build a flagship medical center here. Can you believe it's happening? They'll break ground in sixty days and plan to complete the building by next summer," Amber said, talking faster than usual.

"It's not unusual, Amber. I didn't realize, but after looking into it, I learned the city chooses a facility based on more than price."

"Girl, I'm telling you that Teresa and Bruce knew before all the bids were in and way before an official decision was made. And honey, that isn't legal, especially if money changed hands. I work with this group on the reg, and there is something oddly chummy about those two whenever we get together for a meeting. They hardly used to speak to one another. But then, suddenly, they're drinking buddies. It's like they hit the lottery. Teresa's sporting a new car, and Bruce is wearing expensive shoes."

Reagan could hear how desperate Amber was for her to agree, but she needed to stay open-minded to help her friend. "From the outside looking in, the whole council and the mayor have a harmony that we haven't seen in the city's history. It looks like we'll all benefit from how hard they're working on getting along and on finding resolutions for budget concerns."

"Mayor Regalia isn't as harmonious as you say about some of their behavior. He's diplomatic and works hard to hide it, but I can tell," Amber's voice cracked when she said the mayor's name. *Was she getting upset?*

"For example?" Reagan asked. She didn't want to upset Amber, and the information she had on the city council members made them look suspicious, but there wasn't any hard proof.

"Well, for starters, he wasn't sure that SLCHC was the best fit. He told them that he had concerns about the facility they had planned to build here and whether it would be big enough to make an impact. He had other concerns, too, and they seemed to go unnoticed. He mentioned it to several people in my office and me."

"So, he isn't happy about the specific group coming here? There isn't any proof that it was achieved illegally. And I heard he was pleased that it would get done for the city. I can't see how a compromise over who the city council chose would upset him when it was his original choice. It's still a win."

"Did he tell you that personally?"

The question surprised Reagan, especially when Amber accented the word *you*. "Of course not. You know I'm with Seth and that the mayor and I don't chat regularly."

Amber cleared her throat. "You're just not listening to me, Reagan."

"I am listening. I also have Jerry looking into it. He said that the new CEO and CFO for the Community Health Care Centers couldn't have attended a game, much less games with the council members. Both executives are new, and neither man had visited the city since last summer when they looked at potential locations for the health center. Jerry also checked the parent company out of Texas. He couldn't find any evidence that any of them had ever been to New Orleans. I don't know your sources for the information, but it's suspicious. Jerry will let me know as soon as he has anything else, but so far, he hasn't found anything that could help your case against them. Promise me that you will continue keeping your suspicions confidential for now. Let him finish his investigation."

"I'm telling you that a representative from SLCHC was here in the city at two separate games, box seats, and there has to be video proof," Amber said.

"If there is proof, Jerry will find it. Until then, you keep your head up."

Amber agreed, and they made plans to have lunch together the next day. When Reagan hung up the phone, she sat on her bed. Why was that conversation so difficult? She and Amber had always built each other up, and that conversation felt like an argument. She needed to center herself and put the emotion away. Either Amber was right or wrong about the illegal activity, and Jerry would find the evidence.

She suddenly needed Seth. *Was it too soon to feel that way?*

It had been another long day, and she was emotionally tired. She headed out of the bedroom and found him in the kitchen, but something was wrong with him too. He leaned against the counter with his arms crossed in front of his chest, staring at her.

"Everything okay?" she asked, watching him cautiously.

"You tell me?"

"That was business, Seth."

"You and Amber don't work together."

Was he mad at her for talking to Amber in private?

"You can look at my phone and see she's the only call I've made. What's going on with you?" She tried to smile at him, but she knew something was off. The whole learning-to-read-the-room as a child told her that she needed to be on guard. She wanted to be wrong.

"Reagan, you seem to keep a lot of secrets."

"That's not fair," she said.

"I've never known you to take a phone call in the other room. You used to always talk about business with me by leaving out the names, but now you turn on the television because why? You thought I would listen in at the door? Do you not trust me? I'm not the one having private dinners in my office with the mayor."

Reagan felt the stab of his words in her heart. "First of all, I didn't lie about that dinner. I didn't want you to think it was something that it wasn't, and you were already suspicious of my relationship with Alexavier. I told you because I didn't want any secrets between us. You can't use that against me."

Even he couldn't believe he'd said that to her, but he was hurt and didn't stop there. "Or maybe you didn't tell me because there was more going on between you and Regalia?"

Reagan looked into Seth's eyes and shook her head. "I can't believe you don't trust me."

"He's the one that I don't trust, Rea."

"Well, you can't have an affair going on with just one person. Either you believe me, or you don't. But, honestly, right now, I can't be around you." The betrayal felt deeper than it should.

She'd been honest with him. More open than she'd ever been with anyone, and he used the information against her. It should have been a minor disagreement, but it felt like the world had ended.

How could she ever tell him more?

She walked to her front door and unlocked it, holding it open for him.

"You're kicking me out?"

She nodded and kept the door open until he walked into the hallway. Then, without another word, she shut the door and dead-bolted it. He didn't try to stop her.

Seth walked to the elevator.

What had he done?

He knew her.

He trusted her.

She needed him more than ever, and he let his jealousy take over. He stood there waiting on the elevator, feeling the weight of his tactless words bearing down on him. He saw the hurt on her face when she shut the door. Her strong outer walls had lowered for him that afternoon, and he should have valued the gift. Now he was taking the elevator down to the lobby, and she was alone again.

She always acted strong, and he remembered the conversation with her brother, Ryan. She had a soft center. He knew she had a soft side, and he needed to beg forgiveness for the cruel words he'd used to hurt her.

He did that. He hurt her.

Reagan swiped the few tears that escaped as she put away all the items Seth had set out to cook for dinner. She sure as hell wasn't cooking, and she didn't need the reminder that they almost had another great night together.

She put the last onion away when she heard the melodic knock on her front door. She took a deep breath of relief that he came back to apologize. They might have that spaghetti, after all, she thought as she looked out the peephole.

It wasn't Seth.

Chapter Eighteen

REAGAN OPENED THE DOOR READY to tell the mayor to go home, but he smiled that warm smile, and she saw that he had flowers in one hand and a brown bag that smelled of fried food in the other. She was deeply hurt, the kind of hurt that only happened when someone you loved caused it, and she didn't have the heart to send a friendly face away.

"I heard you were staying home today, and after the vandalism last night, I thought you could use some company," he said, slipping in and giving her a soft kiss on the cheek.

"I'm not really up for company," she said, but it didn't even sound believable to her.

Alexavier nodded. "I figured you'd say that, and I thought I should tell you a story about what happened to me five years ago during my first term in office."

He took off his raincoat and revealed the white button-down shirt and slacks he was wearing. He'd taken off his tie and sports coat when he'd left his office, and Reagan noted that she hadn't seen him casually dressed but a couple of times. He was a very handsome man.

"Would you like something to drink?" she asked.

"Sure."

She picked up the crystal decanter, and half grinned at him. "Whiskey?"

Alexavier nodded. "You never cease to surprise me, Reagan."

"It's been a whiskey kind of day," she said, avoiding his stare.

"I would say it's been a whiskey kind of week where you're concerned," he said, taking the leaded glass she handed him.

Alexavier unpacked the eggplant Parmesan and the ravioli from Mandina's while Reagan got out two plates. They sat at her small table and shared the two dishes along with the warm garlic bread he brought.

As she sipped her whiskey, he began to tell her his tale.

"So, most people don't know the story I'm about to tell you because I begged to keep it out of the press," he said, garnering her complete attention.

"My first term as mayor wasn't as easy as most people believe. I mean, I did win by a considerable margin, and the transition of my team into office was pretty easy on most accounts, but for the first month, I got death threats and threatening phone calls almost daily."

Reagan stared at him, weighing his words. "How did you keep that quiet?"

He shrugged and then gave her that politician smile she didn't trust, but others loved. "It doesn't matter, but after the last administration had such a volatile last year, I thought it was important to have the appearance of an easy-going atmosphere. But, it was anything other than peaceful."

Reagan sat her glass down and crossed her arms in front of her. Alexavier drank the rest of his whiskey as if he needed the confidence, but she knew better. He gave her a sincere look that she knew wasn't rehearsed as he began again.

"The threats were at the office and my home. My car was vandalized, which is why I have a chauffeur still today. But then someone broke into my home and vandalized it while I was at the office. They wanted to show that I wasn't safe anywhere. I had to hire bodyguards, but still, they couldn't stop the threats."

"What did you do?"

"I kept going. Every day, I got up and went to the office like the day before and the day before that. I couldn't let them or him, whoever it was to control my ability to serve the city. It took five weeks, but my security detail found a suspect, and it turned out that he was angry from a contract deal I had drafted up years earlier when I was an attorney. He was arrested and eventually put into a mental health facility."

"Five weeks?"

"Five long weeks," he said.

"I'm sorry that happened."

"I'm not telling you this to make you feel sorry, Reagan. I want you to know that you have options. First, we can hire a bodyguard to watch over you until the guy is caught. There is no reason for you to feel nervous or scared while the investigation continues. We can keep you safe. Secondly, I want you to know that he will be caught. I've already spoken to the police chief and let him know that I want them to pull in the necessary men to help locate your attacker."

Reagan looked into his eyes. "You didn't have to do that for me."

"I know I didn't have to, but I wanted to do it. You are not alone, Reagan. I can help you. I want to help you."

Reagan stood up and made herself a glass of ice water. She needed to stop drinking around Alexavier because all his *I want to watch over you* crap was starting to wear her down. She didn't want him, but he was making a hard case for why she should give him a chance.

Alexavier pulled out a tray of cannoli as she sat back down and offered her one first. She smiled, thinking about how she would end up looking like one of the incredible desserts if she didn't stop eating that way with him. She took a bite and then licked the cream from her lips. The extraordinary dessert wasn't helping her find her strength to tell him thanks, but no thanks.

She watched as he ate two cannoli, licked the cream from his top lip, and then off his finger. He was charming.

"Thanks for dinner, Alexavier. I didn't realize I was so hungry," she said. "And for the encouraging words about my disgruntled fan. I'll have to decline the security guard offer for now, though. I don't want to give everyone the wrong impression, and honestly, if he wanted to harm me, he has certainly had the chance. So far, it's mostly been threats and vandalism. I believe he's heartbroken, and I'm sure he's going to either be caught or turn himself in soon."

Alexavier reached his hand out to pat her leg, and she instantly had goosebumps all over. "You don't need to be alone, Reagan, especially while your *disgruntled fan*, as you call him, is still on the loose. Perhaps he doesn't want to harm you as you believe, or perhaps he wants to torment you first before he does. You can't be sure. I want to know you're safe."

"Thanks, Alexavier. But I keep trying to tell everyone that I'm fine." Reagan stood up and brought the rest of the dishes to the sink. Two weeks ago, she was comfortable and single, and now she had Seth back in her life and Alexavier practically throwing himself at her. It was too much for her to think about on top of the super creepy Salinas. Then there was the investigation for Amber that she had to think about too.

She never thought she would long for a couple of messy divorce cases, but there she was, missing her everyday life.

Alexavier followed her to the sink and stood too close. "If I know anything, it's that when a woman tells you that she's fine, she is anything but fine," he whispered in her ear.

Reagan took a sidestep to put some space between them. She wasn't a cliché, and she didn't like generalizations about women. She didn't think he meant it rudely, though, and she didn't correct him. Alexavier was an interesting man, but Seth didn't have a reason to be jealous. The way he up and left her didn't bode well for their future, but she loved him and couldn't stop loving him just because he was acting like a jerk. She smiled at

Alexavier but held her hand up when he tried to close the gap between them.

"Alexavier," she said and promptly cleared her throat when she realized she was whispering. Seth left without a second thought, but she wasn't the kind of woman to accept the next offer, even if he was the gorgeous single mayor. "I appreciate you coming over to check on me and for the delicious food. You are a sweet man, and I don't meet a lot of good guys in my line of work."

Alexavier put his finger over her lips. "Don't say *but,* Reagan. I know things are crazy right now for you, and besides the jerk who is tormenting you, there is also another man vying for your attention. I presume I met him in your office the other day?"

Reagan nodded.

"I won't ask why he's not here worrying over you like I am. I will say that he should be, though. Nevertheless, I do like you. We would have a great time together, and we could be good for one another. I can give you some time." He leaned in to kiss her on the cheek, and he whispered in her ear, "Call me if you need anything."

He walked over to the couch and picked up his raincoat, and Reagan couldn't miss the swagger in his step. He was a confident man, and Amber was right; confidence was hot. She hurried to the door and unlocked it for him, and he kissed her goodbye again on each cheek before he quickly left.

Reagan locked the door and didn't remember walking back over to her couch and sitting down. How did she have two of the best-looking men in the city jealous and wanting her attention?

She put her head in her hands and tried to think of what she should do next when there was another knock on her door, a frantic knock.

Chapter Nineteen

REAGAN'S STOMACH FELT HOLLOW as she tiptoed to look out the peephole. So, who in the hell hadn't been to her apartment that evening? And why were they knocking so loudly?

Seth was standing there.

She slowly unlocked the door, and when she opened it, he was instantly crowding her. "If I have nothing to be jealous of, then tell me why he was in your apartment the minute I left?"

"Apparently, he's worried about me being alone while there is a nut job out there threatening me," she said to make him even more jealous, and she would admit that later.

"So how much protection did he give you in the forty-seven minutes he was here, huh?" He was furious, and Reagan couldn't believe it. She had never seen that side of him.

"You timed him?"

"You're damn right I timed him. I saw him walking into the adjacent elevator as I was walking out. So, I sat there in the lobby waiting."

"Well, as you can see, he's super-efficient. We got down and dirty the minute he walked through the frigging door, and well, I'm already dressed and everything."

Seth turned and slammed his hand down on the granite

counter-topped island. That's when he saw the containers from Mandina's restaurant and the used dishes on the sideboard. He also saw the two crystal glasses that she used to serve whiskey.

"You drank with him?"

"You would prefer the alternative?" Reagan turned to lock the front door and then walked into her bedroom. Seth followed her and watched as she changed into her flannel sleep shorts and a thermal top. He then followed her back into the living room, where she sat on the couch and covered up with the blanket.

Seth sat down too, and she could see the anguish on his face. "You know I don't want the alternative. I don't want you to see him at all. Do you want him, Rea?"

Reagan stared at Seth. How could such a beautiful and intelligent man be so thick-headed? "Go home, Seth. I'm too tired for this." She was honestly too hurt to defend herself.

"I can't leave you alone until they catch Salinas. It doesn't matter if you want me because I care too much about you. I'll sleep on the couch or the floor, but I have to know that you're safe."

"You don't have to stay. I will be fine. I have a gun."

Seth crossed his arms in front of him as he stared at her. "We both know you're not fine. No one ever means it when they say they're fine."

"Is there some kind of memo that I didn't get?" Reagan tightened her grip on the blanket as Seth looked at her, confused. "When I say I'm fine, I really do mean I am fine."

"Fine," Seth said. "I know that gun is taken apart in a locked box at the top of your closet. What are you going to do? Ask the creep to pause while you go put it together?"

Reagan cut her eyes at Seth. "My brother was a Marine, and he made me put that gun together and take it apart until I could do it in my sleep. I assure you that when you leave, I will get it down and have it ready in case I need it."

Seth grinned at her. She was fierce when she needed to be, but still, he wanted to watch over her.

"I'm not leaving, Rea."

She shrugged and grabbed the remote to turn on the television. Seth double-checked the front door locks and then dug out some of the grocery items he bought earlier and made himself a sandwich. They sat together on the couch watching television without speaking.

They both knew that when you loved someone, it didn't matter if you were mad at them or not; you stayed by their side.

§

REAGAN WAS UP and ready for work by seven. Seth didn't have a change of clothes, so it took him seconds to get ready to drive her to work. They didn't discuss the disagreement from the night before as he bought her a cup of coffee and kissed her goodbye at the front doors of her office building.

The morning went by as usual as any other morning, pre-freak attack, and Reagan texted Amber to make sure they were still on for lunch. Reagan knew how Seth would feel about her going out alone, so she had Amber pick her up, and they drove over to their regular spot for salads. Reagan agreed to sit outside, but they took the tables closest to the door. Amber swore she needed the fresh air to counteract the adverse effects of the fluorescent lights in her office.

They enjoyed lunch and gossiped about shoes and coworkers, avoiding the unfortunate events of the last few days. It was a needed reprieve for them both, and they hugged each other in the car before Amber dropped Reagan back at the office.

The afternoon didn't prove to be as uneventful.

Reagan had a stack of mail, a package, and several messages to return once she got back into the office. She told Nancy that she hadn't ordered anything and to open it and the few pieces of junk mail as she took the rest of the items.

Next, she called Seth and told him about meeting Amber for lunch. Then she agreed to wait inside the office until he picked her up at the end of the day. He seemed happy with her for being agreeable.

The next call was to her detective, Jerry. Jerry had almost decided that the investigation into the city council members was a waste of time. He'd told Reagan that he didn't want to waste her money or his time much longer, but as all of his leads dried up, he discovered something new. No one with South Louisiana Community Health Center had been back to New Orleans in months, but someone previously with the company had. He discovered that the founder and CEO for The Community Health Care Centers had a brother from the area. Supposedly they weren't close, and he couldn't seem to find a picture of the two together anywhere, but Jerry's intuition told him he was on to something. He wasn't going to give up until he discovered who the mystery brother was and if he was connected to anyone on the city council.

Reagan wanted to tell Amber what she found, but Amber had been anxious since it all began. So, Reagan decided to wait until she had definitive proof of what was happening.

Amber was one of the most intelligent attorneys Reagan knew, but she was terrible at keeping secrets outside of her client's privacy. She spoke out of turn, and she said things she shouldn't. It would be terrible if she confided in the wrong person and then lost her job.

Instead of calling Amber, Reagan returned calls to two of her clients and then finally to the detective handling her case whom she'd been avoiding.

"Ms. Gentry, it's good to hear from you," he said as if they were old friends.

"Hi, detective. You have some news for me?"

"I wanted to let you know that we picked up Becky Salinas. It appears that she's been sending money to her husband and helping him since he got out of jail."

Reagan leaned back in her chair, resting her head on the head-rest, as she listened to the detective. It wasn't like the news was noteworthy. She would be rich if she had a dollar for every couple that filed for divorce or a restraining order and then got back together. But, of course, many of them separated again, which was why every case needed to be handled delicately. There was never any way to know if a couple would get back together because it happened randomly, even sometimes after the divorce settlement had gone through.

"We don't want to put her in jail since she has little kids, but we're close to finding him. We're going to watch her a little more closely."

"No problem, Detective," Reagan said, rolling her eyes. He didn't sound any closer to finding Salinas than he did the night of the incident.

Just as she hung up the phone, she heard a scream coming from down the hallway.

It was Nancy.

Chapter Twenty

REAGAN'S HEART SUNK WHEN she heard Nancy's scream. She bolted out of the glass conference room door and toward the office where Nancy sat. She was met at the door by the older woman. "Run! There's a bomb! Run!" she yelled.

Everyone in the office stampeded toward the exits. Nancy had Reagan by the wrist pulling her along, but Reagan worked to peel the woman's fingers off her. "Let me go," she said until Nancy's brain registered what she was saying.

Terrence wore headphones in the afternoon while he worked quietly in his office. He said it was his way of meditating and getting his paperwork done simultaneously. Of course, Reagan would make fun of him as she argued the whole point of meditating was to stop people from multitasking, but he didn't listen to her.

Since Monday, his secretary had been out sick, and Reagan knew he wouldn't have heard the warning or seen everyone freaking out. She had to get to him. But, it was almost impossible to swim upstream as everyone poured out of the doors and hallways. It took all her strength to get past the crowd.

She was out of breath when she pushed through Terrence's door. He looked up and smiled at her until he saw the look on her face. He stood and removed the headphones at the same time. "What is it?"

"There's a bomb," she said in between breaths as the fire alarms screeched.

"You mean a fire?" he asked.

"No. No. I pulled the fire alarm so the other offices would evacuate. It's a bomb."

He jumped up, and they headed toward the exit when a bomb squad member grabbed them and slammed them to the floor. He landed on top of them with a grunt, covering them the best he could with his body and fire-retardant suit. The explosion was deafening.

Reagan's ears were ringing so loudly that she couldn't understand what the first responder was saying, but she also could barely breathe with him on top of her. He looked around before he pulled himself up, and Reagan and Terrence both slowly sat up, assessing the damage around them. It was minimal, considering the loud noise it made.

There was a lot of smoke and tiny bits of what looked like confetti falling from the air. Reagan scooted back to the wall so she could lean there until the ringing subsided. It made her dizzy, and she felt like she might throw up.

Terrence followed her lead, and they sat there together as more firemen and bomb squad techs came through. A fireman came over and checked Reagan and Terrence out, but neither had any severe injuries. Reagan had a scrape on her knee and a small bump on her head from the large man falling on top of her. She and Terrence still couldn't hear anything but the ringing noise.

They sat on the floor for forty-five minutes, watching all the emergency workers do their jobs. Then, when the police detective that had been working her case showed up, Reagan saw him roll his eyes before he tried to act like he was glad to see her.

He held his hand out to help pull her up, and she and Terrence followed him out of the mayhem.

They sat in an evacuated office down the hallway, and a paramedic came and cleaned up Reagan's knee and double-checked her head. She disagreed with him when he suggested she go to the hospital to be checked for a concussion, explaining that nausea and dizziness were from the ringing in her ears.

The local FBI agents on the scene said that the bomb appeared to be in one of Reagan's packages delivered that day. The box had disintegrated, but it was easy to see that the bomb was meant to scare everyone but wouldn't have hurt them.

"You know what I think?" the detective said.

Reagan stared at him. The ringing was still there, but she could hear his voice finally. He was a nice man, but she didn't have a lot of faith in his ability.

"What do you think?" Terrence asked, ever the polite one.

"I think this guy wants to scare you, but I don't think he's as dangerous as he seemed initially."

Terrence spoke before Reagan could ask him if he came up with that all by himself. "Well, if he's not dangerous, then he sure as hell is destroying our office."

The detective looked thoughtful as he nodded.

Reagan wanted to roll her eyes, but she knew it would only make her head hurt worse.

It took two hours before Reagan and Terrence could leave, and that's when Reagan realized she'd lost her phone in all the shuffle. The police officer allowed her to check the conference room and the floor in the hallways. She couldn't find it anywhere.

Terrence grabbed his things, and they walked out together. Seth was standing there waiting as she exited the front doors. She hugged Terrence and then turned and walked into Seth's arms. He held her close as he walked her to his car.

She was overwhelmed. Each day was more dreadful than the day before, and she couldn't understand how things continued to get worse. She was lost in her thoughts which was why she didn't notice Seth wasn't driving her home. Instead, she leaned against the door and watched the cars slowly creep forward on the congested roadway. It was the worst time to go on the I-10, but she didn't care. She was so happy to be away from the disaster of her day.

Seth reached over and held her hand. "Ryan was ready to go all Rambo on that building if you didn't come out soon. We didn't know if you had been injured or killed during that blast, and no one said anything to the crowd for over an hour. Then, finally, I was able to speak to someone from the fire department, and he assured me that you and Terrence were okay. I told your brother we were going to Maisonville as soon as I got you out of there."

Reagan nodded but didn't say anything. She'd created a good little life for herself as a respected divorce attorney, and in the blink of an eye or rather lousy fifteen-minute meeting with a silly woman who wasn't sure if she wanted to divorce her husband, it all had gone to hell. No matter how hard she'd worked or how well she'd done, she couldn't stop the madness around her.

She laid her head back on the seat as Seth drove steadily toward the only peaceful place in her life.

It took longer than usual to get across the lake during rush hour traffic, but Seth needed the time to work through all that had happened. He felt like he was having a heart attack while waiting to hear that she was okay.

He couldn't figure out how she didn't make it out of the office when everyone else had. Nancy told him how she had Reagan by the hand, but that Reagan forced her to let her go. It didn't make sense to him until he saw her there with Terrence. He guessed that she went back in to find him. They were going to have a long talk later about how to evacuate a building.

Seth pulled into Reagan's lake house driveway, and Ryan's truck was waiting there. He and Sydney had picked up clothes for them as Seth had explained that he wasn't stopping until he got Reagan out of the city. They also brought dinner, toiletries, additional groceries and lit a fire in the fireplace.

The warm glow coming from the house soothed Reagan in a

way she couldn't explain. It was a home, and she'd never lived in a real home.

They walked into the house and into hugs from both Ryan and Sydney. Ryan kept his arm around his sister and could feel the stress coming off her in waves. He didn't question her because he knew it wasn't the right time, but he would do it as soon as she was past the shock of it all.

Sydney ran around and pulled out plates and showed Seth the homemade potpie she had made for them. The whole welcome home lasted twenty minutes, and then Seth and Reagan were left alone to decompress.

Seth held Reagan's hand and walked her into the bathroom. He ran a hot shower for her and then brought her comfy clothes to change into when she was done.

He jumped into the shower while she got dressed, and they both finished about the same time. Reagan said she wasn't hungry, so they sat quietly in front of the fire until Seth had to get up and add more wood. He then went into the kitchen and made them each a small plate of the warm comfort food Sydney had prepared for them.

Reagan ate only a few bites but drank most of the water he'd brought her. When he finished eating, she laid across the couch and put her head in his lap. He played with her hair until she fell asleep and then helped her to the bedroom, where they both woke up off and on all night.

Finally, at four in the morning, Reagan got up for good. She'd tossed and turned and couldn't get the bombing out of her head. She needed to think, which meant she needed to pace for a bit.

Seth watched her but didn't get up immediately. He could see she needed some space, and he gave it to her until he heard the outside door open.

"Rea. Hold up," he said, grabbing his shoes and running to the back door.

He startled her at first by running, but he quickly grabbed her hand. "It's me, sweetheart. I don't want you to go outside without me. It's safe and all. I just need eyes on you for a few days. Understand?"

She kissed him and nodded as he held out her jacket to put on, and then they headed down to the pier together. She walked to the end and then back again several times. Finally, as the early morning sun rose, she had a seat at the end of the pier, and he sat down next to her watching her face.

She was finally going to talk. He'd missed her voice. He'd missed talking to her. He had no idea how much she had to say.

Chapter Twenty-One

REAGAN SAT ON THE weathered Adirondack chair and played with her hair, pulling it to the side, twisting it, and then untwisting it. It was long and straight but had some natural wave to it too. She mostly wore it up in a twist or ponytail until late afternoon when it bothered her, and then she took it down and let it free. Focused primarily on looking professional, she'd never spent too much time styling her hair. But even now, when she tried to work out a perplexing situation, just like during her childhood, she fiddled with her dark hair.

She'd spent most of her life watching out for her little brother and herself while their parents couldn't manage a single thing properly. Reagan was brilliant and labeled gifted in elementary school. Kids were nice to her, but she wasn't popular and didn't get treated like one of the pretty girls. She liked it that way. She managed to get a lot done by blending in, and that behavior, plus her brains, had always served her well.

She'd always felt like she was successful behind the scenes, which was probably why her current situation felt more difficult. She kept to herself and worked all the time. So how could she have been that man's target when she'd spent her life staying out of sight?

"I can't believe tomorrow is Friday. This may have been the longest week of my life," she said, and Seth listened to her as she rambled. "It's hard to believe a week ago today that I was minding my own business and working to make partner so that I could get a raise. I didn't go out except for lunches with Amber, and that hadn't started but a few months ago. I had dinner with Ryan once a month and tried to come out here to Maisonville every other month or so. I live a simple life. I make good decisions. How am I a part of all this drama?"

She stopped twisting her hair and pulled her legs into her body. It was cooler outside than she'd thought, and now that she wasn't walking around, she noticed the cold. She unzipped her jacket to pull it around her legs, but Seth took off his coat and draped it over her. He had a long-sleeved white t-shirt underneath, and she smiled at how handsome he was in simple things.

She didn't look like she would say anything else, and Seth prompted her. "You don't always have to go looking for trouble, Rea. It can find you."

Reagan nodded. "You're telling me. I was born into trouble. Lance and Sandy Gentry weren't meant to have children. They resented the hell out of Ryan and me. Probably from the time of conception, but certainly once we were old enough to go to school. Parents have to be careful because their kids are finally away from them and can tell someone if they aren't treated well."

"They mistreated you?"

Reagan rocked back in her chair. He could see she was reconsidering the conversation.

He waited patiently for a few minutes while she looked out over the water, and they both watched as a flock of Canadian geese flew over. Then finally, he whispered, "Tell me, Rea."

"Yes. Yes, they did, but no one knew about it."

She looked at Seth, but his sweet expression encouraged her to continue.

"Mostly, it was neglect. They wouldn't have anything for us to eat, or they couldn't pay the light bill, and our electricity was turned off for a day or so." She worried with her hair again, twisting it into a loose side curl. "I would save my lunch at school sometimes so that Ryan would have something to eat. It was so important when he was a little boy, you know."

"You're only three years older than him, Reagan. If he was a little boy, then you were little too."

She shrugged her shoulders. "I think I was born an adult. I always had this keen sense of what was going on. So, I shielded Ryan from it for as long as I could." She was proud of raising Ryan in a positive environment. He could see it in her eyes as they shimmered in the morning light.

"Did you tell someone?"

"I got caught with the food in my locker. I'd do the other kids' homework if they gave me some of their lunch. It had been one of the popular kids' birthdays, and his mom had brought lots of snacks for our class that day. Fortunately, several of my regulars weren't hungry. We had a four-day weekend coming up, and I was excited about our luck. I planned to stash it all in my bookbag after school and carry my books. It seemed like a good plan. Then the secretary's service dog walked by and started howling. I was called out of class to the principal's office. He had the vice principal, the counselor, even the school nurse there. I think they thought I had an eating disorder at first. I wanted to laugh at how ridiculous they were. I was only ten and one of the smallest girls in my class. I certainly wasn't suffering from bulimia."

Seth had some bulimic patients, but they were adults. Many of them had started it as teens. He couldn't believe Reagan knew what it was as a ten-year-old. Then again, he was shocked that she had the ability to barter for food as a ten-year-old. He considered that maybe she didn't keep groceries in her apartment because she didn't know how to stock a proper pantry.

"Did you get into trouble?" he asked but couldn't imagine the administrators getting mad at her over hoarding food.

Reagan shrugged. "They called Lance and Sandy, but they didn't answer. So, then they called my Uncle Trey. He was the one that paid for us to go to private school. He happened to be in the city, and he got to the school in a flash. I didn't want it to be a big thing, and they let me talk to Uncle Trey alone for a few minutes. I tried to explain to him that I could handle it and that it didn't happen all the time. I thought he was going to cry. I felt terrible. Then they called Ryan out of class, but he didn't know anything. He told them that I always made him his dinner and that we ate a lot of peanut butter sandwiches, but he really liked to eat whatever I made him. I think they must have called social services.

"Uncle Trey checked us out of school and took us out to eat at this big Chinese restaurant. Then we went to the grocery store, and he bought more groceries than I'd ever seen before. When we got to our house, mom was surprised to see us. She and Uncle Trey put up the groceries, and they didn't make me help. My dad got home a while later, and that's when things escalated. They were yelling at each other, and my dad came into my room and pulled me into the kitchen. He screamed at me to tell Uncle Trey that I was making the whole thing up, so I did. But Uncle Trey could see that there wasn't anything to eat at our house when he put away the groceries. He and dad had a huge fight, shoving each other and everything.

"Dad said he could never come back to the house again, and I don't think they spoke after that day. A social worker came by that night, but we had the groceries from Uncle Trey. She talked to my parents about signing up for food stamps and maybe getting some assistance with the utilities, but they smiled and acted like everything was fine and said I was a silly kid. I never saw that lady again, and after she left, they both freaked out on me. They threatened to send me away with the social worker so I would never see Ryan again. I was too young to fight back, and I was terrified they would send me away. That's when I knew they didn't care about me. I mean, I felt like they didn't before, but that night, it was the real deal."

Reagan put her legs down and sat up straighter in her chair. She locked eyes with Seth, but he was a professional, and he wasn't going to let her see him sweat over the details. Instead, he kept his thoughtful expression as she watched him.

"Your Uncle wasn't allowed to come over, but I know you saw him because you said you spent summers in Maisonville with him."

"Yes, but we didn't see him often. I was twelve when our parents divorced, and until then, he couldn't come over to the house. Uncle Trey was lovely, though, and he would sneak up to the school every now and again to have lunch with us. He also continued to pay for our tuition and had groceries delivered once a week. Specifically, things that I could make easily."

"He was a good man."

"One of the best."

They sat there looking at each other until Seth broke the silence. "You said mostly."

"What?"

"When I asked you if they mistreated you, you said yes, mostly neglect."

Reagan nodded.

"It implies—."

"I know. I don't want to lie to you, Seth."

"Then don't."

Reagan stared into his eyes, and he knew she was weighing her options.

"Fine," she said. "When we were driving by my father's old duplex yesterday, it reminded me of when he and my mother separated. He had a bad temper after she kicked him out. He would get mad at the simplest things. If I spilled my drink or Ryan dropped his chips on the floor. And he would throw stuff at us. Somehow, I sensed when it was about to happen, and I would shield Ryan. Mother made me hide the bruises. She would say the drugs made him do it."

"She didn't turn him in?"

Reagan didn't answer at first. Tears lightly fell down her cheeks, and Seth held her hand. He wanted to stop her and tell her it would all be okay, but he knew she needed to tell someone. She needed to tell him.

"She couldn't turn him in because he only did it a couple of times. She knew if she called the police, they would find out," Reagan paused, and when Seth thought she wouldn't continue, she did. "They would find out that she was worse than him."

Seth's jaw tightened as she admitted to having two physically abusive parents and no one there to stop them.

"I'm so sorry that happened. It shouldn't have."

Reagan wiped her face dry and gave him a half-grin, pretending she was okay.

"I didn't spend the night at our father's place again after she found the bruises, but we did visit him at the park or a fast-food place like McDonald's, and he would buy us burgers. He never did anything mean to me again. It was like visiting a stranger, a nice stranger. Our mother was mean as the devil. She slept a ton, but whenever she was awake, she was angry. Thankfully, she never hit Ryan, but she would wear me out with a belt or a wooden spoon. Really anything she could get her hands on. If I avoided her, she would break things in the house until she wore herself out. By the time I was in tenth grade, I was finally big enough to fight back. Ryan was in the seventh grade, and he stopped her too. He was a lot bigger, and he threatened to kill her if she ever touched me again. She either believed him, or she couldn't muster up the energy to do it anymore. So, it stopped."

Reagan stood up and stretched. Her face looked more peaceful than before. "Of course, the summers in Maisonville with Uncle Trey were wonderful, and it made me feel braver when we went back home. I learned to watch for signs that she was losing her temper, and then I avoided her. I got really good at avoiding trouble. At least until this week. This crazy week."

Seth stood up and wrapped his arms around her. He wanted to shield her from the outside world. She deserved to be protected.

All the time they had spent apart, he thought about how she

hid her past. His experience as a doctor told him it must have been awful. He'd prepared for it. But he couldn't have planned for his own response. She wasn't his patient. She was the love of his life. He was angry that anyone would ever hurt her, especially the two people in the world who should have protected her.

"Seth?" she whispered his name.

When he pulled back to look at her, she could see his eyes were red. She had never seen him cry, and she wasn't sure if she could handle it if he did.

"You know I'm okay, right?"

He kissed her on top of her head several times and then on her forehead, nose, and lips. "I know that I'm going to do everything in my power to make sure of that, Rea."

Reagan kissed him and then turned her head, so she didn't start crying too.

They headed into the house to shower and dress for the day.

Seth scrambled some eggs and made some toast, but Reagan had coffee.

"It's too early for food for me, thanks," she said as they sat down at the table together.

He ate and watched her.

"What, Seth?"

He set his fork down. "Do you think your childhood made it harder for you to trust people?"

Reagan lowered her eyes at him. "I told you that stuff because, well, I'm not sure why, but you seemed to want to know that crap. But I'm not here to be psychoanalyzed, Seth Young. I had an awful childhood. Big deal. I'm a grown-up now, and I don't have to depend on anyone for anything."

"You don't have to depend on anyone, but wouldn't it be nice to have that as an option?"

Reagan avoided looking at him. It was too much. "What do you want from me, Seth."

"I want you to know that you can depend on me. If you get a flat tire, lock your keys in your car, or have some crazed clients threaten you, then I want to be the one you call. I don't want to hear about it from your brother or your secretary or even hours later from you."

Reagan reached her hand out across the table to hold his. She didn't want to be strong all the time, but she didn't know how to let go of all that control. She would try for him, but it was going to take time. "I appreciate you saying that, I really do. But if someone is threatening me, I will call the police first, then call you. Is that okay?"

Seth nodded and then leaned across the table to kiss her. They had a long way to go in learning to communicate with each other, but they had made some progress. It was a big step for them.

He was going to marry her one day. He just didn't think she was ready for him to tell her that yet.

He finished his food and then made himself a cup of coffee while Reagan started on her second cup. They moved into the living room and sat on the couch together.

"Can I ask you something, Seth?"

He was so happy to hear those words out of her mouth he almost forgot to answer her.

"Of course, baby. What is it?"

"Does it seem strange that a man who fights with his wife, who otherwise has no history of violence, has suddenly turned into this crazed stalker? I mean, if she is helping him hideout, then it doesn't make sense that he is still coming after me. Right? I mean, he's threatened me, and I guess he was the one that bombed my office. But he went from a restraining order to now certain prison time. I don't understand."

Seth shook his head. "I was so busy worrying about you and how to keep you safe that I hadn't thought about the progression of his violence. It could be that he was hanging on the ledge, and this sent him over, but you're right. His jump from fighting with his wife to bombing an office is a hell of a stretch."

"Maybe it's not him," Reagan said, tilting her head back and forth as she weighed the words. Then she turned sideways on the couch and crossed her legs to look at Seth. "I don't know who else in the world it could be if it wasn't him, but what if it's not Salinas?"

Seth nodded. "It all points to him, babe."

"I guess you're right. I've never had as much as a prank call before the Salinas guy. It doesn't make sense, but if he's unstable, then it probably wouldn't make sense to anyone but him." Reagan sighed.

Their conversation was interrupted when Seth's phone rang. It was eight o'clock, and she hadn't noticed until that moment that she didn't have a cell phone. She paced while he finished his call, and as soon as he hung up, she asked him if she had the phone with her yesterday.

He confirmed what she already knew; she didn't have the phone when she came out of the building. She sat down and covered her face with her hands. Seth knelt in front of her and was a breath away.

"What is wrong with me? I need a phone for my clients or the office to contact me. I remember looking for it, but I got distracted when we finally left the building. How could I have forgotten that and not even missed it until now? What if one of the partners tried to contact me?"

Seth held her hands. "Rea, I'm sure they would all understand after everything you've been through this week."

"That's just an excuse, Seth. Besides, they all went through the bombing yesterday too. I have to get out of here and get a new phone. I bet Amber is losing her mind." Reagan stood up and headed toward the front door. She remembered she didn't have a car there. She didn't have a working vehicle anywhere.

She was losing everything she'd worked for, and it had all happened in less than a week. She turned to ask for Seth's keys, but he was right there, ready to drive her. "I know there's no use in telling you that you need to rest. You've been through a tragedy, and you haven't had time to process it yet."

"You're right. There isn't any reason to tell me that because I have responsibilities. I'll try to rest later. I have to go."

He reached around her to open the door. "*We* have to go. I go wherever you do, Rea."

She didn't say anything, but she was happy that he was with her.

≈

WALKING into a store and buying a replacement cell phone should've been easy, but nothing worked out that way for Reagan lately. Instead, the salesman immediately tried to up-sell her current model, then proceeded to try and wow her with his technical knowledge about the device. Reagan didn't want to be rude to the sales guy with a ponytail, but he pushed his luck.

She explained that she'd lost her last phone in a fire and gave him all the information he needed to grab a phone from the back and let her pay for it. Instead, he opened it up and wanted to activate it for her. She let him, although she knew how to do it herself. He then attempted to help her retrieve her information from the cloud, and after she'd been patient for ten minutes listening to him give her a tutorial, she leveled her eyes at him.

"I know all the sales guys here are part of the mobile phone brain trust, and you have top-secret information on this magical device written in secret code that only you and your brethren can understand, but I don't give a flying bag of monkeys. I don't normally come into these places and figured they were obsolete with the ease of ordering phones online. Sell me the damn phone, so I can go to work and use it."

Seth could see she was ready to blow, and he stepped in to help. "She's been under a ton of stress with that fire and all. Can we go ahead and purchase the phone and set it up ourselves?"

The salesman nodded and walked straight to the cash register to ring them up as fast as possible.

Reagan stepped up as if she had something more to say, but she simply took the bag with the phone in it.

Seth waited until he got in the car before he laughed at her. Reagan ignored him as she quickly logged into her phone so she could start receiving messages and make a call.

"Flying bag of monkeys? Bad experience at a phone store before, Rea?"

Reagan finally laughed. "How did you guess? I was at the store in the mall one time, and I swear they held me captive for two hours. First, I had to get my name on a list to get help. Next, they called my name to assign me to someone that would help me when they got free. When they helped me, they insisted on getting all my information like ID, phone number, address, blood type, you know the important stuff. Then she opened the phone and showed me everything I already knew about the device. In the end, I found out I could have ordered the phone online, and it would have shipped to me, where I would never have to do that again. Time is money, you know."

"So, I hear," Seth said, trying not to laugh at how fired up Reagan was over a typical retail experience.

As Seth headed back to the lake house, Reagan called Amber. She apologized for not calling sooner but told Amber she had to purchase a new phone.

"Lawd. Please tell me they didn't try to help you set it up again."

"Seth saved them from me."

Amber laughed. "I'm glad you're with him. I've been so worried about you since I heard about the bombing in your office. I couldn't call you either because our office was on lockdown when security heard about your threat. And when it was all over, my phone went missing too."

Chapter Twenty-Two

AMBER EXPLAINED THEY DIDN'T have any warning. "The NOPD, FBI, and bomb squad came running through our building and closed all the entrances and exits. They had bomb-sniffing dogs running everywhere in the building and asked the mayor to stay away from the windows. It was scary."

Reagan looked concerned as they pulled into the driveway and left her bag as she got out of the car to walk into the house. Seth grabbed it for her and then tried to keep up so he could hear the conversation.

"They said it was a precaution until they knew more about your building. I heard local FBI shut down all the government offices for an hour or so."

Maybe it wasn't Salinas? Reagan thought as her friend explained how all of downtown was under high alert for possible bomb threats.

"What did they find?" Reagan asked.

"Nothing. The agent with us said it was a precaution. Then I heard that your building actually had a bomb and that you were inside. I've been sick worrying about you. I still had an old mobile phone, so I had it turned on last night, but when I called you, it went straight to voicemail. When I tracked you, it said that you were in the building. By the time I got over to your office, the whole place was taped off, and the building was closed. They have an armed guard at your office. I rechecked your phone location, and it showed you were in the warehouse district, and then it went out for good."

"The warehouse district? When was that?"

"Six, maybe seven o'clock. I'm not sure. Weird, huh?"

"It must have been a glitch. I lost it in the office before the bomb went off. It was probably destroyed under someone's shoe."

"That's technology for ya, sister. I tried to use my computer and track my own phone, thinking I'd lost it in the office somewhere. It didn't show up at all. I probably dropped it somewhere when the bomb squad showed up and broke it to bits. You would think I'd still be able to track it by GPS. Hell, what are those airplane black boxes made from? They pull them out of the ocean or wreckage from a thirty-thousand-foot drop and still can retrieve information. I can't drop my phone out of my hands without destroying it?"

Reagan laughed at her friend. She sounded good, considering she had been on lockdown in her office for five hours the day before.

"You're sure your office is safe?" Reagan asked.

"Without a doubt. Mathew Nunan from your office was there. Between him and Mayor Regalia, the poor bomb guys didn't have a chance. They made them go through the building three times with the dogs. Mathew even bought me a coke, and we shared some peanuts as several of us hung out in the mayor's private office for hours talking until the ordeal was over."

"Getting chummy with Mathew Nunan over a coke and peanuts?" Reagan teased.

"Don't say it like that. Matt's a great guy to have around in an emergency. I was so nervous, and he got my mind off the bomb scare."

"I'm sorry, Amber. I know it was a difficult afternoon."

"I'm saying he's a better man than I originally thought, and maybe you should give him another chance? But you are the one that has been through hell. I was nervous over the potential threat, girl, but you survived a bomb in your office. It would take a lot of margaritas to calm me down afterward."

"You and I will catch up over Rita's. For now, you stay in the office where your safe today," Reagan said, thinking about how she wished she had the distraction of work. *Would she ever feel safe there again?*

Amber felt terrible for all that Reagan was going through. Reagan worked harder than anyone else she knew, and she didn't deserve anything dangerous happening to her. "It won't be long before your office is redone and things get back to normal, Reagan."

"Are you sure about that?"

"Hell, yes. I'm sure. Your office brings in some serious money over there, and I know those attorneys won't let their superstar new partner get picked on. I bet your office is ready to go on Monday."

"I can't wait," Reagan said, trying to put on a happier demeanor for her friend as she tried hard to cheer her up. "We need a girl's night and at least two margaritas."

"How about I promise you a private yacht and as many margaritas as you can hold?"

Reagan rolled her eyes. "Sure. Where in the world are you going to score a private yacht?"

"Girl, I have skills you haven't ever seen before."

Reagan laughed out loud. She needed that phone call with Amber, and she needed some one-on-one time with her girlfriend.

"Seriously, Reagan. I need you to be my plus one a week from Saturday."

"Private yacht? I'm in," Reagan said, not genuinely believing their luck.

Amber squealed over the phone. "I knew you would be excited. It's Mayor Regalia's birthday party. It will be an intimate group of one hundred and fifty, and it's on a huge sailboat yacht thingy. Sexy dress attire." Amber's excitement was undeniable.

"Are you sure this isn't a people from work deal?" Reagan knew better because Alexavier had already verbally invited her, but she was second-guessing the whole thing.

"He knows we are best friends, and he invited both of us." Reagan didn't know what else to say because she wanted to support Amber, but she also knew that Seth would hit the roof when he found out it was a party for Alexavier.

"You know Amber—."

"Don't you dare ditch me, Reagan Gentry." Amber knew Reagan was about to try and decline, and she interrupted her first.

"No, I was going to say that maybe I shouldn't attend something with the mayor as long as I have a target on my back. If I learned anything, it's that this person will stop at nothing to get to me. I put my entire office in danger, and I can't do that again." Reagan shuddered, thinking about being on a boat at night with a bomb going off.

"Oh, Reagan. I'm sorry. I'm insensitive talking about a party while you're going through all this mess. But a lot can happen in a week, and I'm sure by next Saturday, this will all be behind you. What are the police saying? Any idea where Salinas is hiding out or if they're closing in on him?"

"You're not insensitive. I've tried to put it out of my mind, but the jerk won't stop. The detective thinks Salinas and his wife have reconciled, but she's not giving him up. She says he couldn't have done anything else but hasn't said how she knows that or where he's hiding."

"Do you want to stay at my place with me? I have a buff fireman that lives next door," Amber said.

"I remember your neighbor crush. Um, no thanks. Seth is sort of my unofficial bodyguard. He and my brother have been conspiring, and I think they have worked out a schedule to make sure I'm never left alone. I'm about to have the fight of my life when they figure out that I'm planning to go into the office for a couple of hours this afternoon."

"Oh-oh. My money's on you, girl. But still, you better get a head start. I know Ryan will track you like a bloodhound."

"Right now, Ryan's the least of my worries."

Amber's laughter transcended the phone. "Seth's with you now?"

"Of course. Which part of I-am-never-left-alone did I not make clear?"

"Yeesh. Call me when you escape this afternoon. I'll bring you a coffee."

Reagan waited for Amber to say goodbye, and then she sat her phone down. She was certain Seth would start the conversation.

"Do you really think going into the office is wise considering what has happened this week, Rea?"

She shrugged but didn't answer him.

"What happened at Amber's office? Did they have a bomb threat too?"

"No. Apparently, security locked them down until they figured out that the threat at our office was an isolated event. That's all."

"And what is this party?" Ah, the question she had been waiting for from the beginning.

"It's a birthday party for Mayor Regalia."

Seth didn't say anything else about the party or ask her any more questions. He stepped out of the room and onto the back deck to talk on his phone. Ten minutes later, Ryan knocked on the door.

Chapter Twenty-Three

SETH SHOOK HANDS WITH Ryan and then invited him inside. He looked at Reagan and, without a word, left her alone with her brother. Ryan walked straight over and sat down on the coffee table directly in front of Reagan.

"Reagan, what's going on?" he asked.

"It would help if I knew what you were specifically referring to, Ryan." This was where being a good lawyer was helpful. She knew when to answer and when to play dumb. She didn't speak to hear herself talk, and she didn't necessarily have to have the last word.

"I heard that you wanted to go into work today, and I wondered if you think that's a good idea? Have you spoken to Terrence? They probably haven't cleared the office to open today. Besides, it's harder for us to protect you if you're there in an open building with multiple entrances and exits and hundreds of people coming in and out of the entire building."

"I understand, Ryan. But I won't let this situation keep me from living my life. If the police can't find him, do you think he'll run out in the open to try and get to me? I mean, he's had opportunities to hurt me, really hurt me, and he hasn't. He just keeps doing things to annoy me."

"What he's doing is threatening you, and each time it's a little more serious than the time before. If he keeps it up, he will eventually hurt or kill you. Rea, I can't let that happen." Ryan moved to the couch to sit next to her and put his arm around her shoulders.

Reagan could feel her eyes watering and had to look away from him before he really got to her. He knew it was a fear of hers to be left alone since their uncle died. It was his too. She'd told him that same thing when he had difficulty assimilating into civilian life after ten years in the military.

"Nothing will happen to me," she said, just like he had told her when she'd lectured him.

He nodded and then smiled at her. He wasn't going to let her out of his sight.

"Fine. When are we leaving?" he asked.

"You don't have to go with me. Seth took off today, and I'm sure he will drive me," Reagan said, feeling more confident that he understood. She figured if he agreed with her, she couldn't be in as much danger as everyone was making out.

Ryan stood up and zipped up his jacket. Seth walked back in from outside and nodded at Ryan.

Reagan was confused. "What are you two doing without telling me?"

Seth stepped forward to lock eyes with her. "I told you that I'm not going to let anything happen to you. Ryan is my backup."

Reagan shook her head. She didn't want her brother back in the protection business. He'd served his time for their country, and it almost took his life. "No-no-no, that is not happening."

She headed toward the front door, but Ryan stood in front of her. "I appreciate the concern, but big sister, this is not your decision alone. I am going. I am setting up a perimeter around you, and as long as you are in that building, I am in that building. Seth will stay with you, and I am the lookout."

Reagan lowered her voice, "Ryan, you have a new career. You

don't have to do this. The police are actively looking for this guy. I don't want to jeopardize your progress."

"I know you can see that I'm not progressing because I'm well now, Reagan. No more excuses. Either you stay here, or we're all going."

Reagan looked back and forth between the two stubborn men. She could debate either one of them into the ground, but no way could she do it when they were teaming up against her. She had to go into the office for a couple of hours to check in with Nancy and a couple of crucial clients. At least she wouldn't be thinking about Salinas and what he could be planning next. She understood that Seth would protect her at all costs, and Ryan would take down the bad guy faster than six of the best NOPD officers.

They piled into Seth's SUV and were downtown in forty-five minutes. The traffic was heavier midday on Fridays, and Reagan always joked that the whole town took the entire day off after lunch every week. Seth pulled into the parking garage but didn't park in a regular space. He pulled up to the stairwell door, and that was when the parking attendant stepped forward.

"Mr. Gentry?" he asked, and Ryan stepped out of the car. He gave the man a wad of cash and opened Reagan's door. She saw that Ryan had a black bag over one shoulder and looked around the garage as she stepped out.

Seth stepped in front of her and led the way into the stairwell as Ryan walked behind her. It was so far from her everyday life that she would laugh as the scene played out like a bad action movie, but it scared her more than she wanted to admit.

They climbed the first flight of stairs, and that's when Reagan cleared her throat loudly and grabbed Seth's arm to stop him. "This is a little much Chuck Norris 1 and 2. They moved our offices temporarily onto the second floor, and no way in hell am I letting you two escort me in like this. Everyone is already watching me, and if I show up with armed guards, I'll have to change my name and practice law somewhere else. Remember, I'm about to make partner, and I have to act like I have some moxie."

Both men smiled at her as Seth resumed his position in front until they got to the second-floor door. Instead of walking through first, he held the door open for her as he peered around the area. Ryan didn't say a word as he followed her into the hallway and then into the large office. Movers had most of the furniture set up, and it looked like their regular law office, except it was brighter and lighter with painted walls instead of all that wood paneling. It was a little too cheery to be a law firm, Ryan thought and then smiled that he would use that joke as soon as he had the opportunity.

Walking into the office, Reagan saw how the secretary stared at her, and she halfheartedly introduced Seth and her brother. She then strolled down the hallway as if she'd been there a hundred times before. When she got to the end, she knocked on a massive door.

It was Terrence's office, and she held the door open for Ryan and Seth. "Sorry about this, Terrence. Frick and Frack forced me to let them come, but I won't be here long. I hope it's not too much of a distraction?"

Terrence stood up and shook their hands, thanking them for coming and looking out for Reagan. "All this excitement is starting to make me rethink my career choice," he said.

"Let's see if I can help make this the same boring office you had a week ago," Ryan said, winking at Reagan and moving out of range so she couldn't swat his arm.

"I'm going to check out the lobby and figure out all the ways someone could get in here while you make the magic happen, Reagan. Make it snappy."

"Watch that bossy tone, little brother, or I'll work all night."

"She means that, Ryan. She's logged more hours than anyone this year." Terrence crooked his eyebrow and added, "Make that last four years in a row."

Reagan shook her head at all the testosterone around her and then exited the office, shaking her head. They were picking on her, and she didn't mind, but she also didn't want Seth to get on his high horse again lecturing her about having a life. She loved her job, and she had a happy life, usually.

Reagan couldn't help but notice how few people were working and when she found Nancy, she asked her if she'd heard anything. "Not yet. The gossip train has been silent this afternoon."

Reagan grinned at Nancy. She always knew what was going on before most everyone else. Reagan had received a text from her that she would be in the office at noon. The head secretary had contacted them all at seven a.m. to let them know it was not a paid holiday and the new office would be open.

Nancy could have stayed home. She didn't need the money, and she knew that Reagan would have understood. But Nancy wasn't about to miss a word of gossip by staying home when she was perfectly fine. She lived to stir things up amongst the staff.

Nancy had already called all of Reagan's appointments and rescheduled them for the next week. She'd also had Reagan's mail scanned in the lobby so she could verify they didn't have anything to worry about. She was the perfect secretary for Reagan, even if she had the hots for Reagan's brother.

When they first walked in, Reagan laughed to herself when she saw Nancy staring at Ryan. The woman had twenty-five to thirty years on her brother, but she flushed from head to toe and licked her lips every time he walked anywhere near her. It was hilarious to Reagan.

Seth kept to his word and followed Reagan everywhere she went in the office, and when she found her area and desk, he sat quietly in a chair. "If you need to make any confidential calls, I can step out into the hallway, Rea. Just let me know."

She caught the inflection in his voice and knew he was teasing her about the ridiculous argument they'd had the other day. He'd felt bad for hurting her, and it was his way of still trying to ease the pain.

She stood up and walked over to him so she could plant a kiss on his lips. He pulled her close, "Hurry up so I can take you home and have my way with you, woman."

Reagan locked eyes with Seth, and he could see the desire. She couldn't wait to get home with him either. A slow grin crossed her face as she walked back to her desk.

Seth continued to stare, and when she glanced up, he winked at her. All of the craziness around her had made her feel closer than ever to Seth. She may have protested having him follow her around, but honestly, she was comforted by having him and Ryan there with her. She focused on what she needed to get done for the first time in days and finished a few things. She called a couple of her biggest clients to explain what had happened and felt like she was back in control of her destiny.

Amber called, but they agreed that it would be too much trouble to try and meet for coffee. Then Amber told Reagan that she had heard some more information about the two city council members that she suspected of bribery. "I can't tell you my source, but trust me when I tell you that he is reliable, Reagan. I know that Teresa's mother raised her on her own and that she didn't have much, if any, retirement money. The nursing home that she moved into is more like a resort than an assisted living place. It costs $10,000 a month. Where did she get that kind of money?

"Also, Bruce has a mistress. His wife found out and whooped her ass. She was going to file a suit against Mrs. Cannon, but Mr. Cannon paid the mistress off to make it go away. How the hell did he have enough money to do that?"

"Just because they are spending more money than you think they have, that doesn't prove anything. Perhaps Teresa has great insurance that helps pay for elderly care? Maybe Bruce's wife has money."

"Reagan, you're not listening. I'm telling you that you have to follow the money if you ever want to catch these people."

"I am listening, Amber. My detective is doing the best he can, and he is thorough."

"Well, you and I are going to be thorough too."

"What does that mean?" Reagan had watched as Seth walked out the office door to stand in the hallway while she talked with Amber.

"I double-checked, and both the city council members have invitations to the mayor's party. I know if I can get them drinking, then they will open up."

"Look, Nancy Drew, this isn't how we handle things. We are attorneys, and we have people to do this kind of stuff for us. Jerry is looking into some more information that he found, and if the council members need to be questioned, I'm sure he will find a way to do it."

"I'm saying if the opportunity presents itself, we should take it."

"That's not exactly what you're saying, and you know it." Reagan knew Amber was playing with fire, but she also didn't know how to change her friend's mind when she decided to do something. Amber was the most determined person she'd ever known besides herself. Amber also didn't ask for anything, ever, and the fact that she'd asked Reagan for help meant it was necessary. Reagan also knew it was a serious matter, and she would stick by her best friend's side no matter what. She just hoped it didn't turn out as badly as everything else had for the past few days.

Chapter Twenty-Four

SETH HAD A CUP OF COFFEE and a pastry, no doubt from Reagan's cougar secretary. Reagan watched him leaning against the wall, being cordial to the gushing older woman. Was he blushing? He must have sensed Reagan looking as he made his excuses and returned to her office.

"Nice shade of red you're wearing," she teased as he put the rest of the pastry into his mouth.

Seth laughed. "Interesting assistant you have, Rea."

Reagan feigned innocence. "How so?"

Seth looked at her, and right when she thought he would be too embarrassed to tell her, he surprised her and did. "Well, she lured me in with coffee and sweets and then explained why sex with an older woman was so glorious. She has a pretty interesting take on it anyway."

Reagan stared at him, and he continued. "She believes that the reason older women are such good lovers is that they no longer have to worry about getting pregnant. They also don't care how it looks to pick up lovers or even multiple lovers. She also said that women of a certain age also know what they like and have no problem asking for it. Of course, it would have been less shocking if she had used the anatomical names like vagina and penis, but nope, she's really into slang sexual verbiage."

"You're kidding me?" That time Reagan wasn't joking. She had no idea that Nancy talked like that, and now it made a lot more sense why her brother, the former badass marine, was so nervous around her.

She couldn't stifle her laughter as she thought more and more about how many times she'd left Ryan alone in the office with Nancy.

"Nancy could be on to something with her other observations, though. You know retirement communities have some of the largest cases of venereal disease and rival college campuses in numbers."

"Oh, my Lord. Don't tell me more," Reagan said, giving him a stern look.

"Babe, you wanted to know why I might be blushing, and I simply wanted you to understand."

Reagan rolled her eyes. "I'm pretty sure you were trying to shock me into blushing too. You forget that I am a divorce attorney, and not only have I heard some of the wildest stories, many times, there are videos or pictures to go with them. I don't want to think of Nancy that way."

Seth laughed, and she could tell he wished he didn't know so much about Nancy too.

Reagan called her detective, Jerry, and left him a message explaining what had been going on in her office and that he should call her cell phone or email her until further notice. She then called the detective working her case, but he was out of the office.

She let Seth know that she was almost done, and he sent Ryan a text to get the car ready and meet them at her office.

While they waited on Ryan, Reagan figured she needed to talk to Seth about the mayor's birthday party. In that perfect Seth way, he listened to her entire story without interruption. It was his way of making her think he was seriously considering what she was saying and would have a thoughtful comment or even rebuttal.

She confided in him that Amber was going through something with work that she was not at liberty to tell anyone. Then she explained that the event, she tried not to use the word party too much, was crucial in helping Amber get some closure.

Just as she finished with, *she and Amber would be together at all times, and that it would be on a boat, sailing on the water so no chance of any stalker getting close to her,* Seth stood up. She also added that the mayor had his own security team to vet all guests before and during the event, but he stared straight ahead.

She remained seated and watched as he clenched his jaw for a moment and then ran his hands through his hair. When he finally crossed his arms over his chest and leveled a stare at her that would melt steel, her first instinct was to move, but she didn't. It was a practiced calm that came over her, and it was a toss-up as to who was going to break their stare first.

Ryan must have seen what was going on because he looked through the glass, and instead of walking into the office to let them know he was there, he simply leaned against the wall until they came outside.

She wasn't sure Seth even knew Ryan was outside yet. It was as if the entire room was twenty degrees colder.

"Reagan Marie Gentry, do you take me for a fool?"

Right as she was about to answer the question, he interrupted her. *Apparently, it was a rhetorical question.*

"Seriously. I've already told you how I feel about Regalia, and you've assured me that nothing is going on between you and never has, but now you have to go out on a sailboat with him and his followers to celebrate his birthday? Oh, and it's for Amber. To top it off, you have a disturbed man, possibly an abusive husband of a client that has threatened your life, destroyed your office, totaled your car, and sent a bomb through the mail to damage your entire law firm, but you're certain that it'll be safe there because Regalia has security?" he said all of that without raising his voice a single octave. It was scarier than if he'd yelled.

Reagan waited to see if he was going to say anything else and when he didn't, she stood up and ran her hands down the front of her shirt to smooth it out. "I can see that you're not going to be rational."

He took two steps, and he was around the desk and inches from her body. He lowered his head, so they were face to face. If it had been anyone else, she would have been scared. But she knew Seth would never hurt her, nor would he ever lay a hand on her in anger. She watched his face and couldn't help but think about how beautiful he was in every way. He had a strong jawline and nose. His eyes were the color of topaz, and his eyebrows were thick and dark. He had strong kissable lips. She looked down so she wouldn't get distracted from the fact that they were sort of arguing.

He hadn't forgotten. "Rational? You think I'm the one that isn't rational?" he whispered that time, and it made her look at him again, but she didn't last but a second.

She kissed him and kissed him hard. When she pulled away, he was still staring at her, but he wasn't as tense. "Don't think that kiss will get you out of trouble. It is only buying you time, babe. I'm going to tell Ryan too. I imagine it will be a hell of a long ride home tonight with him lecturing you on where you can and cannot go without him. I have to go back to work, but he has already told me that he has all the time in the world to hunt down Salinas."

He grabbed Reagan's hand and kissed it as he pulled her toward the door. Under his breath, he muttered, "The hell you say you're going to Regalia's birthday party without one of us."

Reagan stopped walking before he opened the door. Seth turned to see her level a stare directly at him. "You know I love you, Seth, but you will have to trust me. I am not interested in Regalia. I have told him I am seeing someone else, and he understands. I am going to that party with Amber because she doesn't ask for favors, and the one time she does, I will do it. Now Ryan could probably get on the security team or detail or whatever you call it, and I'll make a phone call tomorrow to make sure that happens if that will make you feel better. But don't think for one minute that you are the boss of me."

Reagan couldn't help but raise her voice a little. He may be hot, but he was making her damn mad, and she had to let him know where the line was in their relationship.

Was it an official relationship yet?

She opened the door, and Ryan searched her face and then Seth's to see if either of them had conceded to the other one. He knew they were disagreeing, but he wasn't sure what about or how serious because they both could hold their tempers like no one else he'd ever known.

"Ready, folks?" he asked and led the way to the stairwell.

Reagan wanted to complain about taking the stairs even though she'd been doing it all week. She was exhausted from all the recent mayhem. She kept quiet, mentally complaining, and walked slower than usual, following Ryan down the staircase, and having Seth follow behind her.

They heard the car being pulled up to the door by the attendant, and as Ryan opened Reagan's door for her to get in and then closed it, he noticed the driver three seconds after his sister.

Seth was still walking around the car, so he was shocked to hear Robert Salinas' voice giving commands. "Please don't make any sudden movements. I don't want anyone to get hurt," he said with a deep, shaky voice.

Robert Salinas was sitting in the driver's seat of Seth's SUV, and Reagan was sitting in the front passenger seat next to him.

Reagan didn't take her eyes off Salinas, and as she studied him, she could see he was still wearing the clothes he'd had on that day in her office. He was scruffier than before and had a manic look on his face. Dark circles rimmed his eyes, and Salinas looked like he hadn't slept in a long time. If he was a man on the edge before, at that moment, he was barely holding on by his fingertips.

Ryan commanded Reagan to get out of the car, but she was too frightened to move. She was frozen in place as she stared into Salinas' eyes.

"You're not getting out of this garage, Salinas. I can promise you that," Ryan said in a deep, controlled voice.

Salinas looked at Ryan for a second and then gave him a nod.

Ryan's stomach felt hollow, but his hands were steady as he pointed his gun directly at the man who wanted to hurt Reagan.

Seth didn't have a gun, but he was on the other side of the car, ready to reach through the door and pull the crazed man to the ground. He waited on Ryan's command.

Salinas had tears in his eyes as he looked back at Reagan. "I'm sorry. I'm really sorry, Ms. Gentry. I didn't mean for any of this to happen."

He was shaking even more, and that's when Reagan saw what Ryan had seen all along. Robert Salinas held a revolver in his hand that was partially concealed by his long shirt sleeve. It looked old, and she was more frightened that it would misfire than she was over him using it on her.

"I know you didn't mean for things to get out of hand, Robert. But they have, and now you need to turn yourself in. Think of your kids," Reagan said.

"I'm sorry I trashed your office and scared you. But I didn't do any of that other stuff to you that was in the paper. I-I wish I were a better husband. God, forgive me," he said, and Ryan leveled his gun at the man's head seconds before Salinas pointed it at his own chin and shot himself.

Reagan screamed as the blood-splattered her face and clothes. Ryan pulled her out of the car and held her against his chest. Seth made it over to her in time to pick her up and carry her over to the curb to sit down. He held her until the police and ambulance got there.

Just as fast as all the threats began, they ended with one single shot. Robert Salinas had taken his life right there in front of Reagan, Ryan, and Seth.

The parking garage filled up with emergency personnel, and the case was closed in a matter of two hours.

Seth and Reagan headed to her penthouse in the city, and Ryan went home to Maisonville.

Reagan's entire world had been turned upside down, and suddenly it would go back to normal. It was hard for her to believe.

Chapter Twenty-Five

REAGAN DRAGGED HERSELF OUT of the police car that drove her and Seth home. It took everything she had to walk to the elevator and then down the hallway to her place. She was still covered with blood splatter from Robert Salinas' head, but it was dried now. She knew she looked scary. She could care less what anyone thought at the moment as she walked through her building and to her penthouse door.

It wasn't late, but it felt like the longest day of her life. Seth followed her into the bathroom, and he turned the water on in the shower for her. She struggled to unbutton her blouse, and he reached over and slowly undressed her. It was the most caring moment she'd ever had. He undressed and stepped into the shower with her. He washed her hair and soaped up her body, gently washing away all the evidence from that afternoon. She shuddered, thinking about Robert Salinas shooting himself. It was tragic. His head was blown all over Seth's car and Reagan.

She leaned into Seth as he took the sprayer and rinsed them both from head to toe. Minutes later, they dried off, and he helped her into a waffle woven robe she had hanging up on the back of the door. She silently brushed her teeth and removed the rest of her eye makeup that had run in the shower.

She looked younger without makeup. Seth watched her as she went into her bedroom and crawled under the covers.

"Rea, I was thinking of making some chicken and stars soup. I know you're ready for bed, but you haven't eaten much of anything today, and I don't want you to get sick," he said and then kissed her on the forehead before tucking the blankets snugly around her entire body.

His mother must have treated him like that when he was a kid, she thought. He was an only child, and it always amazed Reagan when she saw the intense love his parents had for him.

"Do I have soup in there?" she asked. She never knew what was in that pantry, and now that Seth was around, there were the beginnings of a working kitchen in the place.

"Yes. I bought some the other day when we were at the store. I also got some saltine crackers."

Reagan stared at him. As much as she loved him, it didn't feel right to have someone care for her. She wasn't so messed up that she believed she didn't deserve love at all, just maybe not that all-consuming care that he generously gave to her. He was a wonderful person with an open heart. He deserved to have someone like that, too, and she wasn't made that way. At least if she'd been born like that, it was gone before she recognized it. She needed a lot of time alone. She needed to be in control, or she felt too vulnerable, and then fear crept into her bones.

"Thanks. But only make it if you're going to have some."

He kissed her again and left for a few minutes to make her a tray with soup and crackers.

She felt like an interloper watching the scene before her. He helped her sit up in bed and flattened all the blankets so he could then place the large, flat tray on her lap. Seth had made her breakfast in bed like that when they dated before, and no one had done it before then or since. It was such a loving gesture that she almost teared up. He was too good for her. She pulled her wet hair over one shoulder and twisted it to distract her emotions from taking over.

"Thank you, Seth. Aren't you going to eat?"

He sat down next to her. "In a little while. Canned soup isn't my favorite, Rea."

She gave him a half-smile. "I know, but I didn't grow up with a mom who made me homemade chicken soup," she said, teasing him, but it sounded sadder than she'd planned.

"We'll work on homemade soup together," he said and opened the sleeve of crackers for her.

She avoided looking at him and talking while she ate. Her feelings were raw, and she couldn't control whether she would cry or laugh. She was anxious, and her skin felt prickly. She hadn't felt like that in a long time.

Seth could tell she was struggling emotionally. She ate the soup slowly as he handed her crackers, one at a time, to eat. He cleared the tray away as soon as she finished, and then he turned the lights off and sat beside her as she curled up under the covers.

"I'm really tired, Seth," she said, unable to send him away as she should.

He laid down on top of the bed next to her. "Trauma affects everyone differently, Rea. The rush of adrenaline is strong, and the comedown can be overwhelming. You need rest. Honestly, a lot more rest than you've been getting."

She nodded but didn't respond. She didn't trust her words at that moment. She loved Seth, but she would send him away for good. That would be their last night together, but she let him wrap his arms around her one more time until she fell asleep.

When Reagan woke up, she was alone in her bedroom. It felt like she was alone in the apartment, and she immediately searched for her clock because she was sure it was morning. *Had Seth left?* Did he pick up on her feelings the night before and go ahead and leave? He had to go back to work, and perhaps they would simply go on with their lives without each other and without discussing their brief recent affair.

She stumbled out of bed and turned the clock around to find that it was only eleven p.m. She pulled her robe together and walked into the kitchen, where she could see the living room. She didn't see Seth at first, but the television was on. She walked a little further and then saw his feet jutting out from the end of the couch. He was still there, and he was sound asleep.

He was only wearing boxer shorts, and sometime that evening, he'd ordered a large pizza. She took the empty box away and wiped off the coffee table. She cleaned up for him as he'd done for her, and then she covered him up the best she could with a small blanket. He didn't stir, so she sat down on the chair and watched him.

He was beautiful inside and out, and she quite possibly loved him even more than before. She'd wished she was a different person. He'd grown up with a loving family and had an easy-going disposition. Everyone who met Seth liked him.

He was a man's man like her brother, but he felt comfortable showing his caring side too. It was unusual to be around a man so openly loving. He grew up in a traditional home, and she understood that made him self-assured and sweet. His parents were the same way. His mother was a homemaker, and his father was a medical doctor. She kept a beautiful home and baked for fun. Seth would love to create that life for himself, being the head of the household with the little woman at home. He adored his mother and never stopped smiling when he was there eating her cooking.

It would never be like that for them if they stayed together. Reagan worked more hours than he did. She'd never baked a cake in her life. He would want to be the man of the house, but she wasn't sure she could concede any control. It didn't seem like they fit together. Would there always be disagreements? She couldn't participate in all that fighting like she'd grown up around.

Reagan wiped her eyes. She got up to make herself a glass of water. She wouldn't let herself get emotional over something that was inevitable. She'd managed to think things through her entire life logically, and that street sense had gotten her and Ryan through for years as kids and as adults. She was at peace because

Ryan had found the perfect person for him, and he and Sydney would be married soon. They were going to make her an aunt. She didn't have the same destiny as her brother. She knew the rumors about her being a cold fish were based on some truth. She could shut down her feelings to do what she needed to do, especially when it was the most sensible decision.

Seth may not understand it, but he would soon realize that he would be happier with someone else. Reagan had been a loner too long and was set in her ways before she hit thirty. He needed someone meeker and softer than Reagan. She'd had a mentally disturbed man threaten her all week and then kill himself in front of her, and all she could think about afterward was going back to work. There was something wrong with her. Seth would say she probably needed therapy, but she couldn't be fixed. She was permanently broken. Thanks to Lance and Sandy Gentry, she would never be worthy of someone like Dr. Seth Young.

She did love him so much that it hurt her sometimes to look at him. Seth had said he wanted to get married. But it was when he let her believe he'd met someone in Tennessee. She wasn't so sure she was the marrying type, and what if he wanted kids? She struggled over wanting a dog and trying to decide if she could be good enough for one.

She leaned against the counter in the kitchen. She cared enough for Seth not to drag things out. He was a catch. That's what Amber said about him. Men like that didn't last long on the singles circuit in New Orleans. They were a rarity. If you didn't find your man in high school, then your only shot was college because someone else would marry him before he lasted a year in his career. It was a joke made between Reagan and Amber, and they often laughed that the only guys left were the scarred ones or the unsuspecting single men that relocated to The Big Easy. Seth would be snatched up immediately. She remembered how the young secretary in her office looked at him and Ryan that morning when she walked in with them.

Reagan finished her water and then went back to her

bedroom. She couldn't sleep, so she grabbed a notebook and started making to-do lists. She had a full client schedule to makeup, an office to remodel, a new car to buy, and a breakup to orchestrate. Then there was also the mayor's birthday party with Amber that she had to attend and attempt to keep her friend away from any city council members.

It was going to be another hell week.

Chapter Twenty-Six

SETH WOKE UP, FEELING like he had cotton in his mouth. His neck was stiff, and his left leg was asleep from hanging partially off the couch in Reagan's condominium. He immediately noticed the television had been turned off and the coffee table had been cleaned.

He checked on Reagan, but she was back in bed asleep. He saw her notebook on the floor and knew how she paced or made notes when she had something on her mind. She was complex and hard to understand from the outside, but he knew she needed love and lots of understanding. He was ready to love her for the rest of their lives.

He climbed into bed with her and pulled her close as he fell back to sleep.

Seth woke to rain hitting the windows in Reagan's bedroom. He could see her in the bathroom zipping up her dress. She was completely ready for work except for her shoes. She walked out of sight and then into the bedroom wearing sexy black pumps.

He gave her a lazy smile, but she avoided looking into his eyes. Instead, she gathered up her notebook and pen and told him she was in a hurry.

She then walked into the kitchen, and he heard her calling the building valet to ask for a taxi. Seth didn't have time to find his pants, he only had on his boxers, but he had to get into the other room before she took off without him.

"Rea? Is everything okay? What's the rush this morning?"

"No rush. I have a two-page list of things to get done, now that last week's stress is over." She still wasn't looking at him, and he walked closer to box her into the kitchen corner.

"Look at me, babe."

Reagan took a deep breath and then looked at him.

"What's wrong?" he asked again.

She diverted her eyes past him as she spoke. "I already told you, nothing is wrong. I need to reclaim the hours I missed last week due to the Salinas' case."

She gave him a curt smile and a kiss on the side of his mouth that seemed intentionally aloof instead of her normal I'm busy and meant to plant that on your lips.

"He wasn't a case. He was a sick man, and he almost hurt you and many other innocent people. Last night was a lot for anyone to deal with, and I know that you're not over him sitting in the car with you. Maybe we could take this morning slow and go have breakfast together?" He reached his hand out to gently move her chin so she would look at him.

She leveled a stare that was as unexpected as her mood.

"Seth. I appreciate everything you've done. I can never repay you for watching over me and making sure I was safe. It was very sweet. You're very sweet. But I'm not in the right headspace to be in a relationship with anyone. We could be friends with benefits, but this needs to slow down. Way down," she said as she wriggled her way around him to pick up her trench coat and an umbrella.

"Stay as long as you'd like," she said, shoving her house key at him. "I'll see you later to pick up my key." she said without waiting for confirmation from him. She then rushed out and shut the door behind her.

Seth stood there in shock. It was Saturday. She wasn't late, and she didn't have clients to see or court to be in at a particular time. What the hell happened? They hadn't had sex since last weekend. He'd watched over her through the crazy week. She knew he was there because he cared for her, loved her. He tried to reason what could possibly be going on inside the head of his complicated woman, but he couldn't get past the fact that she'd called him sweet, like a kid. That wasn't by accident either. She knew the comment would get to him. He would give her a little space, and then he was going to set her straight on just how not sweet he was.

&

REAGAN WAS out of breath when she got into the taxi. She'd bolted out of there, praying that Seth wouldn't follow her. She needed space so she could think. Space away from Seth. Had he been that manipulative all along? He was so adept at making it look like he was taking care of her, but he was actually making her depend on him. She wasn't the type to be herded around, and she wouldn't fall into that trap again.

She called Terrence to see if he had made it into the building yet. She knew they would call him the night before after Robert Salinas killed himself. Everyone was ready to move on and get things back to normal, but no one would want that more than Reagan except her friend and boss, Terrence.

As she expected, Terrence had a cleaning crew in their old office Friday, repairing, repainting, and restoring things. He told her that her office looked brand new, and her furniture would be delivered that morning.

She didn't rely on anyone, but if she did, it might be Terrence. They spoke the same language. He did things the way she did them. It was Saturday, and when she needed it, the older gentleman would be there. She couldn't work in that temporary office anymore; she needed her own space. Things had to get back to normal.

Reagan went downstairs to get coffee for her and Terrence

from the kiosk, and then she watched as the movers brought in her furniture first. She would be able to close the door to her office while they moved everything else in the firm around. She was grateful, and as a side bonus, she loved the new paint color. It was a light gray, and next to the fancy woodwork, it looked fresh, which was exactly the start she'd needed to her day.

Reagan sat behind her desk and felt the mahogany throne's power. She smiled. It was as if last Friday hadn't happened. *Except that Robert Salinas' family would be planning a funeral.* She had to get her mind off that immediately.

She pulled out her list and then picked up the phone to call Amber.

She laughed at Amber's groggy voice. "Hey, slacker. Don't tell me you're still in bed?"

"Why the hell are you calling me this early on a Saturday?" she asked, whispering into the phone.

"Oops! You aren't alone, are you?" Reagan was used to Amber having company in the mornings. Always different company, but some tall, dark, or not so dark, handsome man.

"I will hunt you down, Gentry—" she began to say, but Reagan interrupted her.

"Good. Come hunt me down at the office. I'm back, but I need a car and a ride. I'll buy brunch?"

"What the—" Again, Amber got cut off.

"I'll explain everything. Come pick me up," Reagan knew her friend was kicking the anonymous man out of bed as they spoke. No way she wouldn't be there to pick up Reagan soon.

REAGAN AND AMBER ate leisurely and drank Bloody-Mary's as Reagan told her about the final scene in the Salinas saga.

"It's too bad you're not a fiction writer. You would have some great material for a book. It would have to be fiction, though, because no one would believe it really happened."

"Not a chance," Reagan said, not drinking the alcohol.

"So, will you tell me what you've avoided discussing since we got here? Where is Seth?"

She knew she couldn't fool Amber. She was always looking for the meaning behind the meaning, and she loved gossip a little more than most. "I woke up this morning a little overwhelmed. I need my space, and honestly, he's a great man, but things were moving super-fast for me."

Amber reached her hand across the table. "I know you love that man. I hope things work out, Reagan."

"Things are going to work out the way they are supposed to, and that's that," Reagan said.

"You and I both know that's not how the world works. Relationships, good relationships, take work."

"Says the woman who has never been in a long-term relationship."

"I might surprise you one of these days," Amber said, and Reagan couldn't miss the sparkle in her eyes.

"What? Wait a minute. Are you telling me that you're dating someone right now? When? Where?"

"Don't lecture me, but we sort of decided to keep it quiet until we know where things are going. No need to get everyone gossiping if it doesn't look like it will be serious."

"How long has this been going on?"

"It's very new, although we've had our eye on each other for a little while. I am happy," Amber said. She had a glow that Reagan could now see, clearly, and there was a calmness that she'd never seen in her friend.

"I'm so happy for you. Are you sure you can't give me a hint?"

Amber shook her head. Then she leaned in and said, "He'll be at the party this Saturday."

"So, he made the cut for this super exclusive party? Impressive." Reagan couldn't remember Amber ever keeping a secret from her, but love did strange things to people. As a divorce attorney, she could attest to that more than most.

"Don't expect to be introduced, and don't go nosing into things and trying to figure it out. We'll tell everyone when the time is right. Okay?"

Was Amber nervous? Reagan would usually work until she figured a secret out. But recently, she couldn't trust her own crazy emotions. Perhaps this one time, she should let one go. Amber was happy, and that was the most important thing.

Reagan leaned in, "I'm so so happy for you, Amber. You tell me when you're ready."

"And you and Seth?"

Reagan shook her head. "It's not the same. I mean, I love him, but he and I are completely different people. Dr. Young is ready for the wife, kids, dog, and picket fence, and I'm quite comfortable in my penthouse."

Amber shook her head, not believing what Reagan was saying. Love changed people all the time. Sometimes you had to put your trust in another person's hands and let go. At least that was what she had done, and the experience was more profound than any relationship she'd ever had, but she didn't think she could say that to Reagan yet.

Chapter Twenty-Seven

REAGAN AND AMBER WENT TO the Mercedes dealership and test drove several cars, but Reagan couldn't make up her mind. When the saleswoman suggested trying the small SUV, she was ready to walk.

"I've had a convertible for years. Do I look like I need a mom car?" she asked, under her breath to Amber.

"I don't know; this thing is loaded. You could live in here," Amber said, sitting in the driver's seat. "Get in here, girl."

Reagan had a seat, and the saleswoman offered to get the keys so they could drive it. She hated to admit it, but it was a comfortable ride and looked pretty hot considering it had a bench seat in the second row and a large cargo area.

"What do I need with all that space?" she asked. "I don't have kids or a dog."

"Groceries?" The saleswoman added.

Reagan lowered her eyes at the woman, and Amber butted in. "Shopping, girl. We could do some serious damage if we had this machine to cart our treasure."

Reagan looked at Amber and grinned. "I'll take it."

It took two hours from when they got to the dealership, picked out a vehicle, and then purchased it.

Amber choked over the price and how her best friend didn't flinch when she picked out the loaded version with heated and cooled leather seats and a sunroof. Amber hadn't spent that much on the last two cars she owned combined, but she was thrilled that her best friend could do it.

They each headed their separate ways, with Reagan returning to the office and her to-do list. She spent the rest of the afternoon putting up all her books and rearranging everything that wasn't damaged into her newly renovated office space.

It was beautiful, and she was wiped out when she sat down in her chair to see that it was seven. She realized she hadn't heard from Seth all day, and although she wanted it not to matter, it did.

She packed up and then picked up dinner through a drive-through window. She started rethinking the idea as they handed her the fries, and she almost dropped them on the floorboard of her new car.

She smiled at the man in the window and asked him to put everything into a larger bag. She pulled forward past the drive-through window, and she could see the highway clearly. She thought about how quickly she could get to the bridge to Maisonville from there. She knew she was doing the right thing where Seth was concerned, but she didn't want to be in her apartment without him. She made an illegal U-turn and headed for the bridge, but she only made it halfway before digging into the bag to eat hot French fries.

Reagan pulled into the drive of her lake house and frowned that the lights were off. She swore if she ever lived there full time, she would make sure to leave a light on. It was very dark at the lake at night. She headed inside and saw the bed was unmade and the groceries her brother and Sydney had bought were still there. She took a deep breath to stop herself from crying. Missing Seth would happen everywhere she went. She walked out on her deck and tried to get him out of her mind.

It didn't work.

She wondered what Seth could be up to, and then she remembered that his car had been impounded by the police the night before, and he was without a car all day. She smiled. He would love her new car. Then she scolded herself for thinking about him constantly.

"Get a grip, Reagan. He deserves the Mayberry life that he wants. You girl are not Mayberry," she said aloud, talking to herself. She looked around at her place and then thought about her new SUV. She was kind of a modern-day version, but she wouldn't admit that to herself.

She went inside and watched television before she went to bed. Seth was still on her mind, and she wanted to be stronger than that but knew it was not possible when she reached over to pick up her cell phone. It was dead. All the trouble she'd gone to for a new phone, and it didn't hold a charge? She shook her head because she didn't have a charger at the lake house. Reagan put the phone down. At least she wouldn't be tempted to call him or invite him over. Having a dead phone would undoubtedly make it easier to stop relying on him.

Tossing and turning all night, Reagan finally got up at six in the morning and made a pot of coffee. She sat out on the old Adirondack chairs that were getting more use than ever before, since she and Seth had been out there twice already.

She couldn't get him off her mind even in the early morning hours.

As she watched the sunlight coming over the lake, she took a deep calming breath, considering how peaceful things were there, unlike the city. She finished her coffee and saw a boat coming around the bend in the lake toward her house. As it got closer, she smiled that it was her brother. Ryan threw the rope up to Reagan, and she tied it off and gave him a hand climbing up.

He gave her a big hug and then asked for a cup of coffee. They walked inside, and she poured him a cup and herself another before they walked back out to sit together. Ryan was quiet like she was in the morning, and it was a few minutes before he finally began talking.

"You know, Reagan, most women that have been through what you've been through, would at least call and let someone know where they are at night."

She stared at him but didn't respond.

"I know you're not most women but come on. You had Seth worried to death, and I was a little concerned after you didn't show up at home during the night either. If you hadn't been out here when I rode up, I would've been in my truck and across the lake putting a search party together."

"I didn't mean to worry anyone," was all she said.

Ryan watched her for a few more minutes as she drank her coffee. "I get it. You need some room to breathe. It's the Gentry way, you know. We're the suffer in silence type."

"I'm not suffering in silence, Ryan. I'm just used to being alone, and I like it."

"Reagan, that's where you're wrong. You're the one that taught me never to complain or ask for help. At least, I learned it from you. If it weren't for therapy and Sydney, I would still live alone and think my life was fine."

"So, your therapy taught you that my life can't be fine if I enjoy being alone?"

"Do you? Or maybe you don't know any different?" He sat his cup down on the arm of his chair and watched her. She knew Ryan, and that was a test. He watched her for the slightest flinch, and if she even squinted a little too hard, he would pick up on it.

Instead, she told him the truth. "I don't know what I want anymore. I see you and Sydney and how perfect you two are together."

"Seth's a good man, Rea," he said.

Reagan shrugged. "He's a great man, and he comes from a good family. He's used to things that I've never been around, and he wants different things than I do. I'm not an easy person to live with, and I know it. He deserves to find someone who will be everything to him like Sydney, and you are to each other. I have work and a busy schedule. I like my life. I'm not looking for a wedding ring and rug rats."

"I didn't think you liked the outdoors either, but you're here and seem to be comfortable."

"It's a good place to think. You know, here in the quiet."

Ryan nodded. He absolutely knew what she meant. The lake was the best therapy he'd ever had, and he'd had a lot of the traditional kind of therapy. He stuck his hand in his pocket and pulled out a phone charger for her. "Seth told me you had a new phone. It's the same kind as Sydney's, so I figured you might could use this."

Seth had to be mad at her, yet he still was worried enough to call Ryan. It was a good thing she went to the lake to escape him. It would be too easy to fall back into the bliss that Seth created around him. Reagan shook her head, who in the world was that happy all the time? She couldn't understand it. He was too nice. She needed someone harder like her so that she could relax. Reagan looked up to see that her brother was staring at her. Had she given too much away? He watched every facial expression or simple body movement, and she swore he could also read her mind.

"Thanks for the charger. I did need it," Reagan smiled at Ryan and then offered to bring his mug into the house so he would feel alright leaving. She knew he didn't like to leave Sydney for too long, and Reagan had already had him with her all day, the day before following her around.

Ryan hugged her goodbye and told her to check in that evening and let him know where she'd be, the city or the lake.

Reagan noticed that he didn't assume she could answer something as simple as that at the moment. He was right. She couldn't answer because she didn't know what she was going to do.

Chapter Twenty-Eight

IT WAS LATE SUNDAY EVENING when Reagan drove back to the city. She had charged her phone and saw all the missed calls and texts from Seth and Ryan made the day and night before. Following Ryan's request, she texted to let him know she was safe and heading back home to New Orleans. Finally, she also sent a message to Seth and told him she was fine and at the lake but didn't want to see him.

Neither of them called or sent her a message back. In fact, she didn't have one phone call or text message the entire day or night. It didn't make her feel bad, but it did remind her that things were getting back to normal. Waiting until the last minute to get back to the city made things seem normal, coming and going as she pleased. It wasn't until she got upstairs to her apartment that she realized she didn't have her house key. She'd given it to Seth without thinking it through.

She was going to have to see him. She shook her head. She would figure out another way to get into her apartment.

Reagan went downstairs to the security guard, and he called the building manager, who was more than happy to help Reagan. She had to wait fifteen minutes for him to come over from another property, but he was prompt and had taken the time to make her an extra key before he got there.

Reagan walked into her dark apartment and felt more alone than she'd felt in a long time. Seth had cleaned up everything before he left. He'd made her bed, picked up her bath towels, straightened the throw pillows and blanket on her couch. He'd left zero evidence that he'd ever been there. Her stomach twisted, and for a moment, she thought she might be sick.

If it was that hard to let Seth go after a couple of weeks, what would it be like if she let him into her life for months or years like before? He wanted a traditional lifestyle. He'd all but described that scenario to her, and she'd never been conventional. She couldn't explain why things around her swirled like a damn dust storm, but that was why she needed so much control in her life. It was the only way to keep things neat. Seth never had to fight for much in his life. It all came easy for him, and there was no way he would be up for the demons that always lurked in the shadows for Reagan.

Her parents had fought with each other and took it out on Reagan, but she had fought for a good life for Ryan. Reagan had fought for summer vacations at the lake with their uncle. She'd fought her way into college, law school, and for the job she loved. She fought for Ryan to live through the injuries he'd sustained in war, physical and mental. She'd fought for her heart after Seth had broken it the first time. And she was fighting to make partner. There was always something, and in her heart, she felt like it would become too much work for Seth to make life with her happy. He had no idea what she had to do to keep going. No idea.

The next three days, Reagan went to work, and her routine seemed intact. After all the week's chaos, everything in the office was restored to better than normal. The facelift was worth the effort as everyone at Williams, Morrison, and Weisnick seemed to have more pep in their daily routines. There was a positive air around the office that Reagan couldn't remember being there ever before.

Wednesday at lunch, Reagan and Amber went shopping for dresses for the party Saturday. Amber had placed several on hold for herself and Reagan, and all they had to do was show up and try everything on. It was more than Reagan had planned.

"Are you sure these dresses are appropriate for a birthday party on a boat?" Reagan asked, staring at the sequins gown with a slit up to her thigh. She hadn't felt like eating much over the past couple of weeks and had lost a few pounds. It made her clothes look sexier.

"It's a yacht, and yes, being the best dressed is always the goal," Amber said, admiring how she looked wrapped in red satin.

"Wow! You look—," Reagan started to say before Amber cut her off.

"Hot!" Amber said, turning around to adjust her cleavage.

Reagan clenched her lips to keep herself from finishing her sentence. The word hooker came to mind, but she wouldn't tell Amber what her friend already knew. The dress was too much.

"I'm buying it and the navy flapper-looking dress. What about you? Black sequins or the royal blue number?"

Reagan laughed. "I think I'm going to keep looking."

"Look, Reagan, you only have two days until the party, and I will be very disappointed if you make me go alone."

"I promised I would go, and I will, but I don't think I'm prepared for the attention those dresses will demand. I like to observe at these types of parties not have the spotlight on me."

Amber grinned. She knew her friend would push back when it came to dressing flashy. But, at least, she'd tried.

As Amber went to the counter to check out, she picked up several old-fashioned metal lighters and smiled. Reagan watched as she dug through the display and found one with a 1950's era pinup girl embossed on it. When Amber saw her friend watching, she grinned. *Was she blushing?*

"It's a gift. I'll tell you more about it later," Amber said, and Reagan understood it must be for Amber's new lover.

They finished up and then grabbed a quick smoothie before

heading back to their respective offices. Reagan was thankful for the distraction because Amber didn't ask her again about Seth. Reagan hadn't heard from him since Saturday morning, and she didn't want to admit how difficult that had been for her.

She knew they needed to end things. Pulling the Band-Aid off quickly was the best way. But it hurt a little deeper that he'd had a change of heart and didn't try to call. She'd figured she'd have to push him away a little harder, but he'd taken off without looking back. It was a repeat of their first breakup, and she couldn't talk about it without getting emotional.

The rest of her day and Thursday were as uneventful as the beginning of the week. It was Friday morning, and when Reagan walked into her office, she saw the mayor there talking with Mathew. It was a glaring reminder that she had his birthday party the next day and still had nothing to wear. Amber was going to kill her.

"Good morning, Reagan," Mayor Regalia said. He was smiling at her as he ran over to open the glass door for her to walk through.

"Morning," she said, tipping her head in his direction, but she didn't stop to talk.

When she walked into her office, she was surprised to see Nancy grinning at her.

"You know something that I don't?" Reagan asked, but Nancy shrugged her shoulders.

Reagan sat her things down and then noticed the large flat box on her desk with a shimmering gold ribbon.

She held the gift and walked back toward Nancy.

"From who?" Reagan asked.

Nancy grinned but didn't answer Reagan.

Reagan walked back into her office and closed the door. Had Seth been in before she'd gotten there? He hadn't attempted to talk to her once all week. She took a deep breath as she opened the box.

Inside was an exquisite strapless dress. It was made of raw silk and looked very sexy. It wasn't anything like Seth would buy. Sure, he'd picked out some trashy lingerie in the past and even a cute sweater here and there, but never a designer dress and in her exact size.

She got up from her desk again, and that time when she opened her office door to speak to Nancy, the mayor was standing there.

"Do you like it? I heard that you didn't have anything to wear, and I didn't want that to be the reason you didn't come," Alexavier said.

Reagan's mouth was dry. It was an exquisite dress and entirely inappropriate for her friend, the mayor, to give to her.

"It's beautiful, but I don't think I can accept it," she said, licking her lips and wishing she had a bottle of water.

He gestured for her to walk into her office and then followed her inside and closed the door.

"Nonsense. You'll look incredible in that dress, and besides, it's as much for me as it is for you."

Reagan shook her head, but before she could respond, Alexavier stepped closer. He was now a breath away from her and whispered, "It is my birthday, Reagan. Please wear it for me."

Reagan couldn't speak. She stared at him, and his eyes twinkled. He'd caught her off guard. He had the upper hand, and he knew it. "Should I send a car for you tomorrow?" he asked.

"I-I'm riding with Amber," she whispered.

"Then I'll send a car for both of you," he said and then kissed her on the cheek before he turned around and left her office.

Reagan sat down on one of the upholstered chairs in front of her desk. Amber wasn't going to believe the mayor bought her a dress or that he was sending a car to pick them up. Reagan had thought maybe the mayor was Amber's mystery man, but surely, he wouldn't also flirt with her? They weren't dating, and they honestly weren't friends, but the mayor insisted on doing things for her. Why was her love life so complicated?

Chapter Twenty-Nine

"WHAT DO YOU MEAN THERE is a car coming to take us to the party?" Amber called Reagan to let her know she was on the way to pick her up.

"I'll explain when you get here," Reagan said and quickly got off the phone, so she could finish getting ready.

She was irritated and battling with the idea that Seth had been right all along. She'd thought it was some harmless flirting, but Alexavier wanted her.

Maybe if she wasn't so confused over Seth, she could entertain going out with Alexavier? She shook her head in the mirror, scolding herself. Who was she kidding? She liked her privacy, and whoever the mayor dated had zero privacy.

Alexavier Regalia was a handsome man, and usually, all that confidence would do something for her. He was forward in a way that she'd fantasized about Seth behaving so many times. But it felt wrong coming from Alexavier. And she was pretty sure he seemed to get a charge out of being bossy when they were alone.

What was that all about?

Reagan hadn't given him any reason to believe she liked that sort of behavior. Sure, she'd been flattered by his attention and embarrassingly charmed when she spoke to him a couple of times which could've been seen as flirting. But they hadn't been intimate or even kissed. He had no reason to believe she liked aggressive sexual behavior. There were signals that he should have waited for or certainly some type of consensual behavior. He didn't.

She was obligated but regretted agreeing to go to the party with Amber, but that would be her last party with the mayor.

Her stomach fluttered again, and she was surprised by her nervousness. It was a ridiculous, over-the-top, extravagant birthday party for a man who thought he deserved it. What was her problem?

She couldn't explain it, but she suddenly wanted to talk to Seth. She'd been fine all week. Resolute in what she needed to do concerning him. But as she was about to attend a party that she knew he disapproved of vehemently a few days ago, she needed to hear his voice. Would he tell her it was okay?

She convinced herself that she should at least call him and apologize for being wrong about Alexavier. She hadn't led him on and hadn't tried to make Seth jealous, but she honestly didn't realize Alexavier thought of her that way.

Well, she did try to make Seth a little jealous that one time, but otherwise, she was innocent. Innocently wrong.

Unlike the mayor, Seth was in tune with her signals. He practically read her mind most of the time, and it was unnerving how he knew things about her before she knew them about herself.

She missed him something awful.

Her eyes watered, and she quickly used the hairdryer so she wouldn't ruin her makeup. As soon as she dried her eyes and touched up her eyeliner, she barely made it to the trash can to throw up.

Missing Seth was hurting her physically.

Reagan brushed her teeth and rinsed her mouth as she gagged a couple more times. When her stomach settled, she slipped into her black heels and moved her essentials into her silk clutch purse. Then she went into the kitchen to place the card she'd bought with the wine and package she had for Alexavier.

She rolled her eyes, looking at the gift. Her stomach fluttered a little more, and she found some ginger-ale in the refrigerator to settle her stomach. No doubt, Seth had bought it for her in case she needed it. She paced the kitchen and then leaned against the counter to make the phone call she wanted but shouldn't make.

The phone rang five times, but Seth didn't answer. Maybe it served her right. She hung up without leaving a message and instantly regretted it.

Finally, she called again and left the message.

"H-hello. It's me. I'm sorry to bother you. I'd hoped you'd be there, but maybe it's best that I just leave a message. I do care about you. It's just that my life is complicated, Seth. It's always been that way, and I don't know how to stop it. You are never complicated, and I'm not sure if you could handle the uproar that seems to always be around every corner in my world. I couldn't take it if one day you woke up and decided I wasn't worth all the trouble. I'm admitting that I'm scared, scared of getting hurt again. Scared of not being good enough or strong enough for a relationship or you. Look, maybe you've already changed your mind, and if that's true, then delete this message, and I won't try to contact you anymore."

Reagan's doorbell rang, and she rushed off the phone. "I wish I didn't have to go to this party, but I promised Amber, and the mayor is sending a car. But I'll be home as early as possible tonight, and if you want to talk, call me."

Her doorbell rang again. "Oh, and you were right about the mayor all along; he is kind of into me and aggressive. Take care, and thanks for the ginger-ale. Bye."

She rushed to open the door before Amber rang the bell a third time.

"Wow, you look great, Amber."

Amber turned around slowly to give her friend 360-degree views then winked at her. "I have never spent this much time getting ready."

They both laughed, and Reagan grabbed her things off the bar when Amber whistled. "You look fine yourself. New outfit?"

Reagan shook her head. "This old thing?"

"It looks brand new," Amber said, and then she saw Reagan's shoes. "I know those are new."

Reagan was happy to discuss her shoes. "You know I'm a sucker for great shoes and handbags."

They headed downstairs to meet the town car that would be waiting. When they got into the car, Reagan told Amber about Alexavier. "I'm not sure why he wanted to do it, but when I told him we were going together, then he insisted." She tried to make it seem innocent, and for once, Amber didn't give her the third degree.

"Well, that was very considerate," Amber said, and that was it.

Reagan wasn't sure if Amber was trying not to make her uncomfortable or if she had other things on her mind, but it was entirely out of character for Amber to not say what she was thinking.

Reagan reached her hand out to touch Amber's arm. "Everything okay?"

Amber nodded and then took a deep breath. "I'm excited about tonight."

"Have you decided to introduce me to your secret boyfriend this evening?"

"I do not promise anything, but I think he might be ready. At least he's hinted to me that he's ready."

Reagan patted her friend's arm. Her happiness was palpable, and Reagan was happy for her. Maybe the party would be more fun than she expected?

They pulled up to a private pier and were met at the car by what looked like bellhops, but Reagan was confident they were private security. One of the men pulled out a clipboard and checked their names against the party list. Then another escorted them down the pier to a massive, beautiful yacht.

The pier lights were subtle, but the yacht sparkled with decorations and clean glass. It was impressive and more than a mayor could afford on his own. Reagan took a deep breath as she followed behind Amber onto the landing. They handed their gifts to a woman who greeted them and then followed another where they could get a drink and mingle with the rest of the guests. As usual, Alexavier would make an entrance once everyone arrived.

Amber handed Reagan a glass of champagne, and they clinked their glasses and laughed at the pompous atmosphere. Reagan took a sip, but she didn't care for the bubbly, and when Amber drank her entire glass, she handed hers over so she could have it too.

"Not exactly my drink," Reagan said, looking at the group of wealthy men standing on the deck having Cuban cigars.

"Oh, I don't know, Reagan. I could get used to all this." Amber sipped her champagne with a smile.

"Then I hope mister wonderful is one of Alexavier's rich benefactors."

Amber was staring at her, and Reagan felt like she was supposed to pick up on some hint, but she was too distracted watching the city's elite chatting it up on the fancy boat. It certainly was going to be an entertaining night. She leaned in, "Don't you want to tell me which one he is, Amber?"

Amber shook her head but looked disappointed that Reagan hadn't figured it out already. "Are you feeling alright, Reagan? Your cheeks are flushed. We're about to set sail, so if you're feeling motion sickness already, maybe you should go inside the cabin?"

"Honestly, I wasn't feeling great before we left," Reagan said. She hadn't eaten all day and looked for a waiter walking around with a cheese tray or some fruit. She snagged a few items from a tray and then smiled at her friend.

Amber was probably right about the reaction she would have once underway on the water since she'd already felt queasy. She excused herself to go to the restroom and asked a waitress to bring her a cup of coffee. On her way around the deck, Reagan ran into another one of the security detail officers and remembered the story Alexavier had told her over the threats he'd received when he became mayor. She'd never paid much attention to it before. He'd always had one or two men as his security detail, but tonight she'd seen ten or twelve men already. Why would that much security be necessary?

She found a waiter carrying a tray of mini sandwiches and grabbed one of them. While she was eating it, the waitress from earlier brought her a cup of coffee with cream and sugar. She felt better as she watched Amber talking with one of her coworkers. It was at that time that Alexavier made his entrance, and Reagan couldn't miss the twinkle in Amber's eyes.

Reagan's stomach contracted again. Was Amber having an affair with Alexavier? He'd flirted with Reagan several times, and he knew they were best friends. How long had he and Amber been sleeping together?

She watched her friend a minute more and then shook her head. She had to be wrong. After all, she wasn't feeling her best.

Amber walked over and asked her how she was doing.

"A little better. Sorry about before. I put in tons of hours this week to make up for my lost time. I think I just needed some food and coffee. Maybe a little dessert later?"

Amber smiled at her. "Me too."

"So, is your mystery man here yet?"

"I shouldn't have mentioned it, Reagan. You know him, so if you've figured it out, please don't say anything."

"I don't know anything, so how could I?"

Amber looked relieved. "He's a private man, and he's not ready to go public."

"And he's not married?"

Amber laughed. "No, he's not married. Give me some credit, will ya?"

"So, I presume he has a lot of money, or he wouldn't be here, and maybe all that money makes his relationships complicated?"

"Exactly."

"Is he wearing a black suit right now?"

Amber looked angry at her friend and turned and walked off.

"What?" Reagan said. "Half the men here are wearing black. It was funny." Amber didn't acknowledge her friend and kept walking until she was out of sight.

Reagan regretted teasing Amber and wished she could take it back. She wasn't used to Amber being sensitive. Reagan recognized a few of the guests but didn't know anyone at the party very well except for Amber. She decided to get some fresh air and set her empty coffee cup down so she could take a stroll along the perimeter of the boat.

She was all alone and looking out at the stars sparkling over the water when Alexavier walked up beside her. "You are a hard person to find."

"I didn't realize anyone was looking."

"Of course," he said as he slipped off his jacket to cover her bare arms. "You look beautiful."

"Thanks." Reagan smiled and avoided his stare. "I thought this pantsuit was more appropriate for a boat ride, and the more I thought about it, I didn't think it was right to accept such an extravagant gift."

"I saw the box on the table and presumed you had returned the dress. I have to say that I am a little disappointed."

"It's a beautiful dress, but maybe you should give it to Amber?" Reagan was fishing, but her gut told her that something was going on between her friend and the mayor.

"I think you are a better fit," he said, and she was sure he wasn't talking about the dress.

"I would never date another woman's man. Especially my best friend."

Alexavier stepped closer, gently pinning Reagan against the railing and him. "I am not her man, Reagan. I think there's been a misunderstanding. I thought I was being obvious. I'm interested in you."

Reagan held the jacket around her body tighter. She was cold but not from the temperature. She felt foolish mistaking the mayor as Amber's love interest and was even more embarrassed that she hadn't realized he wanted her from the beginning.

Now all alone in his arms, Reagan felt naïve and foolish. She didn't like it. She had to maneuver her way out of there. "So you aren't the mystery man that Amber's been dating?"

"This is none of my business, but I don't think your friend Amber is serious with any one man. She seems to—," he cleared his throat before he finished, "Date around if you know what I mean."

Amber did *date* around. However, she was Reagan's closest girlfriend, and Reagan wouldn't let anyone, not even the mayor, imply something negative about her. Before she could correct him, someone opened a side door, and loud music poured out.

Reagan decided she would argue for Amber another time because that might be her only opportunity to make a break for it. She wriggled out of his arms.

"I'm sure a lot of people are looking for the guest of honor tonight, and Amber is probably wondering where in the world I've gone."

Alexavier reached out to grab Reagan's hand and gently placed a kiss on her knuckles before releasing it. "You're probably right. Go ahead. I'll be there in a minute. Save a dance for me?"

She nodded but practically ran through the door and back to the party. She couldn't explain the feeling she had, but ever since she'd walked onto the yacht, the atmosphere seemed off. She'd heard people say they felt danger in the air, but that never made any sense to her. Suddenly, it did. She straightened out her belt and took a deep breath before entering the crowded deck. Maybe it was all the excitement from the past couple of weeks that made her intuition a little off? She bit her bottom lip, trying to keep it from quivering. She didn't know how, but she would have to find a way to get off that boat.

Chapter Thirty

SETH LISTENED TO HIS message from Reagan twice before he got out of his car. How could she think he would change his mind about her? Sure, he was upset initially but knew she needed space so she would come back to him. He'd stopped himself several times that week from forcing her to see him. He'd driven to Maisonville and sat in her driveway for an hour after Ryan called and told him she was safe. He sat inside the cafe she and Amber ate lunch at on Wednesday and narrowly kept her from seeing him when he held the door open for her and Amber at that boutique. He'd also watched her try on the delicate black heels that she bought for the damned party she was attending for the mayor. It was difficult to stop watching over her after she'd been in so much danger. He was borderline stalking her while she figured out what she wanted. He was never going to get over her or give her up. He laughed when she admitted she was complicated. He didn't think she had any idea just how complicated she really was, but he loved everything about her, including the chaos that seemed to follow her. She was everything he wanted and needed in the world, and he wasn't sure he could wait for her to get back to dry land before he told her.

He ran into his apartment and called Ryan.

"She actually said Mayor Regalia was aggressive?" Ryan asked.

Seth nodded though Ryan couldn't see him. "And that I was right about him all along."

"What does that mean?"

"I told her that he was hitting on her, and she didn't believe me."

"I've always known my sister to be a great judge of character. She picks up on things others don't notice about people. Are you telling me she didn't know he was interested? Damn."

"I don't like her out there on that boat with him," Seth said, remembering the sexy shoes he saw her buying for the party. "I wish she wasn't alone."

Ryan smirked. "It's a little more than a boat. And Seth, if the mayor is involved, there will be a hundred guests or more at that party."

"Trust me when I tell you that he'll find a way to get her alone. He has a long game, and he's played it with her for a while. Probably since the night I met her."

"Then let's go get your girl."

"WHERE HAVE YOU BEEN?" Amber slurred her words as Reagan sidled up next to her at the bar.

Reagan hadn't seen Amber sloppy drunk in years. Sure, they had margarita Mondays, sometimes, and met for a few drinks after work other times, but she could hold her liquor.

Suddenly Reagan's stomach was in knots again, watching her friend act foolishly around the city's elite. That wasn't the place for it.

"I thought we agreed not to drink much, Amber?" Reagan whispered into her ear.

"I've changed our mind."

Reagan tried to smile as her friend embarrassed herself by

finishing a shot glass, she was holding full of what looked like tequila.

The night wasn't getting any better.

Amber was half sitting on a barstool but mostly hanging off it. When she attempted to stand up, she fell straight to the floor. Reagan tried to lift her, and within seconds two men, clearly security, were at her side. They looked at each other, and without a word, one of them lifted Amber into his arms and swiftly carried her out the door. Reagan had to jog to keep up.

"Hold on," Reagan said to the two men who ignored her. "Where are you taking her?"

"We have orders, ma'am."

"I asked where you are taking her, not why." She had her hands on her hips, but she wasn't as intimidating in the tight-fitting pantsuit and high heels as she was in a business suit. They didn't slow down.

Reagan hurried up some stairs behind them and finally into a large room filled with a giant bed. Reagan was shocked to see a full-size bathroom through another door and a balcony large enough to accommodate several good-sized lounge chairs. She smiled that she referred to it as a boat to Amber.

Reagan watched as the two men gently laid Amber down onto the bed and then exited the room. She saw one of them talk into his wrist as he was leaving, and she noticed the watch-looking radio that he had strapped there. She couldn't make out everything he was saying, but she did hear, *situation removed from the general population.*

Was drunk Amber a situation? Maybe the mayor or whoever was running the party considered anyone who got that drunk a situation? But Reagan had a bad feeling that wasn't the case. The men seemed to be on Amber super-fast as if they had been watching her all along. It seemed off and more than a little creepy.

The men stood beside the door and talked on their hidden radios, and then one of the men turned toward Reagan. "Ma'am? We can keep an eye on her so you can go back to the party."

Reagan stared at the athletically built man and wondered if he knew how close he was to getting kneed in the groin. Did she look like the type of woman that would leave an incapacitated friend alone with two strange men?

"Not a chance," she said without blinking.

"It's our job to keep the passengers safe," the second man said, apparently missing the point she was making with her stare.

She closed her eyes and shook her head as if to erase the ridiculous comment from her memory. When she turned to look at him, he held up his hands in surrender. He must have understood how stupid he sounded because they left the room without another word.

Reagan walked over to Amber and took her heels off, and then went into the bathroom to get a cold cloth for her face. Amber was going to freak out when she sobered up, but for the moment, she needed some rest. Reagan covered her up and walked over to the balcony to look out over the water. She pulled out her phone but didn't have a signal. The city lights and shoreline weren't visible, and she'd figured it was a long shot. Still, she wished she could check to see if Seth had responded to her message. She took a deep breath. *What would she do if Seth never called her back?*

The party should have at least distracted her for a few hours. But she couldn't think of anything except talking to Seth. The only person that could've talked her out of calling him was lying in a bed unconscious.

Reagan pulled a chair beside the bed and sat down. Amber mumbled in her sleep. How could she have gotten drunk so fast after Reagan left the room? It hadn't been very long.

Pacing the room and then standing on the balcony, Reagan felt like she'd been in there for an eternity. She wished she had another cup of coffee, but before seeing if one of those security guys were still around, she heard a knock on the door. It was Mathew Nunan from her office. *Were they in his room?*

"I thought I would come and check on you and your friend," he said, staring at Amber.

He'd never checked on Reagan before for anything, and she found it strange that he was doing it there. She looked at her passed-out friend and then back at Mathew. Did Amber even know him? She had said he was at their building during the bomb scare lockdown. Still, it was a stretch. But otherwise, why would he, of all people, check on them?

"We're fine. Do you know what time this boat is returning to shore?" Reagan asked, watching him carefully.

"Boat? That's funny."

"I know it's a freaking yacht, whatever. Do you know how long until we get back?"

"I think hours, Reagan. Would you like me to stay with your friend so you can go back to the party?"

Like hell, Reagan thought. What was wrong with all the men on that boat? Did they not understand girl code? "No. I'm good. Thanks," Reagan dismissed him the same way he'd dismissed her so many times in meetings.

He shrugged his shoulders and then left the room. Reagan paced the room some more, hoping the crazy night wouldn't get any worse.

Chapter Thirty-One

"WHERE THE HELL AM I?" Amber asked, still groggy.

Reagan turned and quickly went to her friend's side. "We're in someone's room on the yacht."

Amber managed to push herself up to a sitting position and wiped her face with her hands. "The party?"

"Still going on downstairs, somewhere, while you sleep off the tequila shots."

"Like hell. I had two shots. One with Mathew and one by myself when he left."

Reagan sat on the bed beside Amber. "Mathew Nunan, from my office?"

"Of course. Two shots. That's it."

"Then explain to me why you practically fell off the barstool and face-planted on the floor?"

Amber's mouth gaped open. "Please tell me you're kidding?"

"I was there to witness the whole thing. Are you sure you only had two drinks?"

"Two shots. That's it." Amber repeated.

"Did you take something before we came to the party?"

"Not even an aspirin," Amber said, still rubbing her face. "My tongue feels swollen." Amber stuck her tongue out for Reagan to see.

"It might be a little swollen. Maybe you're allergic to tequila?"

"Please tell me that's not a thing. What about our Monday Margs?"

"I tell you that you face-planted in a room full of the wealthiest people in the city along with most of the local politicians. Then in front of everyone, you were carried away by two hulking security guards like you couldn't hold your liquor, but maybe it was an allergic reaction. And all you're worried about is that you won't be able to participate in our Monday night margaritas?"

Amber winked at Reagan. "What can I say? Some things are sacred."

Reagan shook her head at Amber. "You are certifiably crazy. And I've spent the last hour watching you toss and turn thinking that you drank like a fish the minute I left the party."

Amber rubbed her head. "Some date you are."

"Me?" Reagan's eyes gentled. "Seriously, Amber. How are you feeling? Can I get you something?"

"Not unless you've got a bottle of Benadryl in your purse and maybe a ginger-ale?"

"Sorry. Fresh out. But if you feel okay for me to leave you, then I can find someone who works here that might have access to a first aid kit. I'm sure a fancy yacht like this comes with its own medical staff or something."

"My head feels like a balloon. A fancy aspirin would be okay too."

Reagan hugged Amber and told her she would be back in a few minutes. It took almost twenty-five for her to find someone that could get her the Benadryl out of the first aid station. Apparently, they needed a key, and the person who had the key wasn't answering their radio. Then, Reagan had to wait for the can of ginger-ale. She headed back to the room, wondering how they would handle a serious emergency if the first aid kit were that much of a challenge, and that's when the emergency lights on the entire yacht started flashing.

She was shoved into the wall by workers and security guards and saw them whisk the mayor out of sight. Then she heard some of them excitedly talking about someone that had too much to drink falling overboard. *Maybe they were allergic-like Amber;* she thought until she neared the room where she'd left Amber. The entire hallway was blocked off, and people were yelling out orders.

Reagan stood there speechless when she realized Amber was the one missing.

The security guard who carried Amber upstairs saw Reagan standing there and immediately told someone on the radio that he'd found her. Reagan wasn't sure she heard him correctly until he leaned in, "Ms. Gentry, please come with me."

Reagan followed the muscular man up another flight of stairs and through several rooms and locked doors, but everything and everyone around her was a blur of color, like melting paint. She could hear herself breathing, but no other sound penetrated her ears, not even the alarms still sounding around the boat.

The security guard slowed down, knocked on the door, and then held it open for her to walk through before shutting it behind her. She looked up to see the mayor and Mathew Nunan sitting in sizeable leather chairs next to each other, with security standing around the room's periphery. Nearby were also three of the city council members she saw earlier, but Teresa McDonald was missing. Why were they securing the local politicians away in a guarded room? And if they were worried for their safety, wouldn't Teresa be there too? It was a lot for Reagan to process while her friend was in danger and possibly fighting for her life.

"Reagan, come sit down," Alexavier walked over and wrapped his coat around her again, but it was more to comfort her than to keep her warm.

She sat down, and someone in the room handed her a water bottle while Alexavier knelt in front of her. "We don't know much. Someone saw her out on the balcony, and then another heard her scream right before she went into the water."

"She was in bed when I left her to find some Benadryl."

"I heard she had too much to drink?"

"No," Reagan said and didn't stop him when he held her hand to try and comfort her. "I stayed with her in the room, and she woke up disoriented, but she wasn't drunk. Her tongue was swollen, and she'd had an allergic reaction. She was pretty clear about what she needed, and I wasn't gone long. I had to get the medicine and a drink for her."

Reagan put her head in her hands. If she had hurried a little faster, maybe it wouldn't have happened. She couldn't believe Amber would get out of bed, and she was more than a little surprised that she would have gone out on that balcony after she'd passed out earlier. Surely, they were going to rescue her. "Do you know if they've pulled her out of the water yet? She's a strong swimmer, and it's not that cold."

"We haven't heard anything yet."

"Nothing?" Reagan stood back up. "They should have spotted her by now, though, right?"

The mayor pulled Reagan into his arms, but she didn't let him comfort her. Instead, she took a step back and raised her voice. "She was the flipping swim team captain when she was in high school. You've seen her. You've all seen her. She's stronger than most of us in this room, and I know I could swim out there." Reagan's voice was higher than she'd planned, but they were all hiding in the room like they were in danger, and no one seemed to be concerned about the actual event. She didn't have time to be upset; she had to do something.

She put her arms through the coat the mayor had wrapped around her and took charge like she knew Amber would've done if Reagan had gone overboard. Who in here has a radio? You need to call up the captain or the head Bosun on this boat."

She lowered her eyes at Mathew, who she knew was about to

correct her over the fact that it was a yacht. She stared him down, and he looked away without saying anything.

"Ma'am, I think they're preoccupied with the rescue, but—" The burly security man stopped mid-sentence when she held up her hand.

"I need to verify a rescue is actually underway, or I need to call the coast guard and get a helicopter here five minutes ago. Do you understand me? This is the city mayor's birthday party guest we're talking about. I am certain with the high-profile people on here they will do everything in their power to save her."

He made the call, and once the captain answered, Reagan held out her hand for him to hand over the radio. He did. She was horrified when the captain explained they did not have Amber and could not locate her in the water. The coast guard had been alerted, but that was not enough. Reagan demanded they send everything and everyone they had.

Next, she called her brother, who for some strange reason, was already on the water in his boat and nearby. She didn't take the time to ask why. She simply told him what she needed, and he assured her that his fellow friends in what was known as the Cajun Navy, local men who volunteered in a crisis on the water, were already on their way.

When Reagan went up top to assess the situation, the night sky was lit up like daytime. Two helicopters had swooped in, and there were boats of every size in the water surrounding them. Reagan refused to give up on saving her best friend. She and Amber would retire together one day in Florida, no matter what their future husbands thought. They had planned it out already. It wasn't her time to go.

Twenty agonizing minutes ticked by when suddenly the searchlights moved away from the yacht. They seemed focused on a dark area of the water, and one of the coast guard helicopters hovered over one particular spot.

Ryan called her on the radio. "She's been found, Rea. It's not good. Their working on her and are about to helivac her out of there. The other woman didn't make it."

"What? There was someone else?" As soon as the words left Reagan's mouth, she knew it was Teresa McDonald. She leaned against the railing as her brother said her name a couple of times.

"Rea? Reagan!"

"Yeah?"

"I'm coming to get you."

"Okay," she said, not registering what he'd actually said to her. All she could think about was Amber fighting for her life. And how had the city councilwoman she'd suspected of impropriety gone overboard at the same time as Amber? The events had to be related.

Time slowed as Reagan waited for news about Amber. When she couldn't take it any longer, she heard Ryan raising his voice out on the deck.

Was her brother there?

There was a line of security guards preventing Ryan from getting on board. And there were at least fifteen more people behind him also trying to get on the yacht for their loved ones. It was chaotic as the security guards yelled at the party guests that they were not allowed to leave.

What was going on?

"I'm sorry, everyone, but we have strict orders that the passengers must remain on board because it is an active crime scene."

"You mean to tell me that there aren't cameras covering every inch of this swanky boat?" Ryan questioned.

Seth stepped forward and explained that Reagan wouldn't leave the premises but that they wanted to make sure she was okay. Reagan couldn't believe her brother and Seth were both there. She stepped into view as soon as she heard Ryan and Seth's voices. Ryan waved to get her attention, and she waved back, but her eyes were locked onto Seth. There was so much left unsaid between them, and the longing was unmistakable.

Before the guard could respond to his request, the mayor walked over and pulled Reagan away from the scene.

It was a toss-up on who was going to pummel Regalia first. Ryan usually kept his cool under pressure, but the anger rippled off Seth in waves as he saw the mayor's hands on his girl.

"I have some news about Amber," Alexavier said, and that's how he got Reagan to walk away with him.

"Please tell me she's okay," Reagan said, and her voice shook as her body trembled over the possibility of more bad news. She usually hid her emotions better, but the real danger Amber was in scared Reagan to death.

She looked away from Alexavier's face as he leaned in close enough to whisper, "She's been taken to the University Hospital. They have the best trauma unit around. That's all I've been told."

Reagan felt the heat of her tears as they slowly fell down her face. She'd made sure her friend was rescued, but now she needed a moment to break down. She wasn't thinking as she let Alexavier lead her into a private area until she looked around the room and saw they were alone.

"Where is everyone going?" she asked, wiping her face dry with her hands.

Alexavier guided her to a small leather sofa, where he sat entirely too close. "They're being briefed on the situation. I told them you're upset, Reagan. They agreed to give you some time."

She tried to wiggle some room between them but couldn't. "Is this about the other woman that they found? Was it councilwoman McDonald?"

The mayor looked surprised that she knew about Teresa McDonald, and Reagan watched as his mayor mask came down over his face. "I'm afraid they found councilwoman Teresa McDonald in the water too. There is a lot of speculation over what happened to cause both women to end up in the water."

"We should go talk to the police. I'm sure they'll want to speak with me since I was the last one to see Amber or at least one of the last people to see her."

The mayor shook his head. "I've already told them everything you told me, and they were satisfied enough to let you rest for a while."

Reagan's head was whirling, but she knew it was strange for them to take Alexavier's word, even if he was the mayor. She wanted to stand up and tell him so, but the dizziness she felt earlier was back, and her stomach was in knots. She kept thinking about Amber and how she looked when she regained consciousness. Had someone laced Amber's drink earlier in order to push her overboard? Had Reagan ruined their plans by showing up when she did and staying with her friend after she passed out? She felt Alexavier's hand on her cheek as he gently turned her to face him.

"I'm sorry for the circumstances, but I'm glad we're finally alone. This was all I wanted for my birthday."

He ran his other hand up her thigh, and she jumped up off the couch.

"What are you doing?" she asked, leaning against the wall for support. How the hell did she get herself into another crazy situation.

Alexavier moved quickly and stood just inches in front of her body. She could feel his body heat scorching her. "Come on, Reagan. Everything has been leading us to be together for weeks. I knew the night we had dinner at your place that it was only a matter of time before we ended up in bed. You know it's true."

"I think you're a nice man—," Reagan said, but he interrupted her.

"I'm definitely not nice," Alexavier said, pushing her against the wall by pressing his hard body into hers.

Reagan tried to push him back with her hands, but he didn't budge. Instead, he kissed her roughly, and she bit his lip.

When he pulled back to lick the blood off, she tried to slap his face, but he grabbed her hand. "I hit back," he said, pushing her roughly against the wall again, and then he kissed her harder. He leaned back again and smiled, "but maybe you like it rough?"

Reagan managed to lift her right knee enough to nail him between the legs, and with how hard his body was when he pressed himself against her, she knew it hurt.

He stumbled backward and placed his hands on his knees as he gasped for air.

"Nothing has led us to get naked, you asshole. My best friend may be dead, and you're trying to get me into bed? I was trying to let you down easily, but since you can't read the situation, let me spell it out for you. Don't you ever put your hands on me again, or you will need a surgeon to put things back together again." Reagan threw his coat onto the floor next to him and tried to leave the room, but the door was locked from the outside.

Alexavier managed to stand, but his face was flushed red. "I'm afraid they have strict orders to leave us alone until morning."

She turned around. "You're a piece of work. Tell them to let me out."

"You don't want to go out there, trust me," Regalia said. "Amber and Teresa were caught up in some illegal activities with another council member. He's being arrested and charged with murder and attempted murder right now. I know you're close friends with Amber, but I don't want anyone to say you were involved."

He looked concerned, but Reagan believed his expressions couldn't be trusted any more than his words.

"You don't have anything to do with it, do you, Reagan?"

She kept silent.

"Was Amber confiding in you?" he asked.

Reagan still didn't answer him. She kept staring instead. It was the one thing that the mayor couldn't handle.

Silence.

He had to fill it, and if she wouldn't talk, she knew he would.

"An internal review exposed some strange messages from Bruce Cannon to Teresa McDonald and then Teresa McDonald to Amber. I wasn't aware of the investigation until they had concrete evidence against them, and honestly, I couldn't believe they had been under surveillance for six months, and no one knew about it."

"Amber wasn't involved in anything illegal. I won't let anyone smear her name," Reagan said and then mentally chastised herself for giving in and speaking.

"So, she has confided in you," Regalia was staring into her eyes, and Reagan regretted giving him any missing information.

"I don't know what you're talking about," she lied. "Amber and I have been friends for years, and she would never do anything illegal. She's a good person, through and through."

Alexavier stared at her as he rubbed the stubble that was beginning to show on his chin. "Why don't I believe you, Reagan?"

Reagan's eyes grew more round, and she pouted her bottom lip slightly. The innocence rolled off her, and he looked confused. He was great at hiding his feelings behind his politician's mask, but she recognized it when he hid his true feelings. He, on the other hand, had no idea about her. She'd learned the skill as a child and perfected it over the years she lived with her parents and then while she was in high school and college. She was the master, and anyone that played poker with her could attest to that fact.

"Amber and I met in Law School. She and I both came from working-class families. Hers was a little better off than mine. She's still close with her parents. She sends them money every month and visits them often. She lives a simple life, and other than going out with different men, she is frugal in every way. She doesn't have a gambling, drinking, drug, or shopping habit. And she still has the same checking account from her small hometown bank that she got when she was a teenager. She is honest and good."

Alexavier looked surprised and crossed his arms as he sat down across from the door. Reagan was still standing in front of the exit, but she was no longer knocking for the guards to let her out. She stared at Alexavier, impressed that he could act calm after she'd kneed him less than five minutes ago.

He managed that fake smile like a champion, but he couldn't

stop the unease vibrating in the room. It hummed in her ears and made her hair stand up on the back of her neck. *Would she have to fight him off again?*

"Ms. Gentry, I don't force myself onto women who don't want me. I don't know how I got my signals crossed, but I thought we had a mutual attraction between us. You don't have to worry about me. I truly was trying to protect you from the negativity outside and then get some alone time with you." He typed on his phone for a minute and then looked up when his security team unlocked the door.

Reagan couldn't help but wonder if Alexavier forced himself on women that *did* want him. She shivered. He was certainly forceful with her, and while Reagan wanted Seth to show her he wanted her, she realized how scary it was when it wasn't mutual. Had she sent mixed signals to Alexavier? She'd thought he was attractive and all that mayorly power was exciting to be around sometimes, but now as she looked at him, she couldn't find one remarkable thing about the man.

Mathew Nunan walked in wearing casual clothes, which she thought was strange, but she figured the party was over. He barely glanced at Reagan before he focused his attention on the mayor. Nothing new about him ignoring her. She'd never liked Mathew, and he never pretended to like her. The bromance between Mathew and Alexavier was odd, though. With the entourage of people around the mayor, why would Mathew always be the one appraising him of the situation?

She watched him lean over to whisper something in Alexavier's ear, and that's when she saw it. The engraved lighter that Amber bought.

No way! Was he the man Amber was hiding?

She couldn't help herself. "Shouldn't you be at the hospital, Mathew?"

He turned to look at her coolly. "What for?"

He said it as directly as he could without saying Amber didn't mean anything to him.

2

Reagan stared coldly into his eyes, wondering between Mathew and his friend, the mayor, how many women had they hurt?

"I'll give her your regards," she said and then whispered asshole as she quickly left to find her ride away from the nightmare party boat.

Chapter Thirty-Two

REAGAN WALKED ONTO THE TOP deck in time to stop Ryan from beating down two of Alexavier's largest security men. Seth had his hands full, squaring up against two more, and she was thankful that everyone agreed to go their separate ways peacefully as long as she could leave the yacht immediately.

Ryan held out his arms to catch Reagan as Seth tossed her over the side to him. Ryan's boat bounced in the waves and would have been a steep climb for her, and they didn't have time to waste. Before she could protest, Ryan looked at her and shook his head.

"We need to get the hell out of here, Rea," Seth said as he jumped onto Ryan's boat deck.

Reagan sat down to take off her heels so they wouldn't scratch Ryan's boat, and as he steered them off into the dark water, Seth wrapped her in his jacket and leaned over to help her remove her shoes. It was a couple of minutes before anyone spoke.

Ryan was the first. "Remember Olivia and Miss Lynn from the diner? Miss Lynn's cousin is a nurse at the hospital where Amber was taken. Miss Lynn doesn't know how to text, so Olivia is sending us messages on how Amber is doing."

Reagan remembered both ladies well. Miss Lynn was in her

sixties and practically mothered all her regular customers. Olivia was in her late twenties and the picture of southern beauty but had the mouth of a sailor. She was hilarious. Neither of them would let a little rule about patient confidentiality stop them from finding out what they needed to know to help a friend. Thankful for the contact, she asked, "Any more news?"

"She's alive, but she's unconscious, and they have her on a respirator."

Reagan put her hand over her mouth.

"We're heading straight there, Rea," Seth said, patting her feet that he'd pulled into his lap so he could warm them.

Forty-five minutes later, they were waiting in the intensive care unit of the LSU medical center, hoping to get in to see Amber for a few minutes. Her parents were driving over from Alexandria, but it would be a couple more hours before they arrived. There wasn't anyone else in the ICU waiting room with them, and Reagan sat down and told Ryan and Seth everything she knew that happened before and during the accident.

The doctor agreed to allow Reagan to step in and see Amber, but she was in a coma.

Reagan wasn't prepared to see Amber that way. Her larger-than-life friend looked as if she had nothing left. There were tubes everywhere, and the worst was the machine that helped her breathe. Her lips were dried and cracked around a large hose in her mouth, and Reagan bit her lip so she wouldn't cry as she watched Amber's chest go up and down with the sound of the machine.

A nurse walked in and checked a few of the monitors. "Some people believe comatose patients can hear you when you talk to them."

Reagan nodded her head and reached out to hold Amber's hand until the nurse left.

"Oh, Amber. I'm so sorry this happened to you. I should never have left you in that room." Reagan's tears fell hard after that, and it took her a few minutes until she could speak again. "I don't know what happened to you out there, Amber, but I know that you didn't fall off that balcony. They're saying that Teresa McDonald was there too and that maybe Bruce had something to do with you two falling in?"

Reagan squeezed Amber's hand gently. "I'm sorry I didn't believe you about those two."

She braided Amber's hair and then sat quietly, holding her hand. She thought about everything she'd done with Amber since she'd moved back to New Orleans and how funny it was to see men following her around like children to the Pied Piper. She then thought about Mathew Nunan. "By the way, Amber, I figured out your mystery man. Girl, we will talk when you get out of here about your choices in men. Hurry up and get out of here, okay? I need you."

At that moment, Amber squeezed Reagan's hand. It didn't last but a second, but it was real, and it felt like she meant it. Reagan kept talking after that about their time in Law School and all the studying they did. She reminisced over getting drinks together after work and how they usually ended up having coffee which, if it got out, it would ruin her party-girl reputation. She kept up the one-sided conversation until the doctor came in and told her she should let Amber rest.

She looked at her friend lying there unresponsive and considered arguing with him. Instead, she told him about her hand movement. He agreed that the hand squeezing could be a good sign, and it gave Reagan hope that she clung to over the next few days.

Seth and Ryan stayed at the hospital with Reagan until Amber's parents arrived. Reagan didn't want them to show up and not have anyone there to tell them what had happened. Reagan offered for them to stay with her at her apartment, but they said they couldn't impose. So she did the next best thing, putting them up at the closest hotel to the hospital.

Ryan dropped Seth and Reagan off at the Starbucks parking

lot where he'd met Ryan and left his new car. Then Seth drove Reagan home.

They pulled into her parking garage, where he parked next to her new SUV. "Nice choice, Rea," he said.

"Strange that I chose an SUV, and you went for the convertible sports car," she said.

"Apparently, we've had a lot of influence over each other lately," he answered and then walked around his car to open her door.

She was still the most amazing woman he knew, but even superheroes needed to recharge. It was four in the morning and silent in the garage and the elevator up to her place. Inside, he walked with Reagan into the bedroom, where he unzipped her jumpsuit as she stripped out of it and then climbed under the covers.

She looked at him expectantly, and he followed her into bed. They had so much to talk about, but that wasn't the time. She leaned over and put her head on his chest while he wrapped his arms around her. They slept that way until noon.

Seth dragged himself out of bed and into the kitchen for coffee. Neither one of them slept great, and when Reagan stepped into the kitchen wearing her bathrobe, he handed her his cup. She took a sip while he made her a cup the way she liked it with cream and no sugar.

Reagan took her coffee with her into the bedroom and bathroom as she showered and dressed so she could go back up to the hospital. Seth drove her, and they spent the afternoon and evening there keeping Amber's parents' company, but there was no change in Amber.

The evening news had reported councilman Bruce Cannon was in jail for the murder of fellow councilwoman Teresa McDonald and attempted murder of a local attorney. Amber went unnamed, but Reagan knew it was only a matter of time before they identified her.

Monday morning Reagan dragged herself to work, but she

felt like a robot going through all the motions of her day. Seth brought her lunch, but she barely touched it.

Monday afternoon Reagan finished in court early and headed back to the office for her last appointment. When it was over, she sat there staring into space until the phone rang. It was Jerry.

"Well, it looks like your friend was on to something," he said, and Reagan swallowed back tears.

What if she had believed Amber sooner? Would Teresa and Bruce both be in jail? Would Amber be healthy and happy as usual?

"What did you find, Jerry?" she said barely above a whisper.

He'd never heard her sound so deflated, but he didn't dare ask her what was wrong. Reagan was a tough cookie, and he knew she would bite his head off if he wasted his or her time. "Remember when I said the founder of that health center had a brother here? Well, it was his younger half-brother."

"Yes," she said, and he could hear the irritation in her voice.

"It seems he and his half-brother used to get in all sorts of trouble when they were kids. They were kicked out of several private schools for vandalism and cheating. They were terrible kids, and yet they grew into responsible adults." She heard Jerry laugh. "I amuse myself sometimes."

Reagan nodded her head, but he was on the phone and couldn't see her. He kept going. "He and his brother haven't gotten into any trouble, or at least they haven't been caught for anything in a long time. They see each other a couple of times a year. I'm still looking for the proof, so don't quote me yet, but I believe they are the sort to offer kickbacks and bribes to get a healthcare facility they own a ton of shares in, to build another facility in the city. Follow the money, I always say."

Reagan couldn't stop her tears as he used Amber's exact words regarding the bribes. "Thanks, Jerry. Keep looking for the money trail. You know what I need for proof."

"Will do, little lady. I'll call you as soon as I find the next bit of evidence. I'm sending you the pictures of the brothers. It was taken fifteen years ago, but I imagine they still look similar."

Reagan hung up the phone and looked at her calendar. She didn't have another appointment. She looked at her clock to see that it was only three-thirty. The day couldn't have dragged on any slower.

She drank her diet coke and then gathered her things to go. She would stop by the hospital for a couple of hours before heading home. She felt like she could sleep for a year.

She left a message for Seth, told Nancy to go home early, and then headed out.

Mathew was standing in the lobby talking with a courier. He'd avoided Reagan all day, and she rushed past him in case he decided he wanted to speak. She glanced over at him while she waited for the elevator, and that was all it took.

He hurried out the door and was standing with her before she could turn and take the stairs. "I heard Amber is still in the Intensive Care Unit."

"Don't act like you care, Mathew."

"I think there's been a misunderstanding."

"No. I'm pretty sure I understand."

"What did she tell you?"

Reagan rolled her eyes at Mathew, and the elevator finally opened. She walked inside, and much to her surprise so did he. Once the doors closed, he hit the emergency button to make it stop.

"What the hell are you doing?" she asked. She was more worried about the stopped elevator than the jerk that was in there with her.

"I wanted to talk to you a second. Look, I liked Amber. She was a great woman—."

"She's still a great woman."

"No, I know. That's not what I meant. Amber and I had fun together. But she took things a little more seriously than I did, that's all."

"Amber has never been serious with anyone. If she thought you wanted more than a hook-up, then you must have made her believe it. In fact, you would have had to prove it to her before she would have fallen for your words. I can't believe you got her to keep it a secret. I understand wanting to keep your private life private, but you took it too far. What are you hiding?"

Reagan really wasn't suspicious of Mathew. She honestly thought he had the personality of wet paint. His behavior toward Amber got under her skin, and so she said what popped into her mind. She had no idea how four simple words would set him off.

Mathew shoved her into a corner of the elevator and lowered his face to hers. She'd never thought about how large of a man he was, but then again, she'd never really thought about him at all.

"I'll admit Amber was a nice piece of ass, but that was it. Now you listen to me, and you listen hard, you better forget everything she told you about me. Women with big mouths fall overboard in the river or get dangerous packages in the mail. Do you hear me?" he said, and for the first time, Reagan noticed how dead his dark blue eyes looked.

"Answer me!" he yelled while he was still only inches from her face.

She didn't flinch. He was a crazy bastard, but she'd had scarier moments in her childhood. She knew all they wanted was to scare her.

She kept her eyes locked onto his but reached out and hit the elevator button so it would move again. As soon as it jolted downward, she started breathing again. She'd been holding her breath since he got into her face.

He took one step away from her and looked straight ahead at the doors. When they opened, she stepped out into the lobby and turned around to see him still in the elevator. Thankfully he wasn't going to follow her further.

"I heard you," she said, and they locked eyes until the doors closed again.

Chapter Thirty-Three

REAGAN GOT INTO HER CAR, locked her doors, and called Seth. She hoped he wasn't in a session with a patient, and as she waited for his secretary to take her off hold, she searched the parking garage for any signs that Mathew was watching her.

She slowly pulled out of her parking spot and then raced out of the garage, waiting impatiently for the metal arm that blocked her exit to raise and release her.

"Hey, Rea. How was your day, baby?" Seth asked.

"Thank goodness you're there."

"Reagan? What's wrong?"

She didn't know why she was crying. She hadn't lost it the entire time she was in front of Mathew, and he threatened her. As soon as she heard Seth's voice, though, she couldn't stop her emotions from taking over.

"Did something happen to Amber? Baby, talk to me."

"N-no. I-I'm heading over to the hospital now."

"Are you driving? Reagan Marie, pull the car over. I'm coming to get you."

She could hear him running out his office door.

"I'm okay," she managed to say but hiccuped at the end.

"You are not okay. Please, baby, pull your car over. You shouldn't drive when you're crying."

"Kay," was all she could say.

"GPS says you're on Canal Street. Is that right?"

She nodded her head.

"Rea?"

"Yes. I'm on Canal."

He stayed on the phone, but it only took him a few minutes to get to her. He pulled in behind her car and jumped out quickly toward her driver's side. When he opened her door, she leaned into him. He managed to get her to climb over the console into the passenger seat so he could drive.

She watched as he used his key fob to lock his car and then used his phone to pay for the parking meter. He reached over, picked up her hand to kiss it, and held it warmly against his chest. "Where to, baby?"

"Home?"

He nodded and then pulled into traffic to get her home, out of the car, and into his arms.

Reagan calmed as soon as Seth was with her. She'd spent a lifetime taking care of herself, and the moment he offered to do it, she'd turned to mush. There was no reason to try and understand it; she just let him hold her hand and sat quietly, considering everything Mathew Nunan said to her in that elevator.

"What happened, Rea?" Seth asked as he pulled into her designated parking space.

Unlike at work, where he could let a patient take her time to tell him what was wrong, he desperately needed to know what had happened to rattle Reagan. It was the first time she'd called him in need, and he'd worried until he had eyes on her.

She looked around the garage, and that was when he knew someone had threatened her. It was something in her eyes, like when Salinas had done it.

He held her hand until they got into her apartment, then he sat next to her on the couch. She told him everything that happened with Mathew, including how she kept her game face on even though she'd been scared to death.

He pulled her into his lap and held her tightly. "I don't think he was only threatening you, Rea. I think he was admitting something."

"You think he pushed Amber overboard? And maybe Teresa McDonald too?"

"It doesn't make any sense, but it also sounds like he might have had something to do with the bomb sent to your office."

Reagan leaned into his chest and cried. She'd trusted Seth and let her guard down. Knowing that he wouldn't run away when things got tough made her even more weepy.

"I don't know what to do," she finally said after her tears stopped.

"We should probably call the detective who worked on the Salinas threat."

"But it's his word against mine, and no one will arrest him over hearsay."

"I don't want you in the office near him, Reagan."

"I don't want to be around him either, but what choice do I have? He's a partner at my firm. I can't imagine him doing any of those things. I mean, what would be his motive? First to come after me and then hurt Amber or Teresa? And then what, frame Bruce?"

"Maybe he wanted to scare you? What secret did Amber tell you about him?"

"That's the thing; she never told me any secrets about him. She wouldn't even tell me who she was seeing. I figured it out when I saw him with the lighter she'd bought."

"What lighter?"

"Amber told me she had a new man, but she wouldn't tell me who he was. She's never had a serious relationship or kept someone she'd slept with a secret. She seemed happy, though. Amber told me they would lay around and share a cigarette after sex, and it felt like she was in one of those old movies where everyone enjoys hard liquor and a smoke. She bought him that lighter as a private joke, and I saw Mathew with it, so I knew it was him."

"Did you say something about the lighter to him?"

Reagan shrugged her shoulders. "When I saw him with the lighter on the boat the other night, I couldn't stop myself. They'd pulled Amber out of the water, and he acted completely indifferent over the situation. I told him I would give her his regards, and I guess he figured she told me."

"He must also think she divulged something else."

"Amber's a straight shooter. She wouldn't tolerate anyone doing anything remotely illegal. If she had any idea that he was doing something that he shouldn't, she would have confronted him and turned him in. Maybe that's why he hurt her?"

"It doesn't explain why he would have gone after you before."

Reagan stood up to pace the floor. "Or why he would have gone after Teresa McDonald or blamed it on Bruce Cannon."

"Plus, sending a bomb to your office could have harmed him too."

Reagan stopped pacing to look out the window across the city. "But you know, he wasn't in the office that afternoon. Mathew was visiting the mayor and on lockdown there with Regalia and Amber while our office was evacuated."

"It's all a little too convenient," Reagan said as she headed to answer her ringing cell phone. Before she could get there, the ringing stopped. She didn't recognize the number, but before she could call it back, her home phone rang.

It was Amber's mother.

Reagan cleaned herself up, and she and Seth hurried to the hospital. Amber had finally woken up, and she'd asked for Reagan.

It looked like her best friend would be okay, and Reagan couldn't stop smiling. That force of nature that made her days a little brighter wouldn't let a fall from a balcony into the dark water stop her. No way. Reagan also knew Amber would tell them who was responsible for pushing her into the water and whatever secrets she had on Mathew Nunan.

The excitement of seeing Amber awake and talking made Reagan practically run through the hospital parking lot. Seth almost laughed at how hard it was to keep up with her, and he was a foot taller than she was and didn't wear stiletto heels.

When Reagan and Seth walked into the room, Amber was sitting up in her hospital bed. The majority of the life-saving machines had been taken out of the room. She only had a blood pressure cup and a heart monitor left. She was sipping on a straw and talking with her mom.

Reagan smiled through her tears. "It's so good to see you awake, sweet friend."

She hugged Amber tightly and then sat on the side of the bed so she could hold her hand. Amber's father explained that the doctors got back Amber's blood work, and it showed she'd been drugged. It was a reaction to the drug that eventually put her in a coma. They flushed out her system, and once they removed all traces of it from her body, she'd woken up.

Reagan hugged her again. Amber's parents decided to go down to the cafeteria to get something to eat so the friends could visit. Once they left, Seth sat down in one of the extra chairs and watched the two women hug each other again.

Reagan sat up and wiped her tears away. Amber had never seen Reagan cry, and it made her emotional too.

"It must have been something in the tequila shots," Reagan said, looking at Amber for confirmation. When she didn't say anything, Reagan added, "I should have stayed right beside you the whole time."

Amber smiled at her. "None of this is your fault, Reagan."

"I wish I felt that way. When you passed out and we went to that bedroom, I should've called someone else to get the Benadryl and water. Maybe I could've stopped whoever did this." She looked at Amber and quietly asked, "Who did it, Amber?"

Amber shook her head, and her eyes watered. "I'm afraid I don't remember anything from that night."

Reagan looked at Seth and then back at Amber. "Nothing? You don't remember going over the balcony?"

"I'm still shocked I could've fallen off the deck of a giant yacht."

"Not exactly. It was a bedroom balcony, but people said you screamed."

Amber shrugged her shoulders. "I don't even remember driving there or what I wore to the party."

Reagan and Amber looked at Seth, but he hesitated to give his thoughts.

"The doctors here said it could've been the drugs or the accident that caused me to forget everything. They also said I may never remember what happened."

"Never?" Reagan asked in disbelief.

"They said sometimes the memories come back in a day or so, but the longer I go without recalling them, the more likely they will be lost forever."

"What about Mathew? Do you remember something he might have said before the night of the party? Like a secret or something?"

"Mathew Nunan from your office? Why would he tell me any secrets?"

"Maybe because you were secretly dating each other?"

Amber laughed at Reagan. "I think you fell off the balcony and hit your head. Mathew's not my type, plus we've barely even spoken. He comes over and talks to the mayor, but other than a hello or goodbye, he's not a talker."

"You definitely dated him. It was in secret. He told you to keep it a secret. Remember?" Reagan said.

"Why would I date a dude who would want to keep the relationship secret? Sounds like a loser to me."

"You bought him a lighter when we were out shopping."

"I seriously doubt that," Amber said, looking at Reagan like she'd been the one in a coma.

Reagan took a deep breath. She could tell she was upsetting Amber. Her precious friend didn't know anything that could help explain what was going on with Mathew, and he wasn't worth worrying her friend. She changed the subject, and they talked for thirty minutes about the good-looking doctors that worked at the medical center.

Seth went to find a cup of coffee so the women could talk with abandon. His girl had called him for help that day, and he knew it was a turning point for them.

Chapter Thirty-Four

REAGAN LEFT THE HOSPITAL happier than she'd been in days. Amber lost a few of her memories, but otherwise, she would make a full recovery.

Seth was beside her, and she wasn't freaking out anymore about whether or not they belonged together. It was right for the time being, and she could work with that.

He drove her to his place so he could pick up some clothes and toiletries to keep at her house, and she unloaded his dishwasher while he gathered his things. When Seth came out of the bedroom, she was singing quietly. He walked up behind her and wrapped his arms around her. He hadn't heard her singing like that since he moved away to Tennessee.

He kissed her ear and then her shoulder. She turned in his arms, and the kiss she gave him was heated. He managed to steer them to his large leather sofa, where they made out and removed most of their clothes. It was an incredible hour of them exploring each other's bodies and making love on the couch and the living room floor.

They didn't talk as they each dressed and moved the coffee table back into place. Reagan held his hand as they walked to her new SUV, where he kissed her warmly again. They drove to Canal

Street so he could get his car and then followed each other back to her place.

Seth made the spaghetti he'd promised a week earlier, and they laid around the rest of the evening next to each other. It wasn't until the following day that either of them brought up Mathew Nunan and his threats.

Reagan had an entire morning of court and wouldn't get back to her office until the afternoon. Seth suggested they have lunch together, and then he would go with her into her office.

"What are you going to do, Dr. Young? You can't confront Mathew in public. I mean, I don't want you to have a physical altercation. I wouldn't want anything to happen to you."

Seth sat his coffee cup down and pulled Reagan forcefully into his arms. "That will only happen if he says anything to you, Rea. But make no mistake, I won't hesitate to kick his sorry ass if I have to, in public."

Reagan stared at Seth as she worried her bottom lip with her teeth.

"If you don't stop looking at me that way, we're going to be late for work," he said and ran his hand down the length of her back and then bottom.

He was really hot when he acted protective, and she scolded herself for second-guessing him to his face. He was in great shape, tall and muscular, but she'd never seen him angry. The kind of anger she figured a person would need to win a physical fight. He was intelligent and highly educated. She didn't mean to stereotype him, but she didn't think of him as someone that would throw his brawn around. But he was holding his own next to her brother on the yacht against the security team.

Then there was Mathew Nunan, who was a heavier scrappy looking man. He wasn't in good shape but had probably been in more than a few fights. She didn't want to think about them throwing punches, but she agreed to let Seth come with her that afternoon.

Reagan finished with her court cases and met Seth for a quick lunch. Afterward, he accompanied her into her office but found that Mathew was out for the rest of the day. Seth stayed, accepting a cup of coffee from Nancy and laughing when she flirted with him.

"I don't want to know what she said, do I?" Reagan asked, looking up at Seth when he walked into her private office with a cup of coffee for her.

"Nope," he said and shook his head. Reagan rolled her eyes. She considered saying something to Nancy about her raunchy mouth, but she was older and only said those things to Seth and Ryan. Honestly, it was pretty funny seeing both men get embarrassed.

Seth agreed to go back to his office since Mathew wouldn't be in that afternoon, and Reagan told him that she was going up to the hospital to see Amber that evening.

They made plans to meet at Reagan's place at nine.

The rest of her afternoon seemed normal as Reagan finished up some paperwork and talked to a couple of clients on the phone.

It was almost six when she called Amber to check on her. "Thanks for the flowers," Amber said, surprising Reagan when she picked up the phone.

"I'm glad you got them."

"You know I love purple, and my mother does too. She's been talking all morning about how extraordinary the arrangement looks."

"Any word from the doc on when they'll spring you?"

"As for the doctors, I found out that charming one is married. No playing house with him. He said they will let me go either tomorrow or Friday."

Reagan's eyes watered. She was thankful for the excellent news. Finally, things were turning around for the best.

She told Amber that she would be by in an hour and offered to bring her something good to eat, but she declined. She said she had a male nurse who would deliver her dinner in bed.

Reagan laughed at her friend and how she must be getting better because her sense of humor was back. She got off the phone, so she could wrap up her work and visit her friend.

Right on time, forty-five minutes later, Reagan packed her briefcase when her phone rang.

"I'm glad I caught you," Jerry said.

"Hey, Jerry."

"Did you take a look at that picture I sent you yesterday?"

It wasn't like Reagan to forget something like that, but she'd been so distracted over Amber that she'd forgotten to check the file. "I'm pulling it up now, Jerry."

Well, I have the men's names, and I think you will be surprised," he said, waiting on her.

Reagan pulled up the email from Jerry and opened the file. She couldn't believe it. "Where was this taken, Jerry?"

It was the grand opening of the North Texas Community Health Center, and it's the owner and his younger brother. The Community Health Centers are named for the area in which they are located.

Reagan stared at the picture on her computer. It was him. He'd gained a few pounds and had more facial hair, but the younger man was undoubtedly Mathew Nunan.

His brother was the previous owner of NTCHC, South Texas CHC, Mid Texas CHC, and North Louisiana CHC, which had just secured the go-ahead to build a flagship facility in New Orleans. He probably still had a substantial stake in the company, and if she looked closer, would she find that Mathew did too? He'd become super friends with Mayor Regalia, and she'd seen him talking with Teresa McDonald and Bruce Cannon. Could they have all colluded on this venture with Amber discovering only a piece of the puzzle?

Reagan's head was reeling, and Jerry wondered if he'd lost her.

"You know who that is in the picture, right?" he asked.

"Yes. Yes, I recognize one of them."

"I thought you'd be interested to see that one of your partners was related to the previous head honcho."

"Yes, things are making a lot more sense now, Jerry. Call me if you get anything else."

Reagan quickly grabbed her things and headed out of the building. She wasn't sure who was involved in the bribery scheme, but she was confident that Amber's accident was related. In fact, there was no telling the lengths they had gone to in order to cover up their crime. She thought about Mathew's threats and how they had more weight now that she understood what was at stake for him. It was more than the local police department could handle, and she shivered over the significance of the white-collar crime.

She scanned the parking garage as she hurried into her SUV and locked the doors. As she started her car and headed toward the hospital, she was overcome with the need to call Seth and talk through what she was about to do.

Chapter Thirty-Five

REAGAN CALMED THE MINUTE she heard Seth's voice. "Hey babe, still at the office?" he asked, and she could hear the smile in his tone. She loved him.

"I'm pulling into the hospital parking lot and wanted to run something by you."

"Amber is okay?"

"Yes. It doesn't have anything to do with Amber or, at least, not anymore since she's lost her memory of the events. Look, I can't tell you all the details, but I need to talk something through with you."

Seth could tell this was serious and was concerned. But he loved the fact that she needed and wanted his support. He'd wished Reagan would lean on him and that one simple change meant everything.

"I've been looking into something for a friend, and my detective, Jerry, has uncovered some information that might incriminate powerful people in the city. I can't say much more than that, but I need to call the FBI and turn over everything I have so they can investigate things."

Instantly he knew the friend was Amber, and he wondered

who else was involved. "Does this have anything to do with Mathew Nunan's threats against you?

She sat there for a minute before she answered. "Yes, I believe it does."

"Do you need me to go with you to talk to them?"

"No. I'm not going in person. I'm calling the local office and giving them everything I have on it and walking away. I'm not really involved. I happened to be in the right or, depending on how you look at it, the wrong place at the right time. I want to step out of this craziness and focus on my own work."

Seth was relieved. He didn't want Reagan involved in anything risky, and he felt like Mathew Nunan was dangerous. "I think that's a good idea, Rea."

"I honestly don't think there is any other way to handle it, and I've talked to special agents regarding cases before. I'm sure they'll jump on this quickly. I don't want to involve Amber while she's trying to recover."

"Amber will be fine. She's lost some of her short-term memories, but she's still a force of nature, and she can hold her own."

Reagan laughed. Seth had Amber pegged. "You're right. I'm going to make a quick call and then go visit our one-woman hurricane."

Seth told her he loved her and would see her at the apartment around eight. They hung up, and Reagan looked up the number she'd stored in her phone. It took a couple of minutes to get through the FBI telephone system where she could input the extension number she had and finally talk to an agent.

It didn't go as she'd hoped.

First, she was surprised when two agents got on the phone with her. Then after she explained the essential information, they began to question her repeatedly for an hour. It was bad cop and worse cop grilling her with no one playing the good cop at all.

She remained calm as she repeated the story about Amber's suspicions and the connection that Jerry, the detective, uncovered. She continued with what happened on the yacht at the mayor's birthday party and then the threats Mathew Nunan made against her. She didn't veer from her original story once, but they still questioned her involvement, even going as far as to threaten her if she was less than truthful.

She wished she'd called the local police department and let them handle it or hand it off to the feds. She didn't need to be in the middle of it. She tried to get off the phone with them, but they wouldn't stop grilling her unless she agreed to meet. They insisted on seeing her immediately and wouldn't take no for an answer. She'd had enough of their bullying tactics, so she told them she wouldn't meet them immediately, but they could come by her apartment at 9 pm that evening. She figured Seth would be there, and together they would control the next interview with the agents.

She texted Seth and let him know that the FBI would be at her apartment at nine.

Reagan considered how everything began with Amber's weak suspicions of two council members. That theory had grown into a substantial amount of circumstantial evidence with a murder, an attempted murder, and possibly millions of dollars funneled to an out-of-state health care facility. It looked like it involved a successful local attorney, at least two council members, and the mayor, but Amber couldn't recall the first thing about it.

Suddenly, Reagan was thankful again that she was a divorce attorney. She took a deep breath and tucked the complicated phone call with the FBI aside so she could enjoy a visit with her friend. A few laughs with Amber always made things seem lighter.

She hurried through the hospital lobby and the elevator to the second floor. It was great that Amber was moved to a regular room, and Reagan could visit at whatever time she wanted instead of designated hours. As she stepped off the elevator, she immediately noticed the more relaxed mood in that particular hospital ward. Colorful pictures were hanging on the walls, and the few nurses at the nurses' station smiled at her as she walked past them. A few additional visitors loitered the hallway, laughing and talking quietly. It was much better than the beeping of machines and drawn faces of the intensive care unit.

Smiling as she opened the door, Reagan stopped cold when she saw Mathew Nunan standing beside Amber's bed.

"Where are your parents?" Reagan asked Amber but continued to stare at Mathew.

"They went back to the hotel to rest for a while. They haven't slept very well since they got here," Amber said.

Reagan forced herself to look away from Mathew and over at her friend. Amber gave her a confused smile, and Reagan walked over and gave her a kiss and a hug. "You doing okay?"

"Great. I feel much better today. Um, Mathew here heard I was in the hospital and brought me those flowers."

Reagan looked at the large bouquet that appeared to be from the gift shop downstairs. "That was nice and unexpected."

"They're actually from everyone at her office. I was over there this afternoon. I'm the courier," he said awkwardly.

Reagan stared at him again, which made the situation even more intense. *What was he doing there? Amber didn't remember him, and he didn't care about her.*

"Still no luck remembering what happened on the boat Saturday?" Reagan asked purposefully.

Mathew glared her way, but Amber didn't notice what was happening between them.

"Nada. They ran some cognitive tests today, and I'm pretty solid otherwise. I can quote municipal laws, but I can't remember what I had for dinner last week."

"Still no boyfriends then?" Reagan egged Mathew on with her questions for Amber.

Amber didn't catch on to the innuendo regarding Mathew. Instead, she thought Reagan had seen another admirer. "I guess you saw my hot fireman neighbor as he was leaving? He brought me those roses in the window."

Amber didn't see the looks Mathew and Reagan were trading

right in front of her as she continued, "The mayor stopped by earlier too."

Of course, he did, because the whole crazy group was worried about what Amber couldn't remember. Reagan thought as she believed that her friend was only safe because of her memory loss.

Amber continued talking. "He met my parents and stayed and talked to my dad for a while. It's incredible who comes out to see you when you're down." Amber looked over at Mathew, but he hadn't stopped giving Reagan the evil eye.

He crossed his arms as he replied to Amber's comment. "Everyone wants to make sure you're taking care of yourself, Amber. We wouldn't want anything else bad to happen to you."

Reagan crossed her arms as she stared at Mathew. She knew he was threatening her friend and needed to get him away from her. "Mathew, is your brother still in town?"

"I didn't know you had a brother," Amber said as she wondered if they were verbally sparring with each other.

Mathew took an aggressive step toward Amber, but Reagan stood up to draw his attention toward her.

"I'm sorry to run so soon, Amber. I need to let you get your rest. I'll try and stop by your apartment tomorrow after you get out," Reagan said as she headed toward the door. She was going to find security.

Mathew stepped back, and under his breath, he said goodbye to Amber. When Reagan stepped into the hallway, he was right behind her. "Let's take the stairs," he said through gritted teeth.

"Like hell," Reagan replied as she darted toward the opening elevator. Mathew was quicker and grabbed her by the arm.

She looked around, but there wasn't a single nurse at the little station where she'd seen three earlier. And the family that had been in the hallway were gone too. Reagan wanted to scream but he shoved her through the stairwell door before thinking of it.

"Did I not make myself clear yesterday?" he asked as he stepped into her space.

"She doesn't remember anything, Mathew. Leave her alone."

"I needed to see for myself, but I think you're right. She couldn't remember my name when I first got there."

"Then now you know, so you can leave her alone. She's not going to tell anyone."

"She's not, but you clearly will. Ain't that right?"

Reagan turned and ran down the stairs as fast as she could. She hit the door at the bottom with force, but it opened to the outside and not into the hospital lobby as she'd expected. She was fast in high heels, but Mathew was faster. He grabbed her and threw her into his car as hard as possible. She hit her head on the console and was instantly dizzy.

He reached past her to the glove compartment, where he pulled out a gun. "Now sit there and shut up," he said.

He made a call as he pulled out of the parking lot, and she figured it must have been to his brother. He drove toward the warehouse district and finally pulled up to a rusted-looking building and honked his horn. Someone from the inside opened the large metal door so Mathew could pull his car inside, and Reagan understood she was in the worst kind of trouble.

Everything Ryan Gentry had taught his sister to do in that type of situation, she'd remembered too late. *"Never let them put you in the car, Rea. Go down fighting. If they're driving, wait until they look at the road and open the door, then jump. You have a better shot of making it out of there alive if you don't let them get you away from the crowd."* He'd said those words to her a hundred times. Yet, there she was in what looked like a deserted metal building away from everything and everyone.

Mathew got out of the car and came around to her side, dragging her out by her arm. Her shoulder ached with the force he was using. She looked up, and the first person she saw walking toward them was Mayor Regalia.

It was dark, but he was still wearing his suit jacket and tie as he walked into the small lit area where she and Mathew were standing.

She couldn't believe he was actually involved. Everything

pointed to him helping Mathew, but she still couldn't believe it.

As he got closer, she could see the split in his lip and another above his left eyebrow. His jacket sleeve was ripped on one side, and it looked like there was some dried blood on it. At first, it didn't register what was going on until she heard another voice coming from behind him. "So that's your girlfriend? She's a looker. I get it," The voice said to the mayor, and then he shoved Mayor Regalia in the back to direct him to walk closer toward Reagan.

Reagan looked at Mathew and then past Alexavier. Coming out of the shadows was a man about Mathew's height, but he was balding and probably ten years older. She recognized him from the photo that Jerry sent. It was Richard Nunan. "The gang's all here?" he said, clucking his tongue like a fool.

Alexavier stepped closer to Reagan. "Are you okay?" he asked, and as much as she wasn't a fan of Alexavier's anymore, she was happy not to be alone with the Nunan Brothers.

"He's not my boyfriend," Reagan said, and Mathew laughed. "Of course, he isn't. You're the Ice Queen. But we needed it to look like he was, and everyone saw you on the boat together."

"He's played me the entire time, Reagan," Alexavier said. "He doesn't care about the city or anyone else but himself."

Mathew held his gun up toward the mayor.

Richard intervened. "Don't shoot him, Mathew. We need it to look like an accident. Lovers on a boat going down in the river. He can't have a bullet in him."

"I've listened to his *'let's make the city great again'* speech until I'm sick to death. He's such a freaking boy scout."

Reagan remembered how Alexavier threatened to hit her back after he kissed her roughly, and she tried to slap him. He was no boy scout.

"What's wrong, Ice Queen? You don't think Mayor Regalia is a goodie-good?" Mathew smirked. "Sure, he'll play along with that dominant thing behind closed doors, but out in the real world, he's an irritating do-gooder. Of course, I may have led him to believe you were into that kinky shit too. It was hilarious feeding him stories about you all the while I knew you were frigid as a snowstorm in the Arctic."

"I'm sorry, Reagan," Alexavier whispered.

She felt light-headed and figured it was from hitting her head. She took several deep breaths and then turned her head quickly to throw up in the shadows.

"The idea of sex turns your stomach that easily?" Mathew tormented Reagan while she was ill.

"That's enough, Mathew," Alexavier said, and Mathew hit him in the face with his gun.

Alexavier fought back and landed several good hits into Mathew's ribs, making him fall to the ground.

Richard stepped in between them. "Mathew. Stop. Bruce will be here with his boat soon enough."

Reagan wiped her mouth with her sleeve and then kept her hands on her knees, trying to calm her churning stomach. Bruce Cannon had made bail, and now she knew who had the deep pockets to make that happen.

Alexavier tried to check on Reagan, but before getting closer to her, Richard and Mathew grabbed him and secured his hands behind his back with large black zip ties.

Richard then stalked over to Reagan and zip-tied her hands roughly too.

"You two are aggravating the hell out of him, and I'm trying to make sure you make it to your watery graves alive," Richard said, and then he made that ridiculous clucking sound again. Reagan shook her head. It was something out of her worst nightmare. She'd just gotten back together with Seth, and her life couldn't end before she got to any of the good parts.

Richard grabbed her arms and shoved her and Alexavier to get them to walk into a darker part of the building. He unlocked a closet door and then pushed them inside, locking them in.

"Feel better?" he asked Mathew. Mathew nodded. "Good. Now call Cannon and see what's taking him so long."

Chapter Thirty-Six

THE CLOSET WHERE REAGAN and Alexavier were held was small and warm. Reagan's head felt heavy, and she prayed she wouldn't be sick again.

Alexavier could hear her breathing erratically. "Reagan, are you okay?"

She nodded her head without thinking about them being in the dark.

"Reagan?" he repeated her name.

"Yes. Yes, I'm fine. I hit my head, and I'm feeling dizzy. That's all."

"If I lean against the wall, I can slide down and sit on the floor. I know the closet isn't big enough for both of us, but you could sit in my lap. It might make you feel more comfortable," Alexavier offered.

"I'm not sitting in your lap, Alexavier," Reagan said, wishing she could wipe her face with her hands. "We need to try and break out of this closet. They're going to kill us, and this may be our only chance to escape."

Alexavier sighed. Then Reagan heard him rubbing his hands against the metal in a fast rhythmic motion. The dark seemed to enhance all of their sounds and movements.

She jumped when she felt his warm hands touch her wrists. "It's okay. I'm going to free your hands," he said, and then he gently pulled her tethered wrists over toward the metal door frame. He lifted her hands until he found the jagged piece of metal and then began to tear the plastic tie in half using the metal frame as a saw. It took a couple more minutes to remove hers because he was careful not to hurt her.

"Thank you," she said, wary over his thoughtful behavior.

"They locked me in here for several hours before you got here. I found that broken piece of metal when I scraped my arm across it earlier. It took me a while to stop the bleeding, and when I couldn't hear them outside anymore, I used my entire body weight to try and push through the metal door and walls. It was no use; they've been reinforced with something. I couldn't make a dent in it. We'll have to try to escape once we're out of here."

Reagan shivered, thinking of being locked in the tiny room for hours. It was going to take all she had to keep calm. And her dizziness wasn't getting any better. She tried to lean against the wall, but she bumped into the mayor's body.

"I'm sorry. I'm trying not to get sick. The last thing I want to do is throw up in here."

"Let's sit down then," he said calmly.

Reagan didn't have a choice. She had to sit down, or she would hurl whatever she had left in her stomach all over them.

She heard Alexavier lean his body against the metal and slide to the floor. Then he instructed her. "Turn your back to my voice. Slowly step back until your heels are against my legs. Now lean your back against the wall and slide down."

Reagan tried to do as he said, but she didn't slide down as gracefully as he did. It was more like falling, instead, and she landed on his lap harder than she'd planned.

"Oh," she said and could feel her heart beating rapidly.

"It's okay, Reagan. I've got you. Try to calm your breathing."

He settled her onto his lap and then patted her upper arm.

There wasn't anything sexual about his behavior as he tried to soothe her.

Reagan's imagination was warring with her mind. Who was the real Alexavier? The man she first met was intelligent, considerate, and then there was the man on the yacht. Could Mathew have truly convinced Alexavier that she liked that behavior?

"Feel better?" he asked.

Reagan leaned her head back, trying to find some fresh air in the cramped space. She was terrified of her weakness, and the dizziness plus being locked in the small closet had overwhelmed her.

Alexavier slowly began to talk, and for the first time, she wondered if he was nervous. "I didn't think I'd get the chance to properly apologize to you, Reagan," he said. "I was such a fool. Mathew knew I was interested in you, and he fed me false information about you. I am very sorry if I was too forward. I suspected he was wrong when you returned the dress I bought for you."

"Do you normally do that for women you're interested in?"

"I got carried away. I felt protective of you after all that you'd been through, and after dinner at your place, I thought we had a connection."

"You were sweet, Alexavier, and I did appreciate your words of encouragement."

"But then I came on too strong by buying you that designer dress and insisting that you wear it to my birthday party? Plus, I insisted on sending a car to fetch you and then practically mauled you when I got you alone?"

"I'm not a big fan of that guy," she said.

"Under the right circumstances, *that guy* can be pretty exciting, or so I've been told."

"I can appreciate excitement, but—."

Alexavier finished her sentence. "But you're dating Seth?"

"It's complicated."

"Well, I'm always free for as much uncomplicated as you can

stand," he said, and she couldn't mistake the deeper tone of his voice. He was the very definition of complicated, but he was also overwhelmingly attractive. She was sure he would find someone else that would appreciate as much debauchery as he could dish out. She wasn't the one.

"In the meantime, we can be friends," he offered.

Reagan rested her head on his shoulder and leaned into him. It was exactly what she needed to hear.

They sat like that for a while, and when Reagan's nausea eased, she broke the silence. She explained everything she knew about Mathew and his brother. She then explained how he grabbed her in the hospital parking lot. "Maybe someone saw him throw me into the car?"

"Maybe so," Alexavier said, not wanting to tell her that if anyone had seen it, they would surely have heard something by now.

Before the silence fell upon them again, Reagan asked, "How did they get you here?"

"Mathew told me he'd found several properties that I would be interested in, and without a second thought, I jumped into the car with him. Before becoming mayor, I spent every extra nickel buying up investment properties. He brought me here, and that's when I met Richard.

"You fought with him?" she remembered the cut above his eye and lip.

"I was kicking his ass until Mathew pulled his gun."

Reagan had been wrong about the mayor. He wasn't all polish and shine. He could run with the wealthier class of the city, but that was his charm. On the inside, he was made of something more substantial. He was important to the city and surely had people out looking for him. "Well then, someone is bound to miss you. I mean, if you've been here for hours, then your office has called the police, right?"

"I told my secretary that I would be out the rest of the afternoon. I went to the hospital to visit Amber and then had the appointment with Mathew, which I expected to run into the early evening. I guess while I was locked in here, Richard kept a lookout while Mathew grabbed you.

Reagan felt the tears well up in her eyes, but she swiped them away as quickly as they came. She and Alexavier were on their own. They would have to save themselves. She may be a high-priced attorney, and he the mayor of one of the most famous cities in the country, but she wasn't going to count them out yet.

Chapter Thirty-Seven

SETH LOOKED AT THE CLOCK again. It was almost nine, and he'd expected Reagan more than forty-five minutes earlier. He tried her phone, but it went straight to voicemail. When he checked the cell phone location tracker, it didn't register. *Why was her phone turned off?*

Perhaps her battery died, and she hadn't noticed it yet? But why was she still at the hospital with Amber?

He thought about how rattled she was over the phone call with the feds. It wasn't like her to get nervous. At least not openly. It would take some time to get used to the new Reagan. The Reagan that shared everything.

He smiled, thinking about her calling him for advice and how much he loved it.

The distraction of thinking of her helped until he heard the knocking on Reagan's apartment door. As expected, two federal agents stood there at straight up 9 pm.

By 9:20, Seth and the two agents were standing in Amber's hospital room. They hadn't wasted a minute trying to get to Reagan, and he understood why they had rattled her before, over the phone. He'd insisted on following them over so that Amber wouldn't get upset, but mostly it was so he could give Reagan a hand if she needed it.

Amber may have lost some of her memory, but she was still as sharp as ever. When Seth and the agents walked into her room, she sat up in the bed.

"Has something else happened?" she asked.

The female agent spoke first, "You're friends with Reagan Gentry?"

Amber got out of her bed with her hand over her mouth. "No. I mean, yes. Oh, Seth. What's happened to her?"

Seth stepped around the two suits and calmly looked at Amber. "We're not sure. She hasn't made it home yet."

"I knew it. There was something strange going on between her and Mathew. I wasn't sure at first, but she left kind of quickly, and then he abruptly left right after her," Amber told them.

"Mathew Nunan was here?" Seth asked, and at the same time, one of the agents asked, "Mathew Nunan was here with her?"

Both agents looked at each other.

"No," Amber said sternly. She didn't want Seth to get the wrong idea, and she couldn't imagine why the agents suspected Reagan of anything wrong. "He got here twenty minutes before Reagan did, and she looked surprised to see him. You know she doesn't like him very much. I don't know why she thinks I could have ever dated him."

"You're Mathew Nunan's girlfriend?"

Seth had witnessed agents try and twist things around to catch people in their own lies. He didn't much agree with the tactic, especially when used against his girl and her friends.

Amber was no wilting flower. "Hell, no. I don't find him remotely attractive, and I have many options."

The agents looked at each other again, but that time Seth interrupted their silent conversation. "Something is wrong. I knew it when Reagan wasn't home on time. She's never more than a few minutes late, and I know she had planned to be there tonight to talk with you two."

The agents didn't respond, and Seth made another point. "The GPS tracker I have on her car shows her here. Shouldn't we go look at her car?"

The agents nodded and headed out the door. Seth promised Amber that he would call her as soon as he found something out, and still, she followed him out into the hallway. That was when one of the agents stepped back and told Seth that they would take it from there. Before he could respond, Amber stepped in front of him to address the agent.

"Take it from here? I'll be surprised if either of you can find your way out of the hospital without a map. You don't know Reagan or—." Amber stopped when Seth gently wrapped an arm around her shoulders and began to speak.

"She's obviously worried for Reagan, as am I. Amber, you need to rest. Don't worry. I'm not going to stop until I find her."

The agent began to speak, but Amber's look made him think better of it. Without another word, he headed toward the open elevator, and Seth ran to catch up before they could leave without him. He knew they didn't want to share information, but he was confident they wouldn't find Reagan soon without him.

In the parking lot, Reagan's new car was locked up tight, and there was no sign she had returned to it once she went into the hospital. Her briefcase was still on the seat, and the agents discussed impounding her car so they could go through it.

Seth shook his head at them as they argued over what to do. They both fell silent when they heard him on the phone with his car service.

"They'll have someone here within thirty minutes," he said. Both agents gave him a blank stare. "Reagan is a compulsive note-taker. She can't help herself, but she doodles when she's on the phone or even when she's in meetings. If she figured something out, then she would have scribbled it on a notebook in there somewhere."

It took the roadside assistance truck only ten minutes to get there and open the locked car. The serviceman didn't even check

FALL AGAIN

Seth's ID to verify it was his account or his vehicle. Strangely the agents stood by as Seth opened Reagan's bag and found her notebook. He flipped through pages and saw his name written several times with circles around it or underlined in bold black pen. She clearly thought about him throughout the day, and it pulled at his heart.

He found a page with notes about Amber and her suspicions about two city council members, Teresa McDonald and Bruce Cannon. Reagan had written several big question marks in the margin. *She had questions about something.* Of course, Teresa McDonald was gone, but Bruce Cannon was fine. Did he know Amber suspected him of wrongdoing? Reagan also wrote mayor Regalia's name in the margin with circles around it. At the bottom of the page, she had dates and times when she spoke to her detective and then the names Mathew Nunan and Richard Nunan. In the margin, she wrote the words "brothers" and "see picture," both were circled several times.

He was starting to see a pattern. Reagan's handwriting was neat, and on the page, she wrote concise notes. However, in the margin, she doodled her random thoughts, ideas, or concerns. Things she felt strongly about she circled, so they stood out.

Seth showed the agents, and they agreed she had a method to her scribbling. One of them looked through the notebook page by page as the other called to get information on what kind of car Mathew Nunan drove. He and Seth looked through the small lot, but Mathew's car was not there.

"I don't think Reagan would have left here by her own free will with Mathew Nunan," Seth told the agents who had fallen silent. He could tell as soon as he said the words aloud that both agents had been thinking the same thing.

Seth pulled out his cell phone to try and call Reagan again. It still went to voicemail. "Can't you find out the location of her phone or at least the last place it showed up?" he asked, feeling a little more desperate out in the dark parking lot.

Finally, the balding agent spoke. "It doesn't work as it does on

247

television. It's hit or miss, and honestly, it takes some time to get the information."

Suddenly his partner smiled slyly. As he dialed his phone, he said, "But we can look at red light cameras and see if we can locate Mr. Nunan."

Seth felt a flicker of hope as both agents seemed to show more energy than they'd mustered over the last hour. It was half-past ten, and Seth was anxious to find Reagan. Standing next to her abandoned car, the night sounds of the city amplified to a deafening pitch.

He needed to do something and went back to his car, where he could watch the agents as they paced out of hearing distance. Each agent was talking to different sources and trying to track down a lead on Mathew Nunan.

Finally, one of them walked over to Seth and said they didn't have anything with Reagan and Mathew, but they had mayor Regalia and Mathew in the car together earlier. The cameras showed them leaving downtown and then had them again in the warehouse district. They couldn't pick up exactly where they went but narrowed it down to one city block. There were only three large buildings on the block, so they would be able to search quickly. The cameras never showed Alexavier Regalia again, but it did show Mathew driving alone, heading in the direction of the hospital.

Seth never trusted the mayor but decided that wasn't the time to mention it to the FBI agents. *Perhaps they'll find more motivation if they think the mayor is in danger.*

And just like that, both agents agreed they should go directly to the warehouse district and try to figure out which building Mathew and the mayor visited. It was the only lead they had at the moment. What the agents didn't mention to Seth was that Mayor Regalia hadn't been seen the rest of the day. Although it wasn't unheard of, it was unusual.

Seth's mind was racing as he followed the agents' car. He knew the moment Reagan didn't make it home by nine that something was wrong. It was almost midnight, and he prayed she would be okay. He picked up his phone and made the call to Ryan that he'd been dreading.

"What do you mean she's missing?" Ryan asked as he jumped out of bed and pulled on his jeans. Sydney watched as he wrangled on a t-shirt too. "Reagan likes to spend time alone. She says her brain needs the solitude to recharge or something. She could be at her office."

"Her car is still in the hospital's parking lot, and her phone goes straight to voicemail," Seth said, explaining every detail. His pulse hammered as he told Reagan's only living relative the dire news.

"I'll be there in thirty," Ryan said and hung up.

Seth knew it was a forty-five-minute drive from Maisonville to the warehouse district, but if anyone could get there faster, it would be Ryan Gentry for his sister.

Chapter Thirty-Eight

THE AGENTS CUT THEIR LIGHTS and pulled their car over to the side of the road a block away from the buildings they needed to search. Seth pulled in behind them as he looked around his new sports car and cursed. He'd become too lax as a doctor and didn't have a weapon of any kind in his vehicle. Growing up in South Mississippi, he'd always carried a knife and sometimes a hunting rifle but more than anything, he'd felt prepared for emergencies. At the moment, he had a leather file folder on his seat and some napkins in his glove compartment.

He clenched his jaw as he got out of his car. Reagan needed him, and he would find a way to protect her.

"Our backup will be here any minute. We'll check out the buildings to see if there is any activity but you to stay here."

Seth didn't say a word as he jogged past both men in black and headed for the first building. He heard one of them curse as they ran to follow him. The building was completely dark. The grass was overgrown and other than a couple of rats scurrying around the outside, there wasn't any activity there.

Seth quickly headed toward the next building. The front roll-down door was chained, but as he neared the back of the building, he smelled diesel fuel and heard a loud engine revving. He motioned the agents his way. The windows were located more than twenty feet high at the top of the building, and although they couldn't get up there, they could make out a faint light coming from inside.

Both agents pulled their guns, and Seth felt helpless as they stepped around him to go inside the building. He weighed his options, and that's when he saw the worn fence boards lying in the dirt. He jerked one of them loose and smiled at the sturdiness and the rusty nails sticking out of one end as he quickly headed into the building.

A single fluorescent light in the middle of the ceiling lit the open warehouse. It gave a flickering, almost surreal look to the activity happening in the middle of the large building. Seth couldn't see either of the agents because a black pickup truck with an attached trailer and boat blocked his view of the other side. The loud engine noise muffled some of the sounds, but there was unmistakable arguing between several men.

When gunshots rang out, Seth dove under the truck bed, carefully hugging the gray splintering fence board to his side. From that angle, he could see both FBI agents lying on the cement floor. Blood pooled around both men, and then the yelling began again.

"Your brother's crazy, Mathew. Hell, both of you are crazy. I was okay with shoving Teresa and that lawyer off the yacht, and I'd gladly help drop that other one in the middle of the river, but the mayor and two FBI agents? They will shoot us first and ask questions later. We're not walking away from this."

Seth couldn't be sure, but it sounded like Councilman Cannon speaking. He couldn't see their faces, but three men were still standing. Another two shots rang out, and Seth saw Bruce Cannon fall face-first to the ground. He was shot twice in the head.

"Richard!"

"Shut up, Mathew. We only needed his boat."

"No, idiot. We needed him to take the fall for the others. Now we have two dead FBI agents and two dead council members."

Richard clucked and then corrected Mathew. "You're wrong little brother."

"You and I can take care of them."

Them? Who else was there besides Reagan?

Seth moved back so they couldn't see him. He considered climbing into the boat. He could hide until they got out onto the water and then get the jump on each of the Nunan brothers. It was a weak plan, and he knew it, but they'd already killed two armed FBI Agents, and he didn't have a gun. He would have to outsmart the two brothers if he had any chance of saving Reagan.

He watched as Richard kicked one of the agent's hands, sending his gun skittering across the room while Mathew bent down and picked up the other agent's gun. *Where was Reagan?*

Mathew leaned against the front of the truck as Richard walked toward the other end of the room and out of Seth's line of sight. Seth needed to move, but he couldn't be sure that Richard wouldn't see him. So, he waited.

"We'll need Regalia's help moving those bodies. We can dump them further down the river, so they'll rush out with the current," Richard yelled as he moved further away.

"Great plan, dumb ass. Kill everyone in the room. No one will suspect a thing when all these damn bodies come floating to the shore," Mathew mumbled where his brother couldn't hear him.

So, Regalia was part of it? Bastard. Seth's jaw tensed.

A loud grunt came from across the room, and the sound of metal scraping had Mathew running in the same direction his brother had gone. Seth took a chance and quickly rolled out from under the truck, but instead of getting onto the boat, he hid in the dark near a thick metal post. The single fluorescent light kept the shadows of the building dark, which would help him stay hidden, but it also kept him from being able to see what was happening across the room too.

Seth waited until he couldn't take it any longer. He faintly could hear Reagan's voice, but before he stepped out into the open, she came into view. She walked ahead of Mathew until he shoved her, almost sending her to the floor. She caught herself before she slipped into the bloody mess, and Seth saw tears rolling down her face. Mathew and Mayor Regalia carried semi-unconscious Richard to the truck and sat him on the seat.

Seth's anger reached powder keg strength, and he took a chance that the only one of them holding a gun was Mathew. As Richard leaned his head onto the seatback, Seth charged full force into Mathew Nunan and slammed the gray splintering fence board into his head, breaking it in half. Richard sat up, and that's when Seth took the broken fence board he still held and cracked it across Richard's face causing him to slide to the ground.

Four swat team men rushed the building yelling for everyone to get on the ground, but Seth was a man on a mission, and he pulled Reagan behind him before he punched Mayor Regalia in the face.

Reagan yelled, "Wait!" and Seth wrapped his arms around her, pulling her to the ground with him. They both put their hands up as the armed men surrounded them.

Alexavier sat up, holding his jaw. "It wasn't him, just the Nunan brothers and Bruce Cannon," he said to the swat team as they had their guns on Seth.

"They mentioned your name too, Regalia," Seth said, angered that he didn't break the man's jaw.

Reagan lowered one hand to put it on Seth's face. "It wasn't him, Seth."

Seth looked into her eyes. He knew Regalia wanted Reagan for himself but did she want him too? "They said he would help them dispose of the bodies," Seth explained to her.

Mayor Regalia walked over and asked the swat team to lower their weapons. He reached a hand out to help Reagan and then Seth up off the ground. Seth didn't accept his help but watched as Reagan hugged the mayor and then turned away from him to hold Seth's hand. She leaned into Seth, and the knot he had in his chest loosened.

"Alexavier was taken first. They were going to make it look

like a boat accident and kill us together." She explained how they were locked in the closet for hours and when Richard came to get them, Alexavier jumped him.

Seth looked over at Mayor Regalia. Alexavier stood next to one of the swat team members, talking, but stopped to look Reagan's way and then at Seth. He gave Seth a nod, and Seth nodded back. They would never be friends, but Seth was grateful he'd been there to help Reagan. He probably shouldn't have hit him, but he didn't feel so bad about that part.

In less than fifteen minutes, every type of emergency vehicle available diverged onto the surrounding lot and street. Four paramedics surrounded the mayor and started assessing the cuts on his hands and the bruises on his face. Someone came over and gave Reagan a water bottle and a blanket she wrapped around her shoulders. She wasn't in shock, but the event shook her. As usual, she acted tough, but Seth could see the worry still in her eyes.

Reporters filed into the few empty spaces around the perimeter of the building, but as usual, Ryan found a way to get past them and the police line.

Reagan smiled shyly as her brother walked over and hugged her, picking her up off the ground for a few minutes. He set her down but kept an arm around her as he reached out to shake Seth's hand. "Damn the drama in this city," he said, and Reagan smirked at his comment.

All three of them watched as the coroner walked past them. When he knelt beside the body of the agents, Reagan shivered. Seth stepped in front of her to block her view and reached out to hold her hand.

Next, the police handcuffed Mathew and Richard Nunan. Mathew was silent as he tried to stare down Reagan on his walk outside to the police car. Richard raised his voice and cursed each officer as they dragged him out.

"I think we've seen everything in the brochure," Ryan said, and Reagan rolled her eyes at him. "What? Is there something else I'm missing in this great city?"

"It is a great city," she said, cocking her head and shaking it as she stared at her brother. "Excluding this event, of course."

"Of course," Ryan answered.

"Look, I admit that the crime needs cleaning up, but if larger cities can do it, then so can New Orleans. We have tons of culture and history. I know you guys love the food, but it is the blending of cultures that created that food and makes it an awesome place to live."

Ryan could see the reporters breaking loose and about to head their way. "Look, sis, before you start singing *Do You Know What it Means to Miss New Orleans,* we need to get the hell out of here." He pointed to an area where the police had removed their tape.

"For your information, I wasn't going to sing that. I was going to sing *When the Saints Go Marching In,*" she said as Seth grabbed her hand so they could escape the press.

Chapter Thirty-Nine

SETH DROVE REAGAN BACK TO her penthouse in silence, and Ryan followed them. It had been a firework ending that none of them had expected. It was hard to know what to do or say to ease Reagan's mind since she wasn't talking. She excused herself and went to shower and change her clothes. When she returned, Ryan and Seth were drinking coffee, and there was a cup of hot tea waiting for her.

She climbed onto the couch near Seth, pulling her legs in and covering herself up with a blanket. She sipped her tea as Seth explained to her and Ryan what had happened once the FBI agents showed up at the apartment that night.

When Seth finished, it took Reagan twenty minutes to tell them everything that had happened to her, including what she suspected was the Nunan brothers' motive.

"And the mayor wasn't involved?" Ryan asked.

"He had no clue," she said. "He's a good person, and it almost cost him his life. He trusted Mathew as Amber did, and they nearly died because of him.

"You almost died tonight too," Ryan said, and it hurt her heart when she heard his voice crack as he spoke. He shook his head, and then she saw the familiar smirk on his face. His eyes turned to slits, and he leaned over toward her. "How many times have I told you not to let them put you in the freakin' car, Rea?"

Reagan rolled her eyes and couldn't stop herself from laughing at Ryan. She knew him like a book. She'd spent almost a half-hour explaining the crazy twisted tale of two criminal brothers that were not only thieves but also murderers, and all Ryan was mad about was the fact that she hadn't followed his directions.

"Well, if you're going to laugh at me, then I'm going home to Sydney," he said and kissed Reagan on top of her head, shook Seth's hand, and headed toward the door.

"I didn't mean to hurt your feelings, Ryan," she said, hurrying to the door to hug him before he left.

"Oh, I'm not hurt, but you're going to be when I put you and Sydney through self-defense lessons. She doesn't listen to me any better than you do. I'm done talking."

He looked at Seth. "I'll have things set up next weekend at the lake so the ladies can start boot camp. Have her there early?"

"Absolutely, man," Seth said, smiling.

Reagan put both hands on her hips. "Hey! Don't talk about me like I'm not standing here."

Ryan fake laughed, mocking the way his sister laughed at him a minute before and then winked at her before he left.

Seth shook his head at the Gentry siblings. The love they had for each other was one of the strongest bonds he'd ever been around. He wanted that deep connection with Reagan. He watched her place her empty teacup on the counter and then followed her back to the sofa.

Reagan stared toward the wall of windows like she was looking out at the city, but she had a far-off look in her eyes.

"Are you okay, Rea?"

Reagan nodded. "I'm okay," she said, and then she pulled her blanket around her legs tighter. Seth wanted to pull her into his arms, but she seemed to build a wall around herself with the covers.

He watched as her eyes watered, but no tears fell. He couldn't take it any longer. "Come here, Reagan," he said as he pulled her into his side and wrapped an arm around her.

She wiped her face with her hands and leaned her head into his chest. "I'm fine. Really, I am," she said. She reached her arms around him and hugged him tightly. "At least I will be because of you, Seth. I mean, I might not even be here if it weren't for you."

He felt her trembling. He wanted to tell her he would fight all her demons if she would let him, but she was an independent woman that would want a sword instead of a knight. "I did what I had to do because I love you, Rea. I know you would do the same for me."

Reagan locked onto his eyes. "You took Mathew and Richard out with a warped fence board and were ready to beat the mayor to a pulp with your bare hands. I'm not sure I could've done that."

"Rea, you pieced together the entire crime with some basic facts from Jerry and notes from Amber. You'd do whatever it took, and I know that because you've done it your entire life. But I want you to know that you don't have to do anything alone anymore because I'll always be here for you."

Reagan looked away from Seth's beautiful face. He was ruggedly handsome, had a brilliant mind, and a loving heart. He was everything she'd ever wanted, and she couldn't believe she deserved him. He came for her when no one else even knew she was in danger. He fought for her when the odds were entirely against him. And he offered her comfort and affection when he must have needed comforting too. She was overwhelmed by Seth and his selfless love.

She turned and straddled his lap. Then stared into his eyes before she kissed him with everything she had. It was a claiming and surrender at the same time. He was hers and she was his, and they would be together from that day forward. Seth picked her up and carried her into the bedroom so he could take care of her even more.

Early the following day, Reagan snuggled in next to him, and they discussed whether or not to live together before they got married. He said he refused to live in sin, secretly knowing she would put off an official ceremony if he let her. She told him she wouldn't discuss a wedding ceremony when he hadn't asked her to marry him yet.

❦

IT WAS late Saturday morning when they pulled up to Ryan and Sydney's beautiful new house. There were several cars there already, and Reagan laughed when Seth told her they would be in trouble for being late.

"I've already said I'm not participating in a ridiculous boot camp that my little brother has put together. And, I'm not messing up my new shoes or dress for his nonsense, either," Reagan said as she met Seth at the back of the car to carry in some flowers and a cake she'd bought earlier. He took the cake to hold, and she whispered, "You might be too afraid to tell him, but I'm not." Then Seth chased her to the front door.

He had her pressed against the large wooden door with his hard body as she tried not to smash the flowers and him the cake as he smiled down at her. "I'm the only one that gets to mess up your dress later," he said, making Reagan lean up to kiss him.

It was a good thing he was holding her body so tightly; otherwise, when Sydney opened the front door, Reagan would have fallen inside.

"Whoops," Sydney said, laughing when they adjusted their clothes as she greeted them. "Welcome," she said with a huge smile for the happy couple. She led them into the kitchen, where Reagan helped her put the flowers into some water, and Seth grabbed a beer before he went out back to see Ryan.

Sydney's boys were outside too, throwing a ball into the water for their dog to fetch, and Reagan watched out the window as the dog brought the ball back and then shook water all over Ryan, Seth, and the boys.

"The simple life," Olivia said, walking into the room. Sydney nodded, and Reagan and Olivia said hello to each other. They gathered around the large kitchen island with glasses of home-made lemonade and watched Sydney slice the cake before she put it under the glass cloche to preserve it for later.

Reagan smiled, watching the sweet redhead fuss over napkins, and getting things ready for Ryan to cook on the grill. She was a great homemaker and perfect for her brother. Miss Lynn, who'd been looking around the newly renovated house, walked in, and right behind her came Amber and her date, the hot fireman neigh-bor, Angus. Gus for short. Even Olivia couldn't take her eyes off Gus. He was a hottie. But then, as they all settled outside under the large pergola near the grill, they heard the doorbell ring again. Ryan ran inside to answer it and walked back out with their final guest, Alexavier Regalia.

The mayor of New Orleans brought a bottle of wine and a cheese tray and was seated in between Olivia and Miss Lynn. He would get an earful because Miss Lynn loved to gossip. With the news of everything that had recently happened to the mayor and the city council, she would have a lot to talk about.

Sydney sidled up to Reagan and nudged her with her elbow. "What do you think those two have to discuss so seriously?" she asked, nodding toward Seth and Ryan. They'd been pulling items off the grill for several minutes but had been in a deep conversa-tion for a lot longer.

"Probably how to torture us with that self-defense boot camp Ryan wants to set up," Reagan said.

"I've already told Ryan I'm not doing that," Sydney said, and Reagan laughed as she put her arm around her.

"That's exactly what I told him."

Seth and Ryan brought the burgers and grilled chicken to the table. The group enjoyed a family-style lunch including salad, grilled corn on the cob, and then the marbled vanilla and

chocolate cake that Reagan brought served with fresh straw-
berries.

It didn't take long for the boys to talk Ryan into letting them
go canoeing, and after he helped them pull out all the gear, he
joined the rest of the adults. Sydney stood up and nervously
watched as the boys rowed away, and Ryan promised her that they
would be fine. "Sydney, the boys swim like fish, they've been
canoeing a hundred times already, and they have on life jackets."

She nodded and sat back down next to Ryan, putting his arm
around her. He nodded to Seth, who then stood up and pulled a
small box out of his pocket. Everyone watched as he went down
on one knee in front of Reagan.

"Rea, this is about five years later than it should've been. I
hope you'll let me make it up to you for the rest of your life. I love
you. Please, marry me?"

Reagan looked at her brother. Ryan was grinning ear to ear.
Suddenly, it was clear what they'd been discussing so intently over
the grill before lunch. Ryan nodded at her, and she realized she
hadn't answered Seth yet. "Oh, God, Seth. Yes. Of course, a
million times, yes!" she exclaimed and then let him slide the beautiful oval solitaire diamond onto her finger before throwing her
arms around him.

Miss Lynn teared up as well as Sydney and Amber. Ryan
shook Seth's hand and then kissed his sister. Gus held up his glass
and made a toast to the happy couple, and then Olivia flipped her
long dark hair back over her shoulder before she leaned over to
Alexavier's ear and said, "What happened to people fooling
around? Why do they all have to go and get engaged and
married?"

Just then, Gus pulled Amber in for a heated kiss that was a
little inappropriate for public viewing, and Alexavier clinked his
beer into Olivia's wine glass. "There you go. To all the happy
single people," he said and locked eyes with her before he took a
long drink of his beer.

It didn't take long for Amber and Gus to say their goodbyes

and head for the door. They were followed by Miss Lynn, Olivia, and Alexavier, who walked the ladies to their cars. Miss Lynn hurried out of the driveway, and Olivia slipped her phone number to Alexavier as he held open her car door. She was a beautiful woman, with light blue eyes and thick long dark hair. But there was something about her feisty nature that had Alexavier paying closer attention to her than usual. He wondered about Olivia and her story as he headed toward the city. It would be a while before he trusted his instincts with women again.

After their guests left, Ryan built a fire in the outdoor fireplace so Sydney and the boys could roast marshmallows. Reagan and Seth declined the sticky sweets and sat back together watching the fun. It was cool after dark, even by the fire, but they enjoyed watching the kids sneaking graham crackers to their dog, Beezus when Ryan looked the other way.

Reagan was relaxed and had her head on Seth's shoulder, smiling as the boys laughed and told stories.

"I'd love to have a couple of those," Seth whispered to her and then laughed when Reagan sat up straight.

"I hope you mean the dog," she said.

"I like dogs a lot." He kissed her forehead, and she leaned back in her seat.

Suddenly, Reagan looked worried. "My apartment is only a two-bedroom, Seth."

"Yes, babe. But we could buy a bigger house with a yard or move to the lake. Your lake house is perfect for a bunch of dogs."

"A bunch?"

Seth grinned and nodded. "Two, maybe three dogs would be just right. Plus, Ryan and Sydney want more kids, so there needs to be room for nieces and nephews to come and sleepover."

"Oh," Reagan replied and then bit her bottom lip as she watched Sydney's youngest son, John, who curled up next to the dog in front of the fire and closed his eyes. Eli and Erik, the twins, kept poking sticks into the fire, but the oldest boy, Darryl, took off his jacket and covered up John and their dog to keep them warm. Reagan put her hand over her mouth and her eyes watered at the sweetness in front of her.

"Okay, we can have at least two dogs. The boys might need a couple to run around with when they come over," Reagan whispered.

Seth kissed her hard on the mouth. It was plain to see she was smitten with Sydney's boys and loved the sweet, obedient golden retriever sleeping in front of the fire. Reagan had never had a dog or any pet before, and she seemed fascinated all day watching Beezus' pure love for his family. Seth decided he wouldn't tell her that dogs like children needed a good amount of training, especially puppies.

When the golden retriever snuggled his head under young John's chin to get a little closer, Reagan sighed. Seth wrapped his arm around her and smiled because they would have plenty of time to figure the dog thing out together.

THE END

Million Reasons

BY LISA HERRINGTON

Coming Soon!

*Olivia smirked. "I think you're teasing me. You don't seem
like the type of man who wants kids. You do know they
cramp your dating lifestyle."*
"Is that why you won't go out with me?"
"I didn't say I wouldn't go out with you."
*"Yes, you have. Every time I've asked, you've made up an
excuse."*

Want to learn more about the complicated, alpha male mayor,
who's finally met his match? Read on for the first chapter of
MILLION REASONS, part of the suspenseful, romantic
Renaissance Lake Series.

Million Reasons

The quaint town of Maisonville was considered a haven for most retirees and young adults alike. Surrounded by water from a river on one side and a large lake on the other, there were endless options for those who loved the outdoors.

The small town was a suburb of New Orleans, and there was a long 24-mile bridge over water separating the two. Many believed it was just far enough for residents to partake in crowded city festivals and enjoy the peaceful sanctuary that was Maisonville.

Olivia Dufrene would argue about how peaceful the town was or whether it should be called a sanctuary after her long day at work. She slid down onto the stool behind the lunch counter in the diner, where she'd been a waitress for six years. It was the first time she'd stopped since seven that morning, and she couldn't believe it was Wednesday and not Saturday.

The weekend would bring an even larger crowd, and they would pack the diner beyond reason. It was south Louisiana, and October brought the first reasonable temperatures since spring, and everyone loved to visit the town during that time.

Miss Lynn, who owned the diner, put her arm around Olivia. "I promise to get us more help soon."

They had been short-handed for seven months since their friend and previous waitress, Sydney Bell, had left to work with her now husband, Ryan Gentry. They remodeled old homes and were another example of why Maisonville was popular. It was nicknamed Renaissance Lake because everyone believed there was a little magic to the town. Supposedly, when you moved to Maisonville, you were given a chance to begin again at life, a career, a friendship, or maybe even romance.

"It's fine. I need the hours, Miss Lynn," Olivia said. "Of course, right now, I could use a foot massage."

"I think I know someone who would be up for the job." Miss Lynn grinned as she teased Olivia about her late-night caller.

"Hell—O kitty," Olivia said, covering her curse word as her young son walked through the diner door. Lucas was in second grade, and his school bus let him out in front of the diner each day.

"Mom!" Lucas scolded her.

"I didn't say it, Lucas. I said, hello, kitty." Olivia turned and rolled her eyes at Miss Lynn. She'd tried to stop cursing for months, and it was a lot harder than she'd thought it would be.

During his summer break, Lucas helped his mother put away the clean dishes and accidentally dropped a bowl onto the tile floor, breaking it. He promptly yelled, "Shit," which made Olivia cringe. She explained how crude it was for people to curse and then promised to stop doing it herself. They took an old canister and labeled it as "The Swear Jar," and if she or Lucas said a bad word, they had to put a dollar in it.

She was already up to twenty dollars, and that was just what he'd caught her saying. Focus, Olivia, she thought to herself and then promptly burned her hand on the empty coffee pot sitting on the hotplate. "Sugar-Honey-Iced-Tea!" she yelled and then rushed to the sink to run her hand under cold water.

Miss Lynn hurried over to examine the damage, but Olivia told her she was okay.

"Good save," Miss Lynn said. She was tickled over Olivia's

substitutions for her foul language and ever surprised at what she came up with on the fly. She winked at the younger woman and then cleared a space at the counter for sweet Lucas to start his homework.

That was their afternoon routine during the school year. Every afternoon, Lucas would come in and do his homework while Miss Lynn made him a snack. She loved to dote on the seven-year-old and had felt like he was a grandson ever since the day Olivia walked through the diner door with him on her hip.

It was six years ago when Lucas was only a year old, and Olivia was twenty-two. It was just before closing, and the dinner crowd had thinned out when the raven-haired beauty with cobalt blue eyes hurried into the diner. She was clearly shaken and trying to hide it. She sat at the bar and simply asked for a glass of water so she could make a bottle. Miss Lynn saw she didn't have on any shoes and sat down at the bar with Olivia offering to hold Lucas while she mixed up the formula for him.

By the time the last customer had left, Miss Lynn had found a pair of sandals for Olivia and offered her a room for the night. By morning, she'd given Olivia a job and allowed her to bring baby Lucas with her until they could find childcare nearby.

It was the beginning of a lovely friendship that turned more familial by the day.

Olivia sat next to Lucas as he worked out his math problems and then kissed him on the forehead as she started setting up for the dinner crowd.

Some days Olivia took Lucas home to play outside after school, and on others, he would stay at the diner until Olivia got off.

Miss Lynn enjoyed sitting with him to color until they got busy. Once the diner filled up, she or Olivia would get Lucas set up in the back room where he could watch television or look at books. At seven or seven-thirty, Olivia got off, and they headed home.

At their small duplex, Olivia rushed Lucas through his bath

time and then laid in bed with him to read. He loved reading and insisted on five of his favorite books every night.

Thankful that she didn't fall asleep, she quietly padded out of the room and left the slightest crack in the door so she could peer in on him later.

She had towels to fold and another load of laundry to finish before washing the dinner dishes. She checked her wall calendar and saw the reminder to check Lucas' bookbag for his folder and papers that she needed to sign too.

Rushing through a quick shower, she headed to the laundry room so she could finish her chores and eventually get into bed. She checked the clock on the kitchen wall and smiled that it was nine o'clock.

Alexavier Regalia was in his last term as mayor of New Orleans. He had a little more than a year left on his second term and had spent most of his time helping modernize city hall. He'd changed the landscape for local government, making them more efficient and better able to serve the public.

He was an overachiever and one of the most beloved mayors in the city's recent history. He truly understood how to increase the quality of life for residents and worked tirelessly to clean up crime and give some affordable housing and even healthcare options for its citizens.

Alexavier had grown up in the heart of the city and had strong Italian roots that could be traced back for generations. He'd lost his wife to cancer early in his first term, and after a year of mourning her, he slowly began to date.

The beloved mayor was photographed with local beauties like Miss Louisiana, the local favorite evening news anchor, and various single doctors, lawyers, and real estate agents. He never seemed to get serious with anyone, but he was social and kept local gossip buzzing about him.

However, while he continued to keep up appearances at all the local festivals, farmer's markets, high school theater shows, 10k running events, and various high school football games, Alexavier had been quietly but seriously focused on only one woman.

He'd met beautiful Olivia almost six months earlier at a friend's cook-out in Maisonville, but she had yet to let him take her out on a proper date. Instead, they slowly began chatting over texts and late-night phone calls.

For a couple of months, he'd sent texts to her, or she'd text him a funny meme, but she wouldn't go out with him. He'd figured it was because she had a young son, but he'd offered to take them both to the zoo or the aquarium. Still, she declined, making excuses about work or other obligations.

July and August brought their own excuses, but the texting turned into a few late-night calls.

It gave him hope.

Then in September, things turned even more promising. He'd started calling her almost nightly. They would laugh and talk for an hour or longer about her day at work or his. Sometimes, they discussed music and the lyrics of their favorite songs. She liked to read smut, as she called it, and she would brazenly tell him about those stories. Those phone calls were hot, and he knew she was teasing him but also affected by the naughty conversations. Even so, she wouldn't have lunch or dinner with him.

He'd driven across the lake once a week for months to Maisonville to have lunch at the diner where she worked, just to see her. It took forty minutes one way to get there, but it was worth it to speak to her in person.

He loved her laugh, but to see her do it in person was even better. She had a great sense of humor. She also had a big heart, and he watched her on more than one occasion pay for someone's food because they forgot their wallet or didn't have enough. Alexavier and Olivia clicked on a lot of levels, and the attraction between them was mutual. He could see it in her eyes, her beautiful blue eyes. Still, she wouldn't let him take her out to dinner or even allow him to cook dinner for her.

He would not give up. It was October and a fantastic time to enjoy the city and all the fun it offered. He would find a way to talk her into spending a day or night out together.

Alexavier finished eating a leftover bowl of spaghetti for dinner and then propped his feet up on the coffee table in his living room. He wondered what Olivia and Lucas had eaten for dinner and smiled that all boys liked spaghetti and meatballs.

A notification ring came from his phone and made him laugh. It was nine PM and later than he'd thought, but he could almost set his watch by Olivia Dufrene.

About the Author

LISA HERRINGTON is a Women's fiction and YA novelist, and blogger. A former medical sales rep, she currently manages the largest Meet-Up writing group in the New Orleans area, The Bayou Writer's Club. She was born and raised in Louisiana, attended college at Ole Miss in Oxford, Mississippi and accepts that in New Orleans we never hide our crazy but instead parade it around on the front porch and give it a cocktail. It's certainly why she has so many stories to tell today. When she's not writing, and spending time with her husband and three children, she spends time reading, watching old movies or planning something new and exciting with her writers' group.

Connect with Lisa, find out about new releases, and get free books at lisaherrington.com

Made in the USA
Las Vegas, NV
03 May 2025

21652028R00157